HELL IN REZTA

HELL IN REZTA

AMY FLASHMAN

authorHOUSE®

AuthorHouse™
1663 Liberty Drive
Bloomington, IN 47403
www.authorhouse.com
Phone: 1-800-839-8640

Published by AuthorHouse   08/22/2012

ISBN: 978-1-4772-2615-5 (sc)
ISBN: 978-1-4772-2616-2 (e)

PROLOGUE

When you have nothing in the world, what do you have to lose when you hear a voice telling you to let go of life and there's nothing you can do? Do you simply fight it or welcome it?

There are some like me who no longer have that choice; I can never have that choice, because I'm already dead and in a different world.

When you think you're alone with no one around, do you dream of different worlds, of different lives?

I did, and now I wish I never had.

Chapter 1
Desperate beginnings

I am sixteen, and I wouldn't call myself an "ordinary" girl. I live with my drunken dad, who violently hates me. He's never sober. I always get the full blame for every mishap that happens in our small house. I hardly remember going to school either. I cannot remember the number of times I have been beaten and it doesn't surprise me. Most of my life I spend in my room, trying to avoid my beast of a father. If you are ever told that someone is related to you, make sure they run on blood and not alcohol.

This is why I dreamt of a different life in a whole new world. I always dreamt of one place—Rezta.

I live through someone else's eyes there. I see what I've seen since birth in Rezta, always the same thing: a never-ending cloud of inky black darkness slowly consuming the planet and growing worse and far more vivid as time passes.

This hell like-place is also what comes to my head when I try to think of my mother. My mother abandoned us when I was younger. I don't really remember her, and I only know what she looks like thanks to the one picture of her in my house. She was young, and if it weren't for her dark eyes, that closely resembled my own, I wouldn't recognise her. Her face was happy and carefree, smiling at the long-lost camera, innocent and untroubled. Both my dad and I loved her, but when she disappeared he spiralled into a deep depression, and nothing I ever did or said helped him, but the drinking did.

I wake in sweats every night, seeing this place, Rezta, and its people being haunted by something, leaving a deathly trail wherever it goes. Slowly over the years, I have watched this make-believe place go from bad to worse, and it has burned me every night until I awake, suppressing sobs into my pillow.

"Oy, girl! Get here now!"

My body froze as I heard my father's voice come booming up the stairs, echoing threateningly and stealing me away from my thoughts. He'd been hitting the bottle again of course. He always comes home drunk, and then he attacks me. The hospital doesn't believe me when I come in with my various injuries. Who would though? I'm only a child, and no one ever believes children—especially not when the caring father hugs and kisses his daughter in public and puts my cuts and bruises down to "sheer misfortune".

"Shana!" My father screamed from downstairs. "If you make me come and get you, you . . . you'll bleed for a whole bloody month! So get down here! Now!"

I had no intention of going anywhere. The hospital said if I "fell" again, I would have to go into childcare, so my father stopped taking me to school where the teachers could see my bruises. I was locked in the house while he was out getting wasted, waiting for him to come home and give me another wave of fresh torture.

I should've run when I was at school, but my few friends I had there were what kept me sane. They were a comfort to me, an escape route from my life; but that changed quickly when my father took me in for "home schooling" and never let me out again. But it was too late to do anything now. I'll never have a normal childhood with friends or freedom.

I couldn't take it anymore. I had to run. I had to be free and have a life worth living. And it didn't take much to know that this type of living was wrong and it definitely wasn't for me.

Becoming more and more acknowledging of the fact that my father was growing ever more impatient, I got up and stopped beside my bedroom door. I was sure he'd make good on his promise if I failed to appear, and giving him even more incentive to be angry was something I never needed to do. I slowly pulled the door towards me and looked out across the hall. I didn't want to walk down it and meet my father; I was wild with fear as I crept slowly down the landing.

Moving cautiously across the small landing, my heart pumping loudly in my ears, I stopped at the top of the staircase I had "tripped" down a few too many times. My father's bloodshot eyes flickered to life when they saw me, they were more frenzied than usual; his greasy grey hair hung on his slumped shoulders and his drooling mouth was turned into a sneer. If he hit me on the head in this state, my hair would be dyed a dark shade of red.

His sneer turned into a full blown grin as he watched me. I grasped the bannister as I came down the stairs and was aware that I was breathing heavily and loudly, I tried to silence it, I knew that loud breathing annoyed him and that gave him more reason to beat me. I watched my father's reactions with eagle eyes.

"Hello, Shana dear," he snarled out in a blood-curdling voice as I walked steadily, towards him. He turned away and headed for the soundproof basement I have now become so terrified of, with no doubt I would follow him as I had been doing for years. I hung my head in shame and forced one foot in front of the other, knowing it'd be worse otherwise.

Let's get this over with, I thought, sickened.

As I walked past the front door, rays of sunlight caught something metal, I held my breath. It was a key!

All the windows and doors were locked permanently in my house. I got no fresh air, and my hope dwindled as my life continued. My father was very careful not to let me escape or get near a phone, even if I knew how to use one. But he had finally made a mistake. This could be my chance!

I glanced quickly at my father who was still heading for the basement. I'd get the beating of a lifetime if I was caught. It was stupid—and dangerous.

It's now or never, my inner voice told me. My mind was made up.

As quickly and quietly as I could I turned the key in the slot. It made a faint click, but in the still air of the house, it was equivalent to an alarm going off.

My father's head whipped around, but in his drunken state he failed to focus immediately on what I was doing, which gave me time to fling open the door and stumble across the broken tiles that led to the house.

I urged my frail legs to run, even though the pain jolting through them on every step was excruciating. But the breeze felt so nice on my face that I didn't care that I had no place to go or that my father was probably hunting me down right now. I ran so fast I couldn't even control my legs, but that didn't matter. I was free!

"*Shana! Come back here now!*" My father's hysterical voice shrieked behind me down the street.

What happened next went so fast.

I felt something smash against the back of my head, and pain was travelling down my spine to every muscle of my body. My fingers automatically went to the back of my head and brought back red, sticky blood that gleamed on my hand as I was forced to my knees. I felt sick to the pit of my stomach while the agonising throbbing in my head was deafening me. I fell on my side as a grey haze started to cloud my vision. I was shaking uncontrollably now, helpless. Looking round helplessly, I saw my father staring at me from across the road, shaking with wild laughter. He had thrown the bottle he'd been holding directly at my head, causing me to fight for my life.

Maybe it is better this way, I thought as I lay with the gradually growing pool of blood making a halo around my head. No more abuse from that monster; no more hiding from my own life; no more struggling through this miserable and wretched existence. But I couldn't give up, not after everything I had been through. This can't be how it ends.

I remember hearing a scream from a neighbour and sirens in the distance. I was still fighting to keep my eyelids open as they bundled me into an ambulance and sped me away to a hospital. I had to fight. I had no religion and didn't know if death was the end or if there was some sort of heaven.

My mind went foggy as a strange, rough voice echoed suddenly in my mind.

"Shana, come. We need you here in Rezta."

Wow! Craziness must run in the family, my muddled mind managed to think. Hearing voices was never a good sign, even on the brink of death. No, I wasn't going to give up, not ever.

A deafening silence knocked me into oblivion. White light engulfed me, boiling every atom of my existence. I was gone.

Chapter 2
Welcome to Rezta

It was the most painful experience of my life. That's what getting cremated alive must feel like, I thought groggily. I had no idea why I listened to that voice or even if it was real, but I did listen. I don't know what I was thinking. I'm supposed to be dead, I realised. Perhaps I had just fallen asleep in the ambulance, but I didn't want to open my eyes because I knew what I'd find, all because I'd believed the voice.

"Open your eyes," the strange voice said again, reverberating in my head. "Trust me, everything will be okay."

"I'm dead because of you," I said aloud. "I won't listen to you again." Wait, how did I say that if I was dead?

"You're not dead," a different voice said, answering my question. "At least not here."

I opened my eyes. I was staring at a carved golden wall. I wasn't in an ambulance at all. Then it hit me that I was dead but could still think. I didn't do much of that when I was alive, so why would I do it now if I was dead?

I sat up on a large, comfy bed and stared into the eyes of an old man.

"I was wondering when you'd come around," he said to me. "My name is Grint," he continued, without any interest in knowing who I was.

"My name is Shana," I said anyway in a tone of authority. This seemed to amuse him.

"Yes, I know who you are," he replied almost mockingly. He gave a cheeky grin, which creased his already creviced head. It looked creepy and unusual.

He shrugged. I could see he was one of those wise types that usually get on my nerves very easily with all their "wise" speeches. There was a moment of silence which I was enjoying, as the thumping in my head sang dully.

The old man spoke to me again. "Shana, do you know why I have bought you here?" He sounded a little too curious. After a pause, he turned to look at me, questioning my silence. I shook my head slowly.

"You must rest now," he said abruptly, standing up. "This is your room. Come downstairs in one hour. You're no good to anyone tired." He turned to the door and gave a deep sigh; he was either really tired or really relieved.

When he left me on my own, I sat upright in the bed and studied the room. It was enormous. It had a light creamy carpet and intricately designed wallpaper. There was a gigantic cupboard that took up the entire left-hand wall, its doors complete with mirrors that reflected the light that entered from the large window, scattering rainbows everywhere. I could see out of the window from here. Outside was a vast open meadow with two great fountains and a dark forest at its edge. The sky was a clear blue with only the sun to accompany the mountains that rose high in the distance.

With my head still thumping, I got out of the bed and walked over to the oversized cupboard. I stared at the girl looking back at me in the mirror. I somehow looked different. With the same clear olive skin, my deep brown hair was not as tussled as it usually was, because it was currently in a neat bun with only the fringe hanging loose. Then I looked at the rest of my body and I realised that I was wearing a white dress that draped down to the floor. I had never worn a dress before; it looked somewhat elegant. Around my neck was a curious silver necklace with a tiny amber gem in the shape of an oval. It gleamed brightly in the sun's rays which were streaming through the room.

I looked away and opened the cupboard. The two doors folded back to reveal the large interior. I was in heaven. The cupboard was filled with clothes—lots and lots of clothes. Dresses, shirts, shoes of all kinds, jewellery, and more things I couldn't even see. I wasn't used to having luxurious things (or even nice things), so I automatically thought of money, if that even existed here.

My head still ached and I was feeling dazed, so I climbed back into the lavish bed and fell asleep.

An hour had passed when I awoke. I was convinced I had a really weird dream about extravagant clothes and dresses, but one look at the room I was in told me it wasn't a dream at all. I climbed out of the bed again and slowly opened the bedroom doors—slowly, because they were heavier than they looked—and I was taken aback by the beauty of the house or palace I was in. "Palace" seemed to fit better, though.

I walked out into a spacious hallway, looking from one room to the next. The magnificence of each one astounded me. All the rooms I walked into were enormous, but I failed to see why anyone would need sixteen living rooms with not much furniture other than sofas or thick rugs. Or maybe I had just seen the same room more than once.

I might as well face it: I was lost in a house. Had this ever happened to anyone before?

I stopped in a random room and sat down on a red sofa. I sure hoped someone would find me soon; I don't handle boredom well at all.

I don't know how much time had passed since I started, but I realised I was rocking quickly on the sofa. I jumped when the door unexpectedly swung open, and my eyes darted towards it. Standing in the doorway was a small girl with light blonde hair and porcelain skin with hazel eyes. She was dressed in a white cotton dress and brown gladiator slippers. "Huh, are they back in style?" was my first thought when I saw her.

"Hi," I said. I stood up quickly, and I was aware of a dumb grin on my face. "Do you know where Grint is?"

She stared at me with frosty eyes, making me want to run away. I looked around the room, avoiding eye contact with an ever-growing silence hanging between us. This was an awkward environment to be trapped in.

"Uh, I'm Shana Hale," I said, trying to sound upbeat, but I think it came out more as a snarl, because she was still glaring at me. Had I insulted her by saying hi?

"I'm Mia Green," she retorted finally. "Did Grint say where he would meet you?" Without waiting for an answer, the girl Mia crossed her arms and walked back through the door. I ran after her.

"Um, I think he said something about going downstairs," I told the girl, trying to remember the wrinkled man's words. "Are you new here?"

"No, I'm not," she replied huffily. She blew a piece of hair away from her face and marched to a hallway I hadn't seen on my wanderings.

"Can you tell me where I am? My father threw a bottle at my head and killed me." That's always a good conversation starter with awkward people.

Mia looked like she was trying to suppress saying or asking something.

Just then a lady appeared and stepped in front of us. She was richly dressed and had a stone-like face, her hair in a tight circle on her head. "My name is Mary," she began in clipping tones. "Grint is this way, Miss Green and Miss Hale."

Oh my God, I thought. Was I at a morgue or something? Or is everybody here generally just sad and angry?

We followed Mary through a number of doorways to a landing that linked most of the rooms I had ambled through. The stairs were at the end of the hallway, winding around a dark ebony pole with intricate carvings cut into the wood. I looked closely at them as I descended. They were mainly pictures of a young boy about my own age, clutching a sword. He was fighting a sinister shadow, and when I looked at it, it sent shivers and goose bumps up and down my body. It was a big figure with the shape of a human body, but my instincts told me it was something more. I swear I had seen it before.

"Mia, do you know who this is?" I asked the girl walking in front of me, pointing at the carvings. It was probably a stupid question, but I needed to know.

Her expression paled. "Yes. But I don't think it's *who* you should be asking about. It's *what* it is."

Mary had a grim look on her face, and her eyes were stained with anguish as she looked at the boy on the wood. "This way! Do hurry." Her voice sounded harsher than before.

Mary hurried downstairs and beckoned us to follow. I looked at Mia with a surprised expression. I was thinking that saying this place was 'messed up' could be an understatement. I looked swiftly one last time at the boy battling the dark figure and quickly walked on.

At the bottom of the stairs, Mary continued to walk down a brightly lit corridor, its walls decorated with various tapestries and paintings, and finally stopped outside a tall, cream-coloured door.

"In here," she commanded, and she disappeared inside the room. Afraid to be left alone again, I followed Mia through the door.

I was in another large, richly furnished room. A group of people sat casually on sofas centred on a big area, chatting happily to each other. Grint sat in an oversized chair at the head of the room, while Mary strode towards the empty seat next to him and sat down. They were the only old ones in the room, I noticed.

Everyone suddenly stopped talking and turned to gaze at me and Mia where we were still standing.

There was one other woman in the room, aside from Mary. I had never seen her before. She was young and incredibly pretty. She had clear skin, deep brown eyes and blonde hair. She noticed me looking at her and smiled. I gave a brief smile and blushed, which made her giggle, and I swear Mia was finding this amusing too.

"Mia, Shana, come sit," said Grint from the huge chair. They all turned away in silence. Mia gave me a nervous glance which I returned. "No one here will harm you," Grint said, smiling warmly.

Mia walked gracefully forward, and I quickly followed her. She had reached the centre of the circle, when a burly man, at least six feet tall, jumped up and threw an object in her direction.

Everything slowed down. Mia immediately saw the sword heading for her face and raised a hand, seemingly unafraid. The sword glowed red and came to an abrupt halt in mid-air. I couldn't tell what my face was giving away, but I was sure it was frozen in shock as I watched Mia clench her fist, causing the sword to burst into a ball of blinding flames.

A smaller, younger man stood up from a plush sofa and laughed at the guy who had thrown the sword, slapping him round the head.

"Cough up," he said to him jubilantly.

"Fine!" The sword-thrower dug his hand into his pocket and whacked two gold coins into the other man's outstretched hand.

"One day I'll catch her out, and then you'll pay me double of everything I've ever given you," he mumbled grumpily.

The young man sat down, and Mia plonked down beside him. They high-fived each other and the man reached into his pocket and gave her one of the golden coins. The older man just grunted at them, and then he turned to me.

"Hi," he said with a smile. "My name's Thornton, but my friends call me Thorn." He held out his hand to me.

"I'm Shana," I said in a shaky voice, taking his hand. Thorn was still smiling as he took his place.

Now everyone was looking at me again. I looked at Thorn.

I still didn't understand what just happened or where I was. I still believed I was going to wake up at any moment back at home in my lumpy bed with all my bruises. But everyone's eyes continued to stare at me, and my head felt dizzy and confused. It was fair to say that I knew I was going to have a bad reaction, so I promptly passed out.

Chapter 3
Conference

"She shouldn't be here." I recognised Mia's voice.

"We need her, you know that." Grint sounded strained, as if he had had this conversation multiple times.

I decided to intervene.

"Why am I here?" I opened my eyes to see everyone crowded around me, some with worried expressions on their faces.

My question swiftly caught their attention. Everyone's eyes darted down to look at me lying on the couch—everyone except Mia, who was staring at Grint with expectant eyes. She looked at him as though she wanted him to say something. It was quite annoying. What was she afraid of?

"How much do you know of Rezta?" Thorn asked after a long silence. He was staring at me with a grim expression. Everyone else's head popped up as if this was a very important question.

"Only what I've seen in my dreams. There was no detail, but it looked dark and barren. But the view outside does not seem that way, so I guess I was wrong." I looked around at Thorn, who was shaking his head slowly. The view inside certainly matched my description.

"You saw correctly, but that was a part of Rezta outside my island. Rezta has fallen, with one city still standing. We must fight back against Morphius." He said the name coldly, as if saying it was bad luck.

Everyone shivered at the name.

Thorn's tone sharpened to match his words. "Morphius is why you are here and part of what you have been seeing and the main reason why you're dead—ignoring the daddy issues, that is."

"Thorn should not have been so blunt, but Morphius has brought nothing but fear and destruction amongst my people," said Grint. I noticed he had said "my people".

"What do you mean, 'your people'? Are you their king?" I asked. This brought a smile to his face.

"Shana, you mustn't be so rude." The blonde shook her head.

"No, it is fine, Anna." Grint smiled and his face wrinkled. "We do not have kings and queens on this island. I am just the person they come to if they need help and consultation. They fear me. That is why I live here in such a magnificent palace on an island."

Mia had been quiet all through the meeting, but she was instantly alert after what he had just said. "You! You haven't helped anyone since you were put here. You've been exiled and stripped of your post," she smirked.

"I doubt you could be a big threat to anyone." The whole room gasped. "With a sword you would be slow," I injected into the conversation. "With magic, however, you seem to be talented." I looked over to a bookshelf; on it was a book that read "Spells and Incantations".

Grint stood up, as did the younger man, who had a huge monkey grin on his face. Grint walked over to take the hilt of the sword which Mia had blown up. Grint grasped the hilt with one hand on the bottom and one on the top. As if it were heavy, he slowly brought the hilt up to his waist and turned around to face the man standing at the opposite side of the circle. Mia was also on her feet. The other man gave her a warning glance, as if he was concerned for her well-being.

The hilt gave a bright blue glow, and in a blinding split-second a newly formed blade had appeared at the end of the hilt. All the people sitting down were thrown to the opposite side of the room in their chairs. Mia gave a quick dark chuckle at my expression. This looked wrong! She looked as though she was about to fight them. She raised her hand at a clear space in their midst, and a ball of water and light appeared. It was so pretty that I felt like I needed to watch it forever. Mia clenched her fist shut, and the light exploded in front of them. She and Grint stood their ground, while the power in the circle crackled like lightning. The other man was thrown off balance but remained standing. Mia opened her hand towards a wall where swords were hanging, and a sword was torn from the wall into her hand. It too glowed bright blue.

Then the power surge finished, and they began to fight.

"Hendric, are you all right?" shouted Grint, as if the power surge had affected his hearing. Now I knew everyone's name.

"I'm fine," he shouted back, as if he meant trouble.

Then they both lunged for Mia. I couldn't stand this—she looked so frail. She swiftly moved her sword to block the men's attacking swords. How did she know how to handle a sword? Then there was a flash of red light, this time from Grint. He threw his hand in Mia's direction, and she was thrown across the room and into Hendric. Grint chuckled, put down his sword, and walked over to the bundle. Mia wriggled out of the bundle and helped Hendric to his feet. They were both smiling. It was almost as if they knew they were going to lose the fight against Grint.

Now I knew why Grint was dangerous. During the red blast I could feel the power rippling through the room and the suppressed force that could have made for a deadly blast.

The chairs were put back to form an orderly circle. Thorn high-fived Hendric as he returned to his seat. Mia was smiling as she took her place next to Hendric. I was still in shock, but she and Hendric high-fived. Grint was smiling at me from his seat.

"I am not far out of practice, young one, but I grant you a sword is not my weapon of choice. Shana, I suppose you're still wondering why you're here?" I nodded my head feebly at his question. "You are the one I chose out of your world."

Everybody was looking as though they were in complete disbelief. A moment of uncomfortable silence passed. I wished they would stop staring. It was so rude.

"What for?" My face felt hot. I didn't like where this was going.

"It is up to you to save our world, to take Rezta back to the former glory it once was."

I was shaking. The one to save them? I didn't even have magic. I'm just a human.

"Shana, you possess no power, but you are one of the most important people in Rezta." He sighed. "Long ago before I was born, a creature of darkness and evil was created called . . . Morphius. He is a master of darkness and has a hatred for anything with power that can challenge him."

"Why?" It made no sense to be hateful of what you are.

"How much do you know of destinies, young one?" Grint straightened on his chair.

"They tell you the future."

"No, those are prophesies. Destinies are people's fate. Many years ago before I was born, Morphius had a prophecy that he would be killed by a goddess of magic. Many people have turned up over the years with possibilities, but I have been watching you because of your connections."

Hendric cleared his throat and glowered at Grint.

"Can't anybody else do this?" I said sharply. Mary gave a sharp intake of air.

Grint sighed. I knew he was not yet finished, but I wouldn't do anything until I knew the answer to this question.

"There was someone else, long ago. He was . . . He was taken by Morphius and . . ." he sighed heavily.

Mia leaned forward in her chair slightly. "You sent him to his death."

"No, he is being held prisoner," said Thorn.

"What was his name?" My voice sounded distant.

"Joshua," mumbled Mary.

"I thought you said a goddess of magic? Isn't a goddess a woman?"

"He asked the same question as you did." Mary paled and clutched her stomach. "We told him no, but he went anyway in . . . the . . ." Mary was sobbing hard. Anna walked over to her and knelt down to grasp her hand.

"We will get him back, I promise you." Mary put her hand on Anna's, and they exchanged hopeful glances.

I felt sorry for them, but this place was absolutely nuts. Hey, maybe the bottle hit my head so hard I was now in a coma and having a really vivid dream.

Then a thought struck me. "What do you mean he's *being* held prisoner? He's not still there is he?"

Mary shuddered.

"No," said Grint, "he was cast into a statue. He still has a subconscious, but it will take magic of great strength and willpower to change him back." He looked deep in thought.

"Why can't you do it?" Mia said sharply, standing up.

"Mia you must understand, if I leave this palace Morphius will invade it."

"Mia, he didn't say you have to go anywhere," I said, trying to calm her before she could pick up a sword.

Mia looked at me as if I had pulled a joke then looked at Grint.

"I see you keep out of her head," she accused in a bitter tone.

"I have no business in her head."

"What do you need in my head?!" Note to self: Mia has a quick temper.

"I need to keep in touch from long distances." Grint was smiling at Mia. She gave him a cold glare.

"What do mean, long distances? Where is Mia going?" This made no sense. Mia has to go *far* away. Mia turned to give me a bewildered look.

"You know you're going too, right?"

"What? Where?" Realisation hit. "You're sending me to the same place as Joshua?" I was now on my feet next to Mia. I was about to tell him where to go, but Grint was no longer looking at my face but at my neck. I felt a warm glow on my neck and looked down. My necklace was glowing.

"What are you doing to my necklace?" Mia backed away slowly towards Thorn and Hendric. Grint, Mary, and Anna were backing away from me as if I were a leper.

"Shana, I'm not doing anything. Try to calm down and I will explain everything you need to hear."

I was confused, but I took deep breaths and calmed down. They still kept their distance. I looked at her; she looked sixteen years old but was still so much more mature than me. I couldn't believe it. They wanted to send me away on a suicide mission when I had just got here. I wished I had died and it could all be over with.

"Why send me here when—" A jar flew across the room and books started falling off the shelves, interrupting my train of thought. I ducked out the way of another vase. Holy crap! What was going on? The heat from my necklace stopped, the vases dropped in mid-air, and the books stopped falling. They were all backed against the wall except Mia, who was standing beside me with her hands up, keeping a jar a millimetre away from her head.

"Mia, were you scared of me?" I'd hate myself if I'd frightened her.

"No, I wasn't frightened of you." She shook her head. "Just what you could have done"

"What do you mean?" She sighed.

"Shana, that necklace—it's so powerful you can do anything if you want, and if you lost control, anything could have happened." Everyone had taken their places, but they were still on red alert.

"But I have no power. How is that possible?"

"Shana, that necklace—I don't know if it is what I think it is." Grint fidgeted with his hands. "But it holds so much power. I can sense the power emanating from it, and it's the most powerful thing I have ever sensed. Do you know where you got it from?" I looked at Mia for help. But her face was just as interested as Grint's was.

"I don't know." I was now looking into Mia's eyes waiting for an explanation.

"It's because it's a part of you. Ever since birth, you were meant to have this." She pulled back in to her seat. I turned to face Grint.

"What?" My face was blank.

He looked at me as if I'd just won the lottery.

"That necklace—it can't be!" Grint looked as if he had only just tuned in to the conversation. Enough was enough! They kept changing the conversation, and I was having none of it.

"But why do you want me and Mia to go?" I was so annoyed. He was so frustrating. I felt myself shaking—I already knew the answer on some level.

"I want you, Mia, Hendric, Thorn, and Anna to rescue Joshua and bring him back, because we are in a war." The finality of his words was strong. I didn't dare argue.

"Of course" I looked up at Grint. "Why didn't I see it? Go, all of you."

After being told to go on a suicide mission, Mia and I walked towards the door to go upstairs.

"Do you know the way?" asked Mary.

"Yes, we'll be fine. Come on, I'll show you the way to your room. I know you have some questions for me." Mia turned her head away from me.

We walked towards the staircase, but I couldn't help but stop in front of the pole again.

"This is Joshua fighting Morphius, isn't it?" I asked in toneless voice. I shivered as I looked at the dark figure looming over Joshua.

Mia just walked ahead. I hurried after her, not wanting to lose her and get lost again.

We walked up the stairs and along the landing, taking a lot of twists and turns that I knew I wouldn't remember in the future. We arrived outside my door. I had not noticed before how grand the door was, but it had a huge carving of a woman. She had beautiful flowing hair. She was striking her sword in the air; lightning was carved out behind her as if she was a hero. I almost recognised the face, but the familiarity was too improbable to be true.

"Do you know her?" Curiosity was straining her voice.

"No, I don't."

I looked away and opened the door; Mia followed me in. She walked straight over to the window and sat comfortably on the ledge.

"That lady on the door. Who is she?" Mia didn't seem to think at all before answering.

"A lady called Krystith; she was a powerful sorcerer, also a great hero but a prisoner to her duties in Rezta. She served this world well, until the end." Mia avoided eye contact. Maybe I should change the subject.

"How did you get here?" Maybe that was not a good subject either, considering how I got here . . .

She gave a sigh and sat silently for a moment. "It's too long a story to tell, so I'll show you."

My sight blurred, and I was no longer myself. I seemed to be watching an old woman, dressed in maid's clothes, standing in an old kitchen.

"Hilda!" Another women's voice boomed around the kitchen. A tall slender woman walked through a double door. "Hilda, I must speak with you about Mia." Hilda became apprehensive. "You know I cannot condone what she does, so I would like you to put an end to it. I want you to put this in her drink tonight for supper." She fished in her pocket and pulled out a bottle and handed it to Hilda. "Have it done tonight, and I will make it my personal business that your son gets out of that terrible execution sentence tomorrow and make sure he gets set up nice and comfortable in a cosy little house." Hilda wiped her eyes free of tears.

The women left and Hilda was alone. She hadn't moved for what seemed like ages, when a girl in pig-tails came in the kitchen. "Oh, Miss Mia, how are you today?" Hilda looked pale. Mia giggled; her pale pink face and rosy cheeks made her seem like a two year old.

"I'm fine. Mother just said sorry to me in public for not understanding my gifts. Isn't that great?"

Mia looked so young and sweet. "Yes, honey, absolutely wonderful. I'm making your favourite tonight—chicken and potatoes. So run along so I can get it done."

Mia walked out of the room to a huge, wide hall with lots of large windows. Mia's little pig tails bobbed with each step she took. Her pale yellow dress caught the sun as she passed each huge window, making her look like an angel. I followed her to a huge dining room and looked around at the people. She smiled at someone and waved. She walked up to the lady who had asked Hilda to kill her.

"Mother!" Mia hugged the lady.

Oh my god! Her mother wants to kill her.

"Mia, come sit and dine with us."

Mia and her murderous mother went and sat at the top of the table. The dinner was brought in, and Mia was smiling with her mother. Mia's mother stood up and raised her cup.

"To my beautiful, talented daughter!" Her mother looked lovingly at Mia.

Mia beamed at her mother. It made me sick to think was about to happen. Mia's mother drank from her cup, and Mia picked up her cup to do the same.

"No!!!" I screamed, but no one noticed as Mia put the cup to her lips and slowly drank the poison. After she had drunk the lot, her mother smiled at her, and Mia returned the smile, unaware of what her mother's smile meant.

I watched in horror as Mia's mum sat and chattered with the person next to her. Mia's smile started to waver, and she started to look pale and coughed violently. Mia's mum stood up and went to her daughter and started to pat her back.

"Someone help! She's choking!" She bent over to Mia's ear, making it look like a hug. "I will never love you."

Mia looked at her mother as she walked away. People crowded around Mia trying to help. Mia coughed more violently, blood splattered from her mouth. I watched her glare at her mother, and I saw her hand slowly creep forward on the table and clench her fist. Mia's mum started to become red, and smoke slowly rose from her head. I watched in horror as Mia doubled over and threw up blood all over the table whilst her mother soon became clouded in smoke. The windows started to rattle in their frames, and Mia's eyes started to droop. Mia clenched her fist fully shut, and screams echoed through the hall. Mia's mother stood up and tried to kick the flames out at the bottom of her dress. Mia lifted her hand weakly, and the flames rose to completely cover her mother. Mia gave a weak smile, and her head flopped back on the chair. The windows exploded over the guests, and her mother fell to the cold stone floor.

The scene blurred, and I was back in my room. Mia was sitting opposite me. Tears dripped down my face.

"I'm so sorry." My voice sounded raspy and choked.

"You have nothing to be sorry for." Mia's voice was so faint it was almost like a whisper.

"Are you okay?"

"Yeah, it's just not something I like to re-live." Mia looked at the ground, and for the first time I felt like I had a connection with her.

"How do you have powers like that? How can you do anything like that?"

She smiled to herself and looked at me with burning curiosity.

"Have you not worked out anything yet?" she sighed. "I was born with these gifts—same as that necklace of yours." Her voice cracked. "We can never return to Earth."

I looked at the big cupboard in shock. "My dad. What will happen to him? He killed me and laughed at me while I was on the ground as I was dying." I shook my head. "How could he?" I looked at Mia, hoping for some indication that I was seeing things. I may have hated him, but he was my dad after all.

"He never cared. After your mother left, he drank himself silly and had no cares in the world." She spoke in a chilling tone that sent shivers down my spine. She looked up at me with eyes of stone. "He was going to kill you that day anyway. You cost too much money. He needed more money for the drink." Her eyes softened. "It was not your fault; it was your destiny to die when the time was right."

I quickly changed the subject before I burst into tears. "How do you know all this?"

"Mind reading works both ways." She stood up and walked towards me. Only now did I realise that I was standing. She took my hand and led me towards the chaise-longue. I sat down, but I was still tense.

"What do you know about your mother?" Mia didn't look at me and shifted uncomfortably.

"Only that her name was Tania and that she abandoned me." I shifted my weight uncomfortably. I didn't like talking about my mum.

"Your mother's real was name Krystith and she didn't abandon you. She was stubborn, and she wanted to stay on Earth with you. She was the chosen one, though, and once you're chosen, there is no going back. She was to try and fight Morphius. We know now what a big mistake that was. She is dead, Shana. Krystith was going head to head in a standoff. The army never turned up, and neither did the help she asked for. When it came down to it, Morphius had too much power, but she weakened him a lot. Unfortunately she took a blow from the resontvie, the power of Morphius, and she died crying your name in the arms of Hendric, the man she loved. That's why he said nothing to you downstairs. He misses her." I didn't realise I was crying. I sniffed and rubbed at my eyes. Mia wouldn't make eye contact with me. "Krystith was the lady on the door; she left Rezta and had you on Earth"

"Why are you smiling?" I was on my feet, and so was she.

She was looking at my necklace. I looked down. It was glowing again—brighter this time, except that this time I had it under control. I channelled the energy building up inside me and focused it to my hand.

I remembered what Mia had done downstairs. I moved my hand in front of me at the window, and it buckled in its frame. Then I closed my hand, and it shattered. That was not supposed to happen. Mia moved in front of me and the glass slowed down like in the films. She closed her eyes, and the fragments zoomed back into place in the window. She opened her eyes and turned to smile at me.

"Your emotions will sometimes activate your necklace—which is bad, as you are completely irrational!" She walked over to the bed and sat on the end. I sat down on the chaise longue.

"Does Hendric like me?" Mia didn't even look up.

"He doesn't know what to make of you, but he feels like your protector, so I think you're okay. If you want to speak to him, he insisted on having the room next to yours." I was in shock again. I thought he hated me. Now I had a room next to him, by his persuasion.

"If you want, I can go back to my room, unless you have any more questions?" Mia was standing. I nodded, and she left. I walked to my oversized cupboard and pulled some fuzzy socks out to sleep in. I had a feeling I was going to be happy here. For once in my life I felt wanted.

Chapter 4
Let the Fun Begin

A week had passed and Mia and I were getting to know each other well. There had been no indications that I was to fight. Everyone had said that Mia shouldn't have told me about my mum, but I disagreed. I had to know, and now I wanted revenge. I thought this would help, but Grint said I needed practice. But he hadn't taught me anything yet.

I was in my room, jumping on the bed pretending to be three again, when I heard yelling from outside.

There was a frantic knock at my door. Suddenly Mia burst in. She looked like she had just woken up. It was half an hour to another meeting.

"You have to come!" she screamed at me, while I was still on the bed frozen, she turned back quickly and shouted, "*Now!*"

I scrambled off the bed and ran to Mia, who was already hammering on Hendric's door. He came out quickly, looking dazed. Mia grabbed his hand and pulled him with her as she ran for the stairs.

Waiting at the bottom of the stairs were Thorn and Anna. Mia let go of Hendric's hand as she approached the bottom of the stairs.

"Mia, what's wrong?" asked Anna, placing a hand on Mia's heaving shoulder. Mia just looked into her eyes and waited till she got her breath back.

"It's Mary," Mia panted.

Grint came out of the conference room looking ruffled and annoyed by all the noise. He was shaken and ruffled by something.

"Come in!" He boomed and then he disappeared inside the room.

We walked quickly inside the room. Mary's eyes were open wide. She looked a complete mess, beads of sweat dripped over her eyes and her hair was tangled.

"What's going on?" Thorn asked, his face crumpled in irritation.

Grint was staring off into space. Mia was standing beside me looking at Mary, who had fragile moments when she could see the future.

"Morphius is going to try and wake Joshua, but how? Why?" Grint was mumbling to himself. He looked around at everyone, and his eyes settled uncomfortably onto Mary, who had her eyes closed. The room became silent, and everyone backed off.

Mia was tense beside me. I stepped away from her. I knew she could throw me off my feet if I got too close. I already have a lot of bruises from bad experiences with her.

Every time Mary closes her eyes, she sees white; she describes it as like being under a constant white sheet she is unable to get out of, no matter how far she runs under it. She thinks it's something she is meant to see, but it's not quite clear yet. Grint says it could be a side effect from the light that brought her here—the very same light that brought me here when I died.

Mary opened her eyes and lost her balance. Thorn caught her and held her upright.

"Was it still white?" Thorn asked, sitting her down on a chair. We all took our seats.

"No, I saw him, I saw him again. I saw Joshua." She looked up at our faces. "They need him for information, and then they will kill him." Everything went still.

"When?" I asked.

"Not long." Mary got up.

"We need to get him back here before they have a chance to kill him. If he is alive, we can turn him back first and rescue him." Grint looked up to see if anyone dared disagree with his command.

"But you know you can't leave the castle," said Mary. "You are the only one who can turn him back."

Grint was shaking his head before she finished. Everyone was looking at me and Mia. This wasn't happening. Mia was looking at Grint in disbelief.

"You think I can change him back?" I asked in amusement. This was amazing. Morphius sounded ferocious enough. "I can't even fight, and I somehow doubt he is just going to let us waltz in and rescue Joshua."

"You are capable of summoning emotions, and Thorn, Hendric, Anna, and Mia will, of course, be with you." He looked at Mia, who would, of course, disagree with him. She hated the thought of going to meet someone who wished to destroy her without even thinking.

"I can't. I'm not strong enough to fight. I have only just begun learning basic spells. Don't make me go!"

"You do not give yourself enough credit, Shana. You are very powerful—much more so than I anticipated. You do not yet have the ability to defeat Morphius, but I have no doubt you can do this." Grint was confident; there was no doubt on his eyes. Mia nodded in encouragement . . . I wonder how far I could run from the place before they caught me.

"When do we leave?" Anna was not so confident, but she seemed to have some faith in what was happening.

"Soon, I fear we do not have long." Grint was on his feet again, pacing around. You fear! You fear! That's very funny Grint; I just feared the same thing!

"We leave tonight. Any other time will be too late." Mia looked out of the window, and the rest looked doubtful. Hendric looked at me. I had got to know him better over the past week. He told me I looked a bit like my mum.

"We should start to get ready then." Then we all left, possibly to get ready for death. Whoop-dee-bloody doo!

When night approached, we were in the stable saddling our horses, which we were riding only a quarter of the way, because apparently the horses were under some sort of magical oath to never stray too far. This place is mucked up!

The rest would be by foot. *Oh this should be fun!* I walked my horse to the front gate. I was the last to leave. We had all said our goodbyes to Grint and Mary, who wished us luck, which we certainly needed.

I mounted my horse, and we all looked back at the house. I wasn't sure but I think Grint was in the window.

"Come on, we have a long road ahead."

Thorn was placed in the lead, which I thought was silly, considering that all he could do is fight, even though he did have a great build and looked almost indestructible and terrifying when he wanted to. But someone who had multiple tactics should have been leading us.

We rode across the island for a long time in silence. I had never ridden before, but it was surprisingly natural.

We were only interrupted by birds flying overhead and an icy wind blowing past our faces that brought tears to my eyes. I grew weary and I thought of random things. How was I going to do training with Thorn today? I wonder if they are going to stop riding if I need the loo. Does no one here think about personal hygiene? We were not going to be able to shower for ages. I never thought I would ride to rescue someone I didn't even know. It felt bizarre and irrational. When we had rode for what seemed like forever, we dismounted.

"The horses must go back now," said Hendric. He smacked his horse on his rear and sent him running for the trees. He walked over to me and reached out his hand. I took it gracefully. I jumped off my horse and looked over at Mia. She was still on her horse. She had stopped but looked in a daze. Thorn walked in front of her, cleared his throat, and put out his hand for her to get down. She looked down at him blankly and sighed.

"Miss Mia, we really must be swift," stated Thorn in a serious voice.

"I know, but the connection with Grint is fading." She shook her head in despair and jumped off her horse, ignoring Thorn's hand. Then she whispered in her horse's ear, and her horse turned and galloped away. "He said he would give instructions when we dismounted," she continued, "but they are coming through dimly. Should we progress like he said?" she asked Thorn.

"Yes, though it would give me peace of mind if I knew why the connection was fading."

"Me too. That's what I asked the horse to do." She was smiling to herself. *Great, now she was horse whisperer.*

I had almost forgotten this was an island, so it came as a shock when we had to climb into some boats and row across a river. But due to Mia's wonderful ability to manipulate the water, we were able to quickly drift across it. When we got off we docked on a small beach, the beach was so small it was more like a mini sand pit toddlers play in.

We walked away from the beach and onto a path. We followed the path for a long time and headed into deeper parts of the forest, I didn't know any of these types of trees, I don't think they were the normal kind. I walked beside Hendric and Mia. I was nervous the only thing that eased my nerves was being in the forest; the woodland had been my sanctuary for many years since my father had become abusive towards me. Right up until he followed me in there and then nowhere was safe.

Shivers ran down my spine as I thought of my father alone with no daughter and having to face prosecution for murder. I hope he was having the time of his life.

"Mia, why did your mother try to poison you?" I asked in a feeble voice. However much I liked Mia, she still had a temper issue. She laughed at my expression, but then she composed herself.

"I was from a different time than you. You, as I understand it, were from the twenty-first century, but I was from the year 1541. Magic was forbidden, and if anyone found out, I would have been prosecuted for witchcraft." I gave a gasp as I realised she was talking about the time of King Henry VIII. I knew he had no joy in magic, but I didn't understand why her *mother* poisoned her. It made no sense.

Mia took in my expression with delight, which I thought was odd. "I was from a rich family, and my mother saw me move some water in my goblet without touching it. She didn't tell father. The shame of having a witch for a daughter was too great, so she tried to be rid of such a dreadful thing by means of poison."

"But you're so unladylike!" I'd blurted it out without thinking. I heard Thorn laugh his deep throaty laugh up ahead, and Anna stifled a giggle. I shot an apologetic look at Mia, but she was not looking at me but at Thorn, who was still bellowing with laughter, which echoed among the trees. Just then a thick branch fell from the tree onto his foot. He gave a shriek of pain, and now everyone was in floods of laughter—even me. After all this constant chatter, I started to get tired. The darkness of the approaching night would soon be upon us. I gave a loud yawn and leaned against Hendric, who was riding next to me, for support. I was half unconscious. I peered across to Mia. How was she still going? There were no energy drinks in Rezta!

"Do you want to stop and camp?" asked Anna, shooting a weary look at me. I nodded stiffly. I felt detached from my legs. I stumbled a few more steps and fell on the floor.

"I guess we set up camp here." Mia was sitting by her in the hollow of a tree. She looked at the night sky and the bright twinkling lights in the sky. I stretched myself out on the floor, and the leaves around me blew away to create a bare space for me to lie in. That doesn't happen by accident. I looked at Mia; she had her face hidden in the shadows, but the wisps of her golden hair blew out of the shadows. She was looking at me, and her stare made me put my head down and stare at the stars. Mia was a friend, but she had a strange personality—wild, but friendly. She was the first person to treat me as a friend since my mother had left. The thought of my mother brought tears to my eyes. She was so brave and wise, yet I couldn't remember much at all—just that she was kind to me until that cruel night she had been taken away. I was going to get my revenge on Morphius. I was sure of that.

I was having a nightmare that stirred within me every so often. It was about Rezta, and it was the same one I described at the first conference. Usually, it had been dark and murky, but this time I was seeing it as clear as day. The sky was grey with red smoke. I could see everyone, but I wasn't seeing through my eyes. I was looking down on us from above. There was someone new. It was Joshua. I recognised him instantly. Something was terribly wrong. Someone was missing, but I couldn't see who. Then with a jolt of heart-wrenching fear I realised who it was—Mia.

When I awoke I was sweating. I rolled onto my side and pressed my sweating head against the cool earth. I was telling myself it was just a dream; it wasn't real, but I couldn't help thinking it was real. I gave up on going back to sleep and sat up and looked around for the only person who could tell me it wasn't real, but Mia was gone.

I stood up, shaking uncontrollably. I ran to were Hendric lay and shook him violently awake.

"Wake up!" I commanded. He did so unwillingly.

"What?" he said, still groggy from yesterday.

"Mia has gone," I informed him. He did not respond immediately.

"She woke me this morning and said she was going to the water hole down there." He pointed behind him with eyes still shut.

I ran to where he pointed. The wind whipped at my neck, and the cold sweat covered my face. I came to an opening, and my heart slowed as Mia came into view. Her long hair was wet and dripping down her dress. I walked towards her slowly.

"Morning!" She greeted me with a smile, but her face dropped at the state of me. I must have looked a complete mess. "Bad dream?" I nodded; I was looking at her intently, memorising her features like I would never see them again.

"Can I take a dip?" I nodded my head towards the pool that hadn't been there yesterday. She nodded and pulled her hair into a high ponytail.

I dived in with my clothes still on and went under the water until my whole head was submerged. I washed away the sweat and came up feeling refreshed. I looked around at Mia. She had a dagger in her hand. Her back was towards me. I looked up to where she was looking at the sky, and my heart skipped a beat. What had happened to the sky? It was grey with red smoke. I ran out of the pool and stood next to Mia, who was still holding the knife. My mouth was dry. Was my nightmare real? I stood close to Mia, afraid that if I lost sight of her, she would disappear.

"We have to go." Mia had paled drastically; even her lips were chalky white. She was scared, but her eyes were black. She looked like she could kill.

I pulled her arm and we ran to the camp to find the others on red alert. Hendric looked furious and was kicking out the fire.

"Why didn't you tell me about the sky?" he looked at Mia and me with frustration.

"It wasn't like this when I woke up." Mia stood straight in defiance. "Thorn, I didn't see you when I woke up." Mia looked inquisitively at him.

"I was at the watering hole." He didn't look up. How did he know about the waterhole, Mia had just made it?

I knew he was a lying. Mia had just made that watering hole. Mia threw me look. I knew she didn't want me to say anything, so I didn't, only because I trusted her. She ran to Anna, who was packing, and stood beside her. Anna didn't like using her magic. She didn't have much, but it was enough to help her speed up. Mia stretched out her hand, and everything flew into the bag.

Anna picked up the bag and scrambled to her feet without even thanking Mia. Mia pulled a face behind her back and continued running errands. Soon we were packed and running hastily away from the campsite.

"Why are we running?" I was confused.

"We overslept. We must keep up the pace, and we will get there by nightfall." Hendric spoke lightly to me.

I stopped and so did Mia. I was going to leap to my death tonight? There were so many outcomes.

"Why are you stopping?" asked Mia.

"It's just so soon."

"Are you afraid?" I felt cold and sickly scared.

"No," I am terrified, even my father didn't have me this scared.

Mia took my hand and whispered, "We'll be fine, trust me." She smiled. I let go of her hand and ran towards Morphius' castle.

CHAPTER 5

MORPHIUS

It was nightfall, and we were in sight of Morphius' castle. It was black with huge turrets and few windows which made the castle seem daunting to me; the sky above surged with red smoke moving quietly through the night sky, rippling like water above the castle.

I was surprised that there were so few guards outside. We drew closer and hid in the bushes. Something was wrong, very wrong, why have so few guards?

"Thorn, how do we get in?" I couldn't see a door.

"Mia, Hendric, do you think you could try and get in through the back? Shana, Anna and I will look in the front for a way in." I didn't want to be left alone with him. He had lied at camp, and I didn't know why.

"Actually, Shana and I need to stay together," said Mia. Thorn raised his eyebrows. "If we find a way in, you will wait to get caught. Then I will go and find Joshua and turn him back. I can only do that if Shana is with me."

Mia pulled me towards her and Hendric. I went willingly. Thorn ground his teeth. His temper had changed. Perhaps it was the friction of the situation but he seemed much more sinister in this light.

"Fine!" He spluttered the words and sprayed Mia in the face.

"Get stuffed!" She spat the words at Thorn and sprayed him in the face. Hendric and I turned away and started walking around the corner. Mia trailed behind, looking into the bushes in the dark.

"Stop!" Mia whispered. My heart thudded to a halt. I hoped it was an insect or something and Mia was really squeamish. I looked around at Mia, who had her back to the wall. Her head was tilted up. I quickly looked up and saw a dark face leaning out the window looking straight at me.

"Shana, run!" Hendric grabbed my arm and pulled me away from the dark figure that had vanished, no doubt to tell his master.

"Mia, are you there?" I gasped, using my last puffs of air.

"Yes." She forced it out quickly and gasped for air.

My lungs were on fire. I couldn't breathe. I had never been much of an athlete at school.

There were loud noises coming from inside and I heard the stamping of feet.

"Wait!" Mia stopped and looked up at a high open window.

"Hendric, come here!" Mia pulled on his arm and made him stop.

"What the hell are you doing?" Mia waved Hendric's question aside. They began to whisper quickly, leaving me out of the conversation.

I could feel my emotions building up, heat rising on my neck. I knew what was happening. I felt power rise inside. It looked like fear and hatred of Morphius went well together; perhaps I would get my revenge that night. I raised my arm and lifted my hand flat in front of me in the direction of the window. I pulled my hand down, and the open window floated down the side of the castle. Perhaps when we went through, we would come out on the top floor.

"How did you do that?" Mia was shocked. "You aren't meant to be that powerful yet"

"Surprise," I winked at her.

The window reached the bottom, and we all climbed through into the castle.

I was right. As soon as we were through the window, I looked out and saw that we were at the top of the castle.

"Well done, Shana. You did that exceedingly better than I would have ever expected." The voice came from behind me, but Mia and Hendric were in front of me. I turned and saw Thorn with Anna in front of him. There was something wrong, very badly wrong. I looked at Anna, and her face was pale. I looked down at her hip. It was pushing out slightly. It had a knife against it.

"Thorn, what are you doing?" I walked forward slightly, and Anna gave a sharp intake of breathe as the knife drew blood from her hip.

Mia pulled me back towards her and whispered to me, "Remember, he lied down at the watering hole. That is because he was using his own special magic to turn the sky red and grey. It was an indicator to Morphius."

So why did we walk into a trap?

"But he doesn't have magic," I whispered hurriedly.

"Of course I do, you little fool. I'm far stronger than you." He spat on the floor in front of me, and I flinched back. Hendric stepped in front of me.

"Traitor!" Mia spat the words at Thorn and threw one of his daggers at him. This caught him off guard, and he let go of Anna and ducked. She ran to stand next to Hendric.

Mia was fuming next to me and staring into the eyes of Thorn. I could tell all she wanted to do was to kill him right then.

"You cut off the communication between me and Grint." She spat out the words with venom injected into every one.

"Of course, you really should have tried harder to keep in touch. You're a tricky one, I'll give you that," he chuckled and shook his head. She crouched down ready to pounce on him.

"Mia! Oh Mia!"

We all stood still. No one here had opened their mouths, and the voice was empty and cold, with a mocking tone in it. It turned every bone into my body into cement.

Mia stood up straight and looked around to see who had spoken to her.

"Stay absolutely still." Hendric's voice trembled.

There was a huge gust of black smoke that engulfed us. I flew to the floor and covered my head. The smoke whipped around everyone. I saw arms fly around and heard a shrieking noise. I risked a quick look up. Hendric was on the floor next to me with his arm wrapped tightly around my waist; Mia was still standing with one hand in front of her, shielding herself from the black wind, although her hair blew wildly around her face. The wind screeched, and everything froze for a split second. Then the black smoke blew into one area and it became three pillars of smoke. The pillars started to narrow.

I was lifted to my feet by Hendric and pulled behind him. Mia stepped in beside me, and I grasped her hand, remembering my dream.

The pillars of smoke blew out to reveal three figures. One was about my height, with black wet hair that hung loosely around his neck and big muscles. He looked about my own age. The second was larger, with smears of red blood down his cheek, but there was no cut on his face. He had auburn hair with black streaks running through it, matching his goatee.

The third was the biggest and the scariest. His skin was paper-white and cracked everywhere. His lips looked blood-red. Against his skin he wore a long thin draping black cloak that covered his rotting body, but even through his cloak you could see his chest rotting away. Blood oozed from every rancid crack in his face and chest. The odour of pure death leaked from his every pore. His trousers hung loosely around his legs; he was the epitome of death itself.

I held my breath and tightened my grip on Mia's hand.

"Morphius!" Mia pulled out her sword and gave me a quick look. Thorn was smiling in my direction.

"A new follower?" Hendric indicated the one with the black hair, who stuck his chin out in indignation.

Morphius smirked, and the dry white skin around his mouth cracked wider. Flecks of skin crumbled to the ground.

"This is Diran. He has proven himself beyond all measure to be a very powerful and useful being to have around." I shuddered; he had a light voice that sliced through the air. "You remember Nistal." He gestured towards the tall bloke with auburn hair and goatee.

"You have no doubt come to rescue Joshua, and with that you brought me the help I needed." He was now coming closer to Hendric, egging him on.

Mia stepped forward; I reached out to stop her.

"Young Mia, no doubt, I bet you really want to kill me." He laughed at the idea. "You are powerful, even more so than anyone I have ever met, but not more powerful than me." He waved his hand, and her sword flew across the hall.

"I don't have to be more powerful than you. Neither do I want to kill you. I want to know what you're offering him." She nodded at Thorn, who was talking silently to Nistal.

"Power, my dear Mia. Did you expect me to offer anything less to Thorn? You should think more of me; perhaps we could be friends." I froze. In my dream I didn't see Mia. What if she became friends with him?

Thorn smirked at me. "Your dream, ah yes." He laughed. Was he in my head? "I needed to track Mia down after she disappeared in the morning so I simply invaded your mind while you were sleeping. I knew you would seek her after the dream, so it was a simple thing to do really." You did what? "You led me straight to her, letting me know it was safe to turn the sky red." Thorn's face was contorted into a malice smile. "I needed to know that Mia was going to be out the way, or she would have blown my head sky high." Thorn chuckled at Mia's fuming expression.

Mia surprised no one by spitting in Thorn's face. Hendric grabbed her by the waist and threw her to his side into Anna.

"You will be sorry for that, you little cow!" Nistal picked up his sword and took a step forward. Morphius put out his hand, signalling him to stop.

"You think you can defeat me with these?" He pointed at me and Hendric.

"Shana is more powerful than her mother. You don't stand a chance." I felt my stomach hit the ground and my head go numb. Morphius turned his attention from Mia to me. I looked at him in horror.

"You are no doubt powerful, but you are inexperienced. Your mother was foolish in thinking she could defeat me." He turned his back on me and signalled to Thorn, Nistal, and Diran. They walked towards us slowly.

"Bring them." Nistal grabbed my arms behind my back and pulled them hard. I gasped at the pain. Morphius pointed a finger at Anna, and she was thrown into his arms. Thorn grabbed Hendric by the neck and threw him forward. Hendric did not retaliate. He knew it was a lost cause, but Mia did not. Diran took hold of Mia's hand and pulled her arm sharply behind her. She used her free hand to turn around and punch him in the face. He staggered back, and Mia stretched her arm out and raised her hand. He doubled forward in pain, his handsome features quivering. Then Mia gasped and collapsed forwards. Diran caught her as she fell in his arms. I looked around to see Morphius glowering at Mia.

"There will be none of that here!" He turned his back, and his cloak fluttered around the corner after him. Diran held Mia in his arms for a moment, partially in shock, and then he stood her up. He took her by the waist and led her after Morphius. I felt empty; if she did anything else like that, she would be killed. Diran should be careful, but all things considered, he was being the nicest out of all of them. I should remember, though, that he was on Morphius' side and he wanted humanity dead as well.

We rounded the corner and went into a bright room full of creatures cheering "Morphius" as he took his place on his throne above everyone. He raised his hand to silence them. And they quickly shut up.

"These humans have attempted to rescue the boy." There was laughter and booing. I felt as though I was in a pantomime. I looked around at Mia, who stood on the other side of Morphius' throne. Diran held her close to him. She was still struggling in his arms. "Well I think we should give them a chance, so they don't feel too pathetic." Morphius laughed, chunks of skin fell from his face as laugh lines dug into his flesh. "Bring out the boy!"

Double doors at the back were flung open, and four small green things pushed and pulled a gold statue of a boy into the room—Joshua, no doubt. They pushed him to the middle of the room, formed a circled around him, and started to murmur strange unknown words.

Morphius stood up and beckoned Nistal and Diran forward. Nistal pulled my right arm tighter, making me gasp and blink back tears. He forced me down some stairs that hugged the furthest wall of the room. Mia was down there already, drained of colour and staring at the statue. Diran pushed her, and she stumbled forward and caught herself. Nistal pushed me to the ground and walked away. I hugged the arm he had yanked and sat on the floor.

The murmuring stopped and they all looked towards Morphius. He was now standing at the foot of the stairs with Diran and Nistal on either side of him.

"Mia, Shana, you will turn him back to his pitiful human self." He looked at me and then at Mia.

"What if we don't?" I asked, summoning a lot of courage.

"Then they will die." He pointed a finger up at the ledge where his throne stood. I followed where he was pointing. Thorn was standing on the ledge with both his arms in the air. I looked to see what he was levitating. To my disgust, he had Anna and Hendric both in the air with their hands around each other's necks. So our choices were to destroy Rezta or to defy Morphius and allow Hendric and Anna to die at each other's hands. The choices weren't great, but there was another option. It wasn't going to be easy, but we could try. We could turn back Joshua and escape, but we also had to get Hendric and Anna back. It was going to be hard, but I was going to try.

I pulled myself to my feet and walked across the floor to Mia. She was looking off into the distance, possibly coming up with a plan.

"Don't try anything funny," Thorn boomed, "or they get it!" He squeezed his hands a centimetre tighter, and both Hendric and Anna made a choking sound. I started to panic and looked at Mia; she looked at me with sad eyes.

"You know what to do," Mia said under her breath. I nodded weakly. Was this it? Was this how I was to die? I pushed my feelings to the front of my mind, and my neck warmed up from the necklace, which was now glowing brighter than I had ever seen it.

I took her hand in mine, and we closed our eyes. I started to murmur all kinds of things that just popped into my head. I heard a cracking noise from Mia, and my eyes popped open.

"Mia, what's wrong? Did you see something when you closed your eyes again?"

"The mansion has been invaded. Grint managed to escape but . . . Mary—she's dead."

I stared at her in horror. I couldn't weep; I had forgotten how to. Mary—she had been so kind, and now . . . dead? For so long I had been thinking about getting out. Now Mia, Joshua, and I were leaving.

There was a loud bang and everyone fell to the floor, except for Mia. She was up on her feet and dragging me with her. She ran to the place where the gold statue had once been. Now there was a boy, who looked shaken and stared wide-eyed at me and Mia.

"Thank you," was all he could utter before everyone had stood up again and started looking at Joshua.

He looked around the room and saw Morphius. He froze in mock horror and gasped.

"Why, if it isn't old friends come to say hello!" He indicated Diran. "And, of course, incredibly old friends." He looked at Morphius in mock surprise. "What did he offer you, Diran, for you to turn your back on old friends?"

Diran stepped forward, ignoring Morphius' warning to stay put. "Power, my friend, and lots of it." He winked at Joshua and grinned. Joshua also smiled. Then they walked towards each other and hugged.

"Diran, what are you doing?" Morphius had gone a light shade of pink. It must take a lot to turn his white face pink. Wonder if I could get it to go peach, he might have a seizure.

"Isn't it obvious? We now have equal numbers. Thorn betrayed them, and now I betray you." He took a mock bow, and Mia gasped. Thorn was now fully clenching his fist, while Hendric and Anna had their eyes closed. Mia stretched her hand up, as did Joshua and Diran. I felt kind of left out. Hendric's and Anna's arms dropped, and their eyes fluttered open. Mia dropped her arm, and they fell in lightly in front of me. I hugged Hendric and Anna. Mia came to stand beside me, along with Joshua and Diran.

Then we turned to face Morphius, who had now gone a little bit redder than peach. He had gone a scary coral colour now.

I grasped Anna's hand and stepped back.

"You will pay for the humiliation you have caused me, boy!" Morphius spat every word at the floor.

"You will pay for every life you have ruined!" Mia stood her ground without quivering.

Morphius turned to look directly at me. I quivered, and his glare softened.

"You don't have to die, Shana." His voice was honeyed and hypnotic. "You can join me and be free to do as you please. No one you care about will be hurt anymore." Images of Mary and my mother poured into my brain.

"What about Mary and mother and all other people you killed? Did you give them the same option?" I yelled at him across the tiny space that separated us. I had forgotten my fear and could feel nothing but anger. My head was pounding with rage, and my ears felt hot.

I heard a gasp escape Joshua, Hendric, and Anna. I had forgotten they didn't know. Thorn chuckled, his deep throaty laugh, which made me slightly uncomfortable. I so badly wanted to punch him hard in the face.

"You . . . killed Mary?" Joshua stared at Morphius in hateful disbelief. My temper rose and I felt the scorching glow on my neck, but it was a red glow this time, not orange. I shook in rage and stared in outrage at Morphius. Mia backed off, as did everyone around me. I heard popping noises, but I did not break my stare with Morphius.

He was now staring back hard at me. A black sheet covered his eyes. I pushed my eyelids closer, and a huge rumble came from all around. A huge chunk of rock fell from the ceiling and landed in front of me and Morphius. All around us pieces of rock were falling, and we all knew this was the only chance we were going to get to escape. I ran with Hendric and Anna at my side. We ran through the double doors at the back. Mia flattened a few soldiers that got in the way. I felt sorry for anyone who got on her bad side, I really did.

We followed Joshua as we ran through the halls. I heard loud yells behind us, and we picked up the pace to outrun the soldiers.

"Joshua, where are the real guards?" Diran puffed from up ahead. What did he mean by real guards?

"They only get summoned if we pose a threat."

"Great! So we're not a threat. That means they have us already taken care of." Mia heaved from Diran's side.

"So they think. But they don't have Shana on their side, do they?" puffed Joshua.

We ran through some double doors. Diran, Hendric, and Joshua swiftly closed the doors behind us. There were no other ways for them to enter, and none for us to escape through. We were trapped!

I glanced at Hendric and Anna, who were puffing and panting so hard that they looked as though they would keel over in a minute. I was soon wheezing, and the sounds of footsteps were growing louder. I fell to my knees, and they all turned to look at me while I was on the ground. I felt hot tears sting my eyes. My stomach had gone so tight that I felt like vomiting.

Joshua and Diran pulled me to my feet. I could hardly hold the weight of my body on my shaking legs.

"What are we going to do?" asked Mia, who was standing against a wall chewing her nails.

I looked around at my surroundings. We were in a tall wide room. Apart from a few shelves filled with liquids, there was a pool in the middle of the room filled with clear blue water. This was odd for a filthy castle. I coughed deeply and then threw up. I looked up, and tears spilled out from my eyes as I remembered Mary's death. For the first time since I had come here I felt empty, and everything around me seemed dead and quiet. I stood up straight and went over to the pool. I got down on my knees and peered in. It was so strange. It was so shallow, and yet from a distance it looked never-ending. I dipped my hand in and it went straight through the bottom of the pool. I toppled forward, expecting my hand to hit the bottom that wasn't actually there. I hit the surface of the water so hard that the air was knocked out of me. The water was so cold and dark that it hurt. I tried kicking up but found my legs numb after running. I closed my eyes and tried to find the heat inside that activated the necklace. I opened my eyes, but nothing happened. I was staring at a long passageway in front of me. I clenched my stomach in pure agony as I began to suffocate.

I opened my mouth in a gasp of pain and gagged as water gushed into my mouth. I threw myself back against the wall and hurled my head back to scream in agony, but I couldn't. I saw a blurred shape in front of me dive into the water. As it grew bigger, I could make out Joshua's outline as he drew nearer. I let my head flop as it was now so heavy. My sight blurred over, and my eyes began to close. I had to fight to keep them open, but they continued to grow heavier. Another ferocious rip in my stomach made me try to scream out in pain.

I stared ahead, waiting for death to come. I reached out in one last attempt to swim, but my arms just drifted in front of me, motionless. A shape appeared in front of me and came close to my face. He pressed his lips firmly on mine and blasted air into my mouth. I lost sight of the tunnel as he pulled me firmly to him and began to swim up, blasting more air into my mouth as we went. We finally broke the surface, and I pulled away to gasp fresh air. I still held on to him tightly in fear I would go back down. He swam to the edge, and I was pulled away from Joshua. I trembled fiercely and clung tightly to my legs, rocking back and forth in an attempt to get dry. Mia sat down beside me and cuddled me so I could absorb some of her warmth. I cuddled her back.

She was like my sister now, and there was nothing I wanted more right now than to be comforted and warm.

There was a banging at the door and cries of delight as Morphius' soldiers realised there was no escape.

"Shana, what happened?" Anna was looking down worriedly at me, not even giving a glance at the door.

"I tried to swim up, but my legs couldn't move. I just kept sinking." I remembered the passageway and wondered if it was real. She looked up and went to Hendric, probably to discuss means of escape.

Diran looked at me, puzzled. "What?" Joshua came to stand beside Diran.

"I think I saw a way out. There was a tunnel. It was wide enough to swim down, but I might have been imagining it." I looked away at Hendric; he was looking at me too.

"How far down is the passageway?"

"I don't know," I answered honestly.

Anna walked towards us with Hendric. "It could be our only way of escape." Anna looked at me, probably doubting whether I could make the swim. I knew I couldn't—I felt too weak. I looked to the ground, ashamed that I was the one holding them back from the only possible way of escape.

I tried to stand up, and Mia helped me gain balance. Hell, if I was going to die, it was not going to be in this place.

"I'll try and make it, but if I can't, don't wait. I don't think they'll wait forever to break the doors in." Everyone smiled, and so did I. We walked to the pool, and as we reached the edge, the door started to glow a bright white.

"*Now!*" shouted Hendric. We all jumped, but this time I was aware I would go straight through. I took a gulp of air before my head went under. I opened my eyes and saw five shapes below me. I moved my legs, this time with success. I followed after my friends. I saw them turn and one by one disappear. I hurried after them but found I was still weak. I tried to push my legs further, but I only went forward a little. I saw a figure in front of me. The figure swam closer until I could make out Joshua, even though he was still a blur. I could see his outstretched arm. I stretched my arm out and grabbed his hand. It felt soft, and I clung to it. Even though it was cold, I somehow found it to be warm. He was probably using magic to generate heat. Still grasping his hand, I kicked my legs in a motion to go forward. We swam together to the tunnel I had seen. I had no idea how big it was or if we would be able to reach the end without drowning. I kicked my legs harder, as did Joshua. I found myself once again going dizzy.

I looked ahead frantically for an opening, but I could see none. My heart skipped a beat as I realised we were swimming to a dead end. I looked at Joshua, who had a puzzled expression on his face. He looked at me confused, and we pushed ahead harder than before. I wondered where the others were. I looked around for an opening, but none was to be seen. We reached the end and looked around. I was now turning light-headed. I looked up and noticed the ceiling ripple. I pointed up at the ceiling for Joshua to look at. He looked up and reached out his hand. He turned and smiled, and then we were swimming up and through the ceiling. It was just like the one at the beginning of the pool. I looked up and saw a light up ahead, the surface. I smiled with relief that I wasn't going to drown. We hit the surface, and I gulped fresh air. I looked around to find we had surfaced outside. Mia was ringing her hair and talking to Diran. Hendric and Anna were drying themselves with a spell. My legs felt numb, and I was so exhausted.

I swam to the edge of the lake and climbed out, with help from Mia and Diran. Joshua heaved himself onto the bank with no help and lay panting on his side. Diran went over to talk to him. Mia sat next to me and pressed her dry hand to my forehead, and I began to tingle all over. When Mia took her hand away, I was dry as a bone.

"I won't ask how, but thanks!" I grinned at Mia.

I looked around; we were somewhere quite unfamiliar.

"Where are we?" I turned to Mia, who was turning away from the direction of the two talking boys.

"I don't know." She smiled and walked to Anna, who had been abandoned by Hendric who had gone over to talk to Diran. I was standing by myself and looking at the world around me. My thoughts dwelled on Grint. If Mary was dead, where was he? Was he safe?

I closed my eyes and emptied my mind and thought of nothing until I could feel the glow on my neck. I opened my eyes and smiled to myself in triumph. I walked over to the lake and placed my outstretched hand on the surface. The necklace was glowing, and it became hotter as I thought of Grint and Mary. There was a burst of white light from the lake as a picture started to form. It was of Mary, still and lifeless. I sniffed back the tears and wiped the surface with my hand across the lake. As the picture rippled out, a new picture formed. It was a picture of Grint. He was surrounded by lights and many people. The place was not a place I recognised. I smiled, knowing he was safe. Many of the people were in a discussion with him, laughing and playing. A new figure was appearing. It was that of a girl of the same age as me and Mia. She had thick blonde hair, which shined like water reflecting the sun. I held my breath as she cast her eyes around and looked directly at me. She stared at me as if she knew I was there. Everyone stopped talking to stare at this girl of pure elegance. The water rippled and shook, and the images were gone.

Where was that place? Who was that person?

I got up and turned around, thinking of the bright place. I turned into Anna who was standing behind me. Her brow was furrowed; no one else seemed to have noticed what I had been doing.

"How much did you see" I enquired. Anna didn't say anything. "Do you know who the girl was?"

She shook her head. I started to walk away from Anna and towards the group, who were beginning to argue.

"Don't tell them what you saw," whispered Anna, swinging around and grabbing my arm. "I shall tell them where he is, but you must promise not to tell what you saw." Anna had a look of concern on her face—except it was more than concern; it was fear. I nodded, knowing something must be wrong, because otherwise she wouldn't have said it.

I pulled my arm away and stared towards the loudly quarrelling group.

"We have to move away from here while we still can!" Hendric was blue in the face as he argued with Mia.

"That pool changes course every minute. We are probably halfway across Rezta by now. He can't follow us with that pool; it was designed for an easy escape." Mia crossed her arms and glowered at Hendric.

"Exactly! It's too easy. He could follow us. Why the hell do you think he would give us an easy exit?"

"It wasn't designed for us; it was designed for him. He never thought we would use it."

Hendric fumed, completely at a loss for words.

"Joshua, can you seal off the exit?" Diran looked at the pool as if waiting for a ripple to flow across the surface.

Joshua nodded and turned towards the lake. I watched to see what he did. He closed his eyes and started mumbling.

The water started bubbling and turned frothy. Joshua opened his eyes and came back over to stand beside me.

Joshua smiled at me. I felt a little tingle go through me and gave an awkward smile back. "He won't be coming through there any time soon."

Chapter 6
Anger All Around

We made camp beside the lake. We made up for the lost bags with water beds that Mia managed to create. I don't mean the usual water beds; I mean actual beds made of water which I found to be awesome.

I had so many questions. What tied me to this necklace? ; Why did Anna not want anyone knowing about what I saw in the pool? Where was Grint? Who was that girl?

Anna was sitting on a log, gazing at the full moon. It was time for some answers. I climbed off my water bed and walked over to her. I sat on the log next to her, but she continued to look at the pool, ignoring me.

"Where is he, Anna?" I asked.

"Who?" She sounded like an echo.

"Grint," I hissed the name. She was acting so weird.

"He is in Mulbeta."

"Where's Mulbeta?" I was starting to get impatient.

"It's the biggest city in Rezta, one of the first places Morphius attacked."

"Why did Grint go there then, if Morphius took it over?"

"Mulbeta was won over by strangers, a very powerful family. The girl Etrina, whom you saw, is part of the family. She is the younger sister of two brothers."

"Did she see me?" Anna nodded with a grave expression.

"Why is that bad?"

"It isn't bad. There is just a story that the families of old used to tell about a girl who would come and liberate Rezta. It said she would lose everything. We thought it was the young Etrina, but now you come, so powerful and having lost so much. We know not of whom the story tells."

"Who are Etrina's brothers?"

"The eldest is two years older than you. He is Prince Frederick. The prince is destined to take over Mulbeta when his father dies. The younger, Prince Otius is one year older than you and is the leader of the new army."

"What about their parents?"

She cleared her throat and her eyes softened. "Their mother died and their father takes care of them now. His name is

Sepal Artimos, and he is the king of Mulbeta." Admiration shook her words.

"Are we going to Mulbeta?"

"Not yet!!" She stood and stared hard at me. Everyone stopped talking and looked over at us. We looked back at our staring friends. I got up and looked at Anna. I stared at her for a while and then walked towards the woods.

How dare she yell at me? What the hell was she hiding from me? And why couldn't we go to Mulbeta and get Grint? I had one hell of a lot of questions. For god's sake, she yelled at me, and now everyone would want to know why she yelled at me, and I wouldn't be able to tell because I didn't know why. God, life sucked!

I looked around the clearing I had just walked into. It was sunset, and the woods were beautiful. The orange sky beamed off of the deep green leaves. It was so quiet. I could hear nothing but the sound of my own breathing. I walked on through the woods until I came to another clearing. It was serene. It had a massive lake and mountains just across the lake reaching as high as you could see. The water was clear, manipulating the oranges and yellows of the sun that were dancing on the surface of the lake. I had to go in the water—it was just so gorgeous.

My clothes were black and muddy. I was so tired and cold. I walked to the edge of the lake and jumped into the water. It splashed high above me, and then I was covered in cool water. I opened my eyes and saw just as clearly as I could see on land. How weird I could never see this on Earth! It was so magical, but even when I was dead, why could I never be happy? Why couldn't I just stay here forever in peace?

I thought about my father. He was a twisted psychopath who killed me whilst finding it humorous. I wondered what had happened to him. Perhaps by some happy chance he was lying dead in a shallow grave.

I started swimming up for air. I hit the surface and took huge gulps of air. It was so beautiful as the last beams of the sun were hitting my face.

"It sure is beautiful."

I spun round to see Joshua sitting on the bank, looking at me.

I smiled at him. He looked stunning and rugged on the bank all ruffled with a smile on his face.

"I know it's amazing." I wasn't just talking about the scenery.

"You look beautiful in this light." He smiled, and I felt my face grow hot. "Tough day, huh?" He spoke casually. I wondered if he knew how fast my heart was beating right now.

"Yeah, it was unexpected. I never thought that Thorn would betray us, even though Mia didn't like him." I wondered how much she hated him now. She has a seriously bad temper, I was actually scared for Thorn, as weird as that sounds. Mia was going to do horrible things to him.

"I didn't think Mia did. She was cursing fire and hell about him before Anna yelled at you." He raised his eyebrows and his eyes went soft. "Why did she yell at you? What did you do?" His tone was too sly and calculating for my liking.

Oh damn! He was cute—and a manipulating bastard!

"If that's why you're here, you can bugger off." I went under the water again. I hated this. He was trying to get bloody information out of me. I was so out of this freak show. I decided I was going to go to Mulbeta and get Grint back myself, and then I was going to kill Morphius for all the pain he had caused me and the restless dark nights back home, taking away the only escape I had left.

Home. For the first time I wanted to go home, not to my prick of a dad, but Earth, maybe to a new country where no one would know me and I could have friends and lead a happy normal life.

The water had turned dark. I started to swim away. I was going to do this myself. My powers would help me, even alone, with no questions from everybody else, but also with no answers of my own. I would do this.

I kept swimming until I grew weak. I broke the surface and saw that I was at the other side of the lake. That was a little weird that I had managed to swim over here. Awesome! I grabbed for the bank, absolutely exhausted, and collapsed in a heap.

CHAPTER 7
JAMIE MEETS KIM

Jamie was sitting in his geography class, listening to some girls in front of him bitching about some boy who wouldn't go out with one of them. He lay back in his chair and started his scribbling again. He kept blowing his blonde hair out of his way.

"Hey, that looks good!" Jamie looked up to see his friend Ethan looming over his shoulder.

"Thanks." Jamie looked back at his work and tilted his head. "I'm not sure what it is, though."

Ethan grabbed the book from behind and looked at it. "It looks like a cave with a pool in the middle of it—pretty!" He fluttered his eyelashes mockingly at Jamie.

"Shut up!" Jamie grabbed the book from Ethan.

The class finished, and Jamie packed his books away.

"Hey, are you coming?" Ethan jumped on Jamie's table and crossed his legs.

"I'm coming!" Jamie pushed Ethan off the table and walked out through the back door. Jamie and Ethan walked behind the science block and went to some benches where they normally hung out. They always hung out there because the woods were right in front of them so that they could quickly slip out if they needed to bunk off next lesson, which they both often did.

Jamie looked around and saw the person he had been looking for—the new girl in school, Kim. She was so secretive, but yesterday when Jamie went jogging, he found out why.

Jamie had seen Kim whilst on a run. She seemed to know where she was going, which was strange because she was new to this area, so he followed her. Kim was walking completely off any path and through the densely packed woods. Jamie had never been through these parts of the woods and was surprised that she just knew where to go. The woods thinned out and then there was a huge open area. Jamie hid behind a tree and watched Kim as she walked casually over to a huge boulder. Jamie pulled out a pack of raisins and began to nibble on them. Kim closed her eyes and began mumbling. Jamie stopped eating and watched curiously as this strange girl made herself stranger. Kim opened her eyes, and her eyes turned pure white. Jamie stood frozen to the spot. Kim walked to the boulder and put her hand on it. The boulder shimmered where her hand touched it and shook all over. An ear-piercing shriek echoed around the woods. Jamie covered his eyes and looked around for the person who had screamed, and when he looked back, Kim had gone and the boulder had shrunken into rocks.

"Jamie!" Sarah yelled from across the field, breaking the thought of the frightening memory. Sarah was a petite and irritating thing that you wanted to squish whenever she opened her mouth, but boys liked her for the fact that she was easy.

"Hi, Sarah." Ethan waved at Sarah, flashing a heart-breaking smile. Sarah hugged Ethan and blew a kiss to Jamie.

"Hey, do you two want to go to the village after school?" her voice was shrill and nasal and made you want to punch her right in the kisser. But Ethan seemed besotted with her.

"Nah, I can't. I have to go and train for athletics competition after school." Jamie sighed. He didn't like staying after school, especially when he wanted to go somewhere else.

"What? Is Edgbarrow having another competition?" Sarah looked at Ethan. "Can you come?"

"Yeah, sure, I'll go with you." Ethan winked at her. Jamie rolled his eyes.

Jamie looked over at Kim. She was looking back at him. He must be going crazy, because she looked older today than yesterday. When Kim had vanished so suddenly in the woods, Jamie had walked over to the shrunken rocks and looked around for Kim, but she was nowhere to be seen. Jamie crouched down by the rocks and started to pull them away. He fell backwards, scattering raisins everywhere. He got back up and dusted himself off. He crouched down again and pulled more away. Jamie could see they were covering a hole. He heaved the rocks to the side, scattering dust everywhere, and when the dust cleared, Jamie looked into the hole. When he couldn't see the bottom, he picked up some stones and dropped them down the hole. Jamie waited for five minutes. When he couldn't hear the clang of the rock hitting the bottom, he got edgy wondering about what he'd just seen Kim do. Perhaps he really was going crazy.

After training at school Jamie went home and to his room. He emptied his school bag and started to put in rope, a torch, some cereal bars, and water.

A little rattle at the door stopped him. The door opened a bit, and his little sister Ella stood in the doorway. She was wearing her traditional baggy tracks and white vest; her big round blue eyes stared you into feeling guilty. "Jamie, do you want to play with me?" Jamie fumbled in his bag and brought out a chocolate bar, which he handed to Ella.

"When I get back, I can play." Ella was already attacking the bar and just nodded.

"Mum, I'm going out for a bit!" Jamie yelled into the kitchen and went out without waiting for a reply.

Jamie started to jog through the woods as he did every afternoon. Jamie knew where he was going, and this time he wouldn't hesitate to go through with it, this time. Jamie entered the clearing he had followed Kim to. The ground was still covered with the raisins he had dropped the last time. He walked over to the pile of rocks.

Jamie popped the bag off; he took the torch out and looked down the hole. He couldn't see anything, but he could hear running water. He put the torch down and took the rope out of his bag. He tied one end to the closest tree, which wasn't that close, and the other to his waist. Jamie put his bag back on and walked back to the hole. He picked up the torch again. Jamie turned around ready to abseil down. He leaned back and started to walk down. The hole was narrower than expected, and he found it hard to move, but he kept going anyway. The tunnel suddenly opened up, leaving him dangling from the rope. Jamie looked down and caught his breath; underneath him was a gigantic pool.

Jamie looked back up the rope. The hole at the top seemed further away than he remembered. Jamie's grip was loosening on the rope, and he began to slip. He closed his eyes and let go of the rope. He plunged under the sapphire water. He tried to kick up but only sank further down. Jamie began to struggle violently under the pressure. A pillar of water shot up from the bottom of the pool and covered him. It started to twirl around Jamie, throwing golden specks and getting faster as it spun. Jamie struggled against the water, trying to free himself, but the water spun faster around him, pulling him into the centre of the column. The pillar vibrated violently, and the ground underneath the pillar began to crumble and turn to bronze dust, until a hole formed inside the bottom of the pillar of water. The pillar stopped, and everything went quiet. Then the pool started to rumble, and Jamie was quickly sucked through the hole.

Jamie was pulled through a great maze of rough stony tunnels, scraping his arms along the sides as he was dragged through. An amazing bright light formed at the end of the tunnel Jamie was shooting down. Jamie was pulled into the light.

Inside the light, Jamie gasped in a huge amount of air and found that he was bone dry, as if he had never been in the pool. He was floating on his back through the misty light.

Everything went quiet. Jamie felt something cold against his back; it felt like cold stone. Jamie started to hear noises around him. It sounded like voices. "What happened to him?" cried one voice.

"Who is it?" asked another.

"Oh crap! How did he get here?" Jamie recognised this voice.

Jamie opened his eyes. His vision was blurry, but he made out a number of figures looming over him. "Kim?" Jamie mumbled.

"Kim, how does he know you? Have you seen him before?" A boy's voice came into the conversation.

Jamie felt a cold hand on his forehead. He blinked and his sight cleared. Above him stood a dark-haired boy with the darkest eyes he'd ever seen, and kneeling next to him was Kim. Her long curly hair came down onto Jamie's torso. She was wearing a white tube top, a brown jacket, and brown leather trousers, and strangely enough she had a sword resting beside her.

"Shut up, Spencer." Kim sounded seriously peeved.

"Kim, what happened?" Jamie tried to sit up, but his head was pounding.

"Kim, is it too late to send him back?" Spencer knelt beside Kim.

A huge crowd was gathering behind the two of them. Kim stood behind Jamie and nodded. "It closed when he came through."

Kim whispered something to Spencer.

"He can't stay here," Spencer tried to whisper to Kim.

"I know that, but what other choice do I have?" Spencer sighed and helped Jamie to his feet.

Jamie looked round and found himself on a small stone street with strange wooden buildings on either side that looked like cottages. "Where am I?" Jamie's voice was croaky and hoarse.

"That doesn't matter. It is how you got here that worries me." Kim was walking in front. Everybody moved out of her way and closer to the houses. Jamie was helped to walk by Spencer and was led down the street behind Kim. Jamie was painfully aware that his ribs were throbbing and his arms were in shreds.

Looking around, Jamie could see that Kim stood out a lot. She was the only female here not wearing a dress. Kim turned the corner and walked into a small open area outside a building. It was dark out, but it was an eerily familiar dark. Jamie looked up at the shop. The sign said "Sincos".

"What a strange name!" Jamie muttered this slightly under his breath in case he might offend someone.

"Yes, it is," Kim spoke from inside the shop, and Spencer laughed.

"Oi, Detrix, where are you!?" Kim bellowed across the store.

"I thought I told you to not yell in my store, Kim." A young man appeared from around a bookshelf and lent against its side.

"You did, but I need your help." Kim turned to look at Jamie hobbling into the shop leaning against Spencer. "Quickly."

Detrix stepped closer to Jamie and Spencer. He looked at Jamie and back at Kim. "Is he from that other world?" Detrix's eyebrows closed into a frown.

"Yup, is there any way to get him back?" Spencer pulled Jamie to a settee and turned to face Kim and Detrix.

"Wait, what do you mean?" Jamie spoke drowsily "'that other world'?"

He was ignored by everyone.

"According to my recent readings, there is no way to go back until the next star streaming in six months' time." Detrix moved closer to Kim and Spencer, trying to get a better look at Jamie, who shifted uncomfortably.

Then Jamie realised. "*What!* I have to stay here for six months!?" Spencer and Detrix looked at him with sudden acknowledgment. Kim walked to a shelf and pulled out some boxes.

Detrix walked forward towards Jamie. "Well, the thing is, you were selected by Rezta."

"No, he wasn't." Kim didn't even look up from the boxes; she just continued to fumble in them. "I brought him here." Kim said this as if it was logical and nothing unusual.

"You what!?" all three shouted out at once.

Kim looked up and put the boxes down on a nearby table. "You saw me, didn't you?" She was speaking directly to Jamie. "In the woods." Jamie nodded and felt sick, but he kept a straight face. "Well, I couldn't leave you there to twitter on about me like a mad person. Seeing as I may go back in six months." Kim shrugged and went back to her books.

Jamie shook his head. "What the hell. What is Rezta? How did you bring me here? What the fuck is going on?" Jamie sat up and walked over to Kim.

Kim looked him up and down, wondering if he was going to pass out.

"First, Rezta is the world you will be in for the next six months. Second, if you use the few brain cells you have, you would kind of grasp that I used magic, the same thing I used to shrink the boulder."

Jamie's head was buzzing. "So, you, well, um . . ." Jamie went pale and swayed. Kim rolled her eyes and turned to another box.

Spencer held Jamie and guided him back to the chair.

"Kim, you could have been more delicate with his feelings." Detrix lectured Kim, who was completely ignoring him.

Detrix sighed. "On a different note, I suppose you didn't get it?" Kim didn't reply and continued to fish through some more labelled boxes.

"There is no more information for you to read. Just face it. The only hope we had of killing Morphius was stolen by the thief." Detrix threw his hands up in a flurry of emotion.

Jamie turned to Spencer, who was sitting on the other side of the settee. "Who is Morphius?"

Spencer looked at Jamie with the blackest of expressions on his face. "Morphius is the thing you most fear when you close your eyes. He is a cold-blooded killer with many allies spread across Rezta, none of them known. But we have an ally ourselves in Morphius' army. There is only one thing on his mind right now; he is trying to exterminate all of Reztarians or make slaves of us. Rumours of hope came and went in a couple of months, rumours of a girl known as the chosen one, but she has gone missing. She was said to be our hero. That's why Kim came to your world in search of the missing piece of—"

"Spencer, can you please come and help me with this?" Spencer sighed and looked at Jamie.

"Tell you later." Spencer got up and walked over to Kim and her growing mess of boxes.

Jamie stayed lying on the settee and watched Kim and Spencer rummage through the boxes. Kim threw box after box onto the pile. "Here it is!" Spencer tossed a book at Kim. "Why can you never remember where you put it?"

"Because I am never here long enough to remember. I have other more important things to remember." Kim opened the book and sighed. "No, I got it right. So why—"

"Huh, what are you on about?" Jamie leant up on his elbow.

"Shut up." Kim didn't even look up and kept rapidly turning pages.

Spencer sighed. "Ignore her. She probably hasn't gotten a lot of sleep, and as you may have noticed, she has little patience."

Detrix sighed and walked over to a chair across the table and facing Jamie. "Would you like me to tell you the story, or are you tired?"

Jamie sighed and lay down. "Go ahead. I haven't had a bedtime story for a long time."

"Very well, then." Detrix looked at the book. Kim held the book so tightly her knuckles looked like they would tear through the flesh.

"No, you cannot have it! I'm using it" Kim didn't even look up. Wow, she had a short temper, thought Jamie.

"No matter. I can remember the story anyway." Detrix grinned.

Detrix put on his spectacles and relaxed in his chair and faced Jamie.

"Well here it goes. This story is the legend of Krystith."

Chapter 8
Story Time

"As a young girl Krystith was the most powerful being in the whole of Rezta. She was a true warrior and protector of Rezta. Her entire life was about protecting Rezta; it was all she ever did. Krystith was dedicated to protecting Rezta for many years, using magic to slow her aging down, but she became very tired of war and battle and tried to find a way out of it, so she could live her life the way she wanted.

On a night of star streaming, she was taken to the stars, and there she found an old magician. She asked him, "Is there any way to pass along my powers and make a new protector?" He gave her five clear gems cut into ovals with pinched ends. The magician taught her a spell. She repeated the spell, and the gems turned an orange colour and joined to make a star.

She placed the star into the hilt of her sword, around the gems and on the hilt metal streaks were pressed in to form swirls and spirals all over the hilt.

The gems transformed her sword into the most powerful, lethal, and deadly weapon Rezta has ever seen, but only a hero could

*wield the sword. She took the sword back to Rezta and left,
never to be seen again.*

*Reztarians from all over came to see the sword, but anyone
who came too close felt intense pain and collapsed . . . dead. A
building was built around the sword, and no one was allowed
near it, until one man claimed he was a true hero. He was not
allowed near it and was sent away, but he was convinced, so he
broke into the building and went slowly up to the sword. When
he felt no pain, he picked it up. Guards ran in and saw that
he had it in his hands and was waving it about, gloating that
he was a hero, but the only reason he wasn't killed was because
the sword must have had something else planned for the man.
The sword started to vibrate and grow hot. There was a flash
of pure white light made of pure fire and pure water. After a
split second the light cleared, leaving the sword behind. The
man was more than unworthy of the sword as he had killed
a man in rage, and he was sent away from Rezta. The guards
went to inspect the sword, and when they felt no pain, they
looked closer at the sword. Where the five gems should have
been placed, there were now only four.*

*A huge panic swept through Rezta, and everyone went looking
for the gem and the man. Six months later, a star stream
started, and a magician appeared at the centre of it. It was the
magician who had made the gems. He informed the Reztarians
that the gem was no longer on Rezta and that according to the
white light, it was on a planet called Earth where the man
had been banished to spend the rest of his life; the gem had
gone with him, and the only way to get there was during a star
stream when the stars hit the floor of Rezta. Every six months
since then, a person has been chosen to go to Earth and search
for the gem, but it has never been found.*

Jamie looked from Spencer to Kim to Detrix, waiting to hear "gotcha!"

Jamie just looked astonished. The story shocked him.

"So that's why Kim was on Earth. She was looking for the missing gem."

Kim looked up. "Yes, I have been to your planet many times. I've been everywhere, but I have never come close to finding it until this last trip."

"What?! Are you kidding? What happened?" Spencer hurled himself at Kim and stopped just in front of her.

"In the forest where Jamie followed me, there was a strong pull of magic—the only one I found on Earth that came from our world. So it must have been the area where the stone and the man landed, but the magic is old and I don't know if I can follow it."

Spencer laughed and picked Kim up. "You did it! You did it! I knew you would. In six months we can have the stone back." Kim laughed with Spencer. It was the most natural and beautiful sound Jamie had ever heard.

Spencer put Kim down, and Detrix patted her on the back "That is wonderful news, my dear, truly wonderful."

Jamie got up and walked to Kim. "So you're telling me that back in my little village, you found the only signal of magic from your world, and now you think that the gem is in my village?"

"Yes, because the gem compels you to never go very far from the nearest magic source, as in where it landed, so it must be in your village." Jamie's face went blank, and Kim smiled.

"Kim, my dear, I believe I have found a complication in your search." Detrix ruined the happy mood.

Kim groaned and plonked down on a chair. "Another one? I'll need a frickin' how-not-to-do-it list for the next time."

"Well, this one is one of the worst. The gem cannot be seen and stays with the person for all their life until they die. Then it is passed along to another, but not necessarily a family member." Detrix spoke slowly and carefully trying to give the news delicately to Kim.

Kim laughed a little, set her elbows on the table, and placed her head in her hands, looking completely angelic. "Of course it would be bloody invisible! Why would it be easy?" Kim sighed.

"Do you have any idea who could have had it?" Jamie asked Kim.

"No, not a clue, could be dead all for I know," Kim barked.

This prodded Jamie. Dead? He knew someone who had died. But surely not? He thought he should tell Kim anyway.

"Kim, I think—"

There was a scream from outside, and everyone looked round at the door.

Kim got up, and she and Spencer hurried out of the door. Jamie looked at Detrix, and they followed. Outside there was a huge crowd in the streets. Kim was moving swiftly through the crowd. Everyone looked at her, and she turned to a small boy. "Do you know what's going on up there?"

The boy nodded. "The soldiers are looking for someone, who is needed at the palace by order of King Artimos." He lisped the last word. Kim stood up.

"Thank you." She smiled at the boy and sped through the crowd.

"Kim, *wait!*" Spencer ran through the crowd to catch up to Kim. "Kim, this isn't smart. We need to get out of here now." Spencer tried to stop Kim.

"Look, I know it isn't the smartest thing ever, so I shall just hide out in the shadows, no one will even notice." Spencer scowled at her, but she ignored him.

Jamie lost sight of Kim and Spencer, leaving him standing with Detrix. "Does she want to get herself killed?" Detrix was speaking to himself more than to Jamie.

"Who's King Artimos?" Jamie looked up to Detrix.

"He is king of Mulbeta," Detrix grumbled and murmured in disgust.

"What's Mulbeta?" Jamie's forehead furrowed.

"Mulbeta is the central city of Rezta, the place Morphius cannot penetrate." Detrix looked back to his shop "it's also where you are."

The crowd in front thinned as three heavily built soldiers came marching through. "Get out of my way! All of you!" The soldier in the middle, the largest, was glowering at everyone. He held a small girl in his hands. That must have been the screaming they had heard earlier. Jamie tried to look at the man's face, but every time he tried his vision was pushed out of focus.

"What are you doing with that child, Latsin?" Detrix blew out his chest and stared at the soldier.

"Get out of my way, Detrix! This is none of your concern." The soldier shook the girl, and she screamed.

"No, but it is mine."

Everyone parted to reveal the most beautiful girl Jamie had ever seen. On either side of her stood two well-built boys with strikingly handsome features. Behind them stood a tall young man, and beside him a woman who looked incredibly grave and solemn.

The girl walked forward, trailed by the two boys.

"If you're going to take innocent people off the street, then I personally make it my business." The boy on her right, who had long dark blonde hair and brown eyes, spoke and took out his sword.

"Well, look who's trying to be brave!" Latsin sneered.

Latsin dropped the girl and threw up his hands. Seven more soldiers came forward. "Do you still think you're a match for me, little ones?"

All five of them took out their swords. They all stood their ground, but the woman looked sceptical.

"Fine," Latsin signalled the men forward, and they all pounced with their swords.

All five of them reacted. The girl went for Latsin, which Jamie didn't like. The eldest man was struggling to tackle two men. The girl looked back at the woman and yelled "Anna, behind you!" The women turned to a thug who was swinging his sword at her.

There was a shrill cry from the shadows, and Kim jumped onto the thug and tackled him to the ground. "Surprise, Latsin! Miss me?" Kim kicked the soldier in the face and pulled out her sword. Spencer ran in and punched the soldier in the face. The soldier fell back on the floor and didn't get back up.

"Stop!" Latsin yelled at his soldiers, and they stopped. Latsin had the girl's sword at his throat, and she was drawing drops of blood from his neck. "We'll go."

"Don't come back, or next time I won't stop." The girl smirked at him.

Latsin backed away, but the girl didn't put down her sword. The other soldiers went and got their unconscious comrade and backed away from Kim and Spencer.

They all slowly walked off, pushing Detrix aside on the way out. The five strangers turned to face Kim and Spencer. "You're good." The girl nodded at Kim and Spencer.

"Not bad yourself!" Kim nodded at the girl.

"Kim," Detrix shouted, "we need to go." Kim nodded and walked away. "You're more than welcome to come with us if you so wish," Detrix invited the strangers. Joshua and Detrix exchanged a quick glance, but no one noticed them.

"That would most useful. It seems things have changed round here." The eldest man nodded and walked up to Detrix and shook his hand.

"My name is Hendric. This is Anna, Mia, Diran, and Joshua." Hendric nodded to each of them as he stated their names. Jamie smiled at Mia, and she smiled back.

"My name is Detrix. This is Jamie, and that's Kim and Spencer." They each nodded to their name.

"Well, do come with us." Detrix signalled for them to follow. Hendric and Detrix walked in front, and everyone followed them into Sincos and sat down. Detrix sat at the table with

Hendric and Anna, and everyone situated themselves either on or around the settee.

Jamie watched as Diran hugged close to Mia, and he started to feel like an idiot for thinking he had a chance with her.

"Mia, we need to get to the castle tonight." Joshua lowered his voice and looked up to see if anyone else heard.

"Yes, I know, but how the hell are we going to get into the castle without being seen?" Diran slouched and pulled Mia into his lap. She nestled her head into his neck and sighed.

Mia frowned at Kim "Kim, how is it you just appeared out of nowhere?" Kim smiled and leant towards Mia.

"Put out your hand." Mia put out her hand, and Kim passed a ring to her.

Everyone crowded round Mia to look at the ring. It was clear glass with small bronze spikes going through it. They all looked up to Kim.

"I can hide whomever I want with that ring." They all shared dark smiles with each other and knew what they were going to do that night.

"So how did you come to be in Mulbeta, then?" Spencer slouched against Kim and looked at Diran, who was pulling Mia back into his lap.

Kim frowned at Diran. "Have you seen anyone other than yourselves in the time you've been together?"

Diran kept a straight face. "No one at all." Diran explained that they were here looking for Grint and had been travelling together for a little under a year, but he omitted any reference to Shana.

"Well, tonight we can break in and speak to Grint."

"Why can't we just go and ask for audience with the king?" Everyone turned to face Jamie.

"Because no one can be trusted to know who the magical beings are in Rezta, and we are all magical, so until we know who to trust, no one can know who we are." Joshua looked at Jamie as though he were a complete dumb ass.

"Oh, how silly of me to not know that on my first day here!" Jamie scowled at Joshua and stomped out of Sincos.

Jamie walked slowly to the spot where he had first appeared. "Stupid mucked-up place! I should have gone to the 'rec' with Ethan and Sarah. Now I'm not going to get to see Ella for six months, and who's going to look after Mum whilst I'm gone? I never should have gone." Jamie kicked the floor and kept walking. The houses here looked like they were from Roman times with their crazy mud roofs. Jamie came to the end of the street. A huge area led off into the shrouding woods. It looked incredibly dark and scary.

Jamie felt a prod in his back and swung round and hit something. He heard a groan and looked down. Lying on the floor was a girl. She looked like she had been through hell and back.

Jamie knelt down beside her. "Oh my god. I'm so sorry. I panicked and—"

"It's okay. I'm fine. I was just wondering if you had any food." The girl looked up with her big brown eyes. She had a shrivelled face and a stick-thin body. Her face was shining from tears.

"No, but if you want, you can come back with me, and we can find you some." Jamie helped her up carefully so he wouldn't break her.

"No, that's okay. I can manage." Jamie fished in his pockets and pulled out a pound coin. The girl laughed weakly and took the coin.

"I haven't seen one of these for ages." She looked up from the coin. "You're from Earth. Whereabouts?" She smiled and clenched the coin.

"I'm from Crowthorne. You probably haven't heard of it." The girl laughed. Jamie thought he recognised the laugh, and a lump formed in his throat.

"I know you." She smiled.

Jamie took a step back, and the girl sighed. "No, no, it can't be . . . you died and . . . !

"No. No, it can't be . . . you died and . . ." Jamie fumbled for words "Shana" he whispered.

Shana gave a forced smile.

"I know I should have told you what was going on, but . . ." Shana looked down. "I was so afraid of him." She looked up, and fire blazed through her eyes. "I'm not afraid any more, though. Tell no one you saw me, especially the people in the shop. One of them cannot be trusted."

Jamie nodded feebly. A gush of wind wiped past his face; he shut his eyes and opened them. Shana was nowhere to be seen.

Jamie stood there for a long time, looking at the spot where his ex-girlfriend had stood. He never knew what her dad was doing to her; otherwise he never would have let her go home.

Jamie missed Shana every day. She was the only one who put light in his day and the only girl he had ever loved.

Jamie smiled. "She's alive!" Jamie lifted his head to look at the sky. The moon seemed bigger and brighter tonight.

Jamie had to find her again. He had to speak to her. He was going to . . .

"Jamie!" Spencer's voice echoed in Jamie's head. The voice he wanted to hear was hers.

Spencer came into the clearing. He looked like a nameless god. He had long mucky dark hair that framed his face and intense dark brown eyes that mesmerised you if you looked too long. His porcelain skin reflected the moon.

Jamie didn't notice any of these features. All he could think of was Shana, he just thought Spencer was Kim's lackey.

Spencer stood in front of Jamie. "Look, okay, everyone's sorry. None of them knew that you were new, and Kim was going to follow you, but she's only just come back and I told her to rest. It's been a hard day for everyone, but to be honest, I don't know what it's like to be new, and I probably don't understand how you feel. Kim feels guilty for bringing you here; she has never done anything like this before."

Jamie crossed his arms and sighed. "Why do you care about her so much? She treats you like you're nothing to her and you seem so loyal."

Spencer's eyes tightened. "She does not! You really did just catch on her on a bad day, and she's normally more conscious of people's feelings, unless you . . . Well, just be sure not to frustrate her. And as for the loyalty I feel towards her, she saved my life." Spencer's words poured out in a passionate flurry as if . . . Oh!

Jamie realised what Spencer was thinking and didn't particularly like it. "Sorry, I didn't know." Jamie tipped his head down and went red. Crap! He'd really stuck his foot in it.

"How did she save your life?" Jamie tried to ease the tension between them.

Spencer looked up at Jamie. "Do you know Morphius has an army?"

Jamie shook his head. "I hardly even know what Morphius is." Jamie sat on a log nearby, and Spencer sat beside him.

"Morphius is everything this place fears. He wants to destroy everything in Rezta, every living thing; he wants to replace it with his own kind."

Jamie frowned. "What do you mean his own kind?"

Spencer sighed. "Morphius is from the netherworld, a world which is dying. It is has become too small for its inhabitants, and they need more pain to thrive on. Morphius represents only half of the netherworld. The other half only ever opened itself up once. That period was called the era of the darkness angels. They destroyed planets populated by billions. They feed on tortured souls. They toured worlds for millennia at a time, starving each world but never letting it die, until they had all the pain they could harvest. Then they would leave and go on to the next planet. Only a few live to remember those times, but something happened—no-one knows what—but they stopped. The rumour is that one of the winged beasts didn't like what they were doing and rebelled against them and overpowered them. The story is a bit vague, and I hope it remains so. If we were ever to find out the rest, we would all die."

It was warm out, but Jamie was shivering in the dark.

Spencer continued. "Rumours went round that the winged beast went into hiding but threatened to return if they ever stirred again. The winged beast vanished, never to be seen again, but tales passing from your world said that the winged beast was alive and that many people had seen it.

Your people call it the angel; a symbol of goodness and purity, but that is far from what it is. Morphius, being part of the netherworld, had information that the fallen angel had a human parent and that's where it got its compassion, but the angel is also part of the netherworld and is therefore a bloodthirsty beast that he needs to awaken. But since the angel has never been seen, so Morphius has sent armies round all of Rezta looking for this angel to turn it into his personal slave to wipe out all of the Reztarians so that he can bring his own people in and rule Rezta, and they can do as they please, raining terror on other planets. But no one knows who the angel is, so he sent armies everywhere in order to locate the angel." Spencer's eyes narrowed. "We can't let that happen. We have set up armies of our own in every village in Rezta with defences everywhere. But Morphius is becoming stronger and more powerful. He has one powerful army to take down every village and find this angel. We don't know why he hasn't used it yet, but we must find the angel first and destroy it." Spencer was sitting up straight, and he had flushed red.

Jamie frowned. "But why can't you just hide the angel or find the gem to stop Morphius?" Spencer gritted his teeth, but Jamie showed only concern for the frustration Spencer was showing.

"No, the angel must be killed. If it is allowed to live, more villages will be destroyed." His eyes became sullen. "More families will be lost."

Jamie understood now why he wanted this angel to die. "You lost your family." Jamie leaned back, not liking this. He still disagreed with killing this angel.

Spencer nodded. "It was about six months ago." Spencer looked at the ground. "Morphius' army invaded my village. We were all huddled into a small shed and had locked ourselves in. Nistal, the captain, gave the command to set it on fire. Everyone started screaming and panicking. All around me people were choking. My mum grabbed my arm from behind me. She was coughing so much I couldn't even speak to tell her I loved her, and she died in my arms. I never found my dad or my brother, but they were in there. I could hear them, but I couldn't call out. From outside I heard yells and the slicing of swords. I heard a girl yelling. It all went silent outside, but the raging of the fire continued to deafen and choke me. I was half dead when the doors swung open and I fell out. I had not realised I was leaning against the door. A girl dragged me out. She gave me air and ordered a man to get me away. I never saw my village after that, but I always remember Nistal and how he gave that command. I always blame the angel, Morphius, and Nistal for that day. I will not let any of them live—if ever I can get close to them." Spencer whispered the last sentence, and his voice shook.

Jamie sighed and held back tears. "I can't imagine how you must feel, and I can understand why you want revenge, and I promise I will help you against Morphius and Nistal. But the angel stopped a war and saved millions of lives; I'm sorry but I cannot help you with that."

Spencer's big brown eyes got bigger. "You don't have to. You are not obligated to do anything, but I haven't been able to track any of them down, and I would appreciate the help. Morphius has gone into hiding, and his army has increased in numbers. If you want to help at all, you can join our army and help defend the villages." Spencer got up and dusted himself down.

Jamie got up and looked Spencer in the eyes. "A war is coming, Jamie, and it's going to be big, unless the angel is found and destroyed."

Jamie showed no emotion. Spencer nodded and walked away, feeling like he had done his job.

Chapter 9
Battlefield

I was so cold. The lake water dripped off of me and down my black dress. My wet hair clung to my face. I sat on the ground under a tree and let the silent tears slowly fall down my face. Damn the lot of them! They were all nosy sods and could never agree about anything. They seemed to spend half the time arguing about nothing. At least this way I could try to work out what was going on, but without Mia that was impossible. I looked around the forest. Everything was covered in moss, and the rain made it smell fresh. Everything seemed normal in the woods, but outside a violent hate was brewing in everyone. I was sat up against a huge tree, and I let the rain drench me from head to toe.

I sighed, and cold fog burst from my mouth. I watched the fog get bigger and further away from me. The fog clouded in front me and didn't seem to leave. I blew out into the clouded fog. A heart-piercing shriek echoed around the forest. I covered my ears and watched the fog slam into the floor and push upwards. The shrieking stopped, and I watched the fog curl upwards. I slowly rose to my feet and watched the fog. It seemed to be blowing around a solid figure. Slowly I could see a dress forming, and my neck started burning. I looked down at my necklace. It was glowing red again, and I squinted at the figure. A hand shot out of the fog and grabbed me by the wrist. I pulled backward, but the hand was still holding my wrist.

"Stay calm, Shana." The voice was cool and relaxed, but it didn't calm me.

"What do you want? And how do you know my name?" The hand released me, and I fell to the floor. White light blazed around me, and I covered my eyes with my arm. The light faded.

"Dear Shana, I have known you all your life." I looked up, and in front of me stood the most beautiful woman I had ever seen. Her chestnut hair hung loosely to her waist, and her deep copper eyes moved like cascading water, she had beautiful olive skin. She seemed familiar to me, but her face seemed to be hidden by an invisible dark veil.

"Who are you?" My voice sounded weak and strained, and my throat hurt a lot.

"My name is Krystith." My eyes widened. "I am so sorry." Her voice was calm and soothing.

"Mother" I blubbered in passionate flurry. All my emotions ran into my throat and choked me, and then I realized she was a spirit whom I could not touch. My necklace shook around my neck, and I felt sick. Tears flooded down my face.

"Shana, there is so much you need to know." I lifted my head and stared into her eyes.

"What is it you are sorry for?" Krystith dropped her head and looked at my necklace.

"I apologise for what loss is to come. You are in grave danger, Shana, from friend and foe alike. The necklace around your neck was once part of me in a similar way it is to you, and you must you keep it hidden at all costs. If people were to realise that the necklace is what they have been searching for, then to the others your life would be a small consequence to get the necklace back." I frowned and looked at my necklace. It had turned from amber into bright blue.

"What do you mean, 'the others'?" I was frowning at her.

"I was once captive in the city of Mulbeta, doomed to protect the city until I was dead or out of use. I wanted a life away from war. A chance presented itself when something called a star stream happened. No one knows what a star stream is, but it emanates great power. The star stream gave me one single chance to go where I wanted, and it was able to transport me to the stars, where I met a very powerful magician. I asked of him that I could be separated from my powers and get away from the city and have a normal life—have children and a husband, a life!"

A look of love passed across Krystith eyes almost as if she was a little girl.

"He separated my powers into gems that formed the star of Krystith. This gem allows a sword to have the power I had then, which is not something I would wish upon anyone, not even my enemies. But the wizard didn't mention that only a hero could wield that sword and defeat the coming evil that is now upon us. So for many years the whole of Rezta has been searching for the gem or an alternative means of defeating Morphius. They have found one way that could defeat Morphius, but it is based on legend. They must not use this other way, for it would bring down the whole of Rezta and many other worlds if it's true potential were to be recognised. Morphius looks for this weapon as well, and he will use it to destroy all his enemies, including your friends. The gem in your necklace is but a mere taste of the whole star of Krystith, and it will bring you help wherever you need it, but you must keep it hidden."

I shook my head; this was way too much information.

"What is this other weapon?"

"A fallen angel. She is a dark formidable creature with no loyalties, but she is brave and knows her own morals. She has been banished from the netherworld after a long battle; she turned against her people and stopped them from attacking and destroying other worlds. She vowed to come back if ever they returned from the netherworld. Recent sightings in your world informed Morphius that the angel has been spotted, but she only appears to your world every so often and then appears to be here as well. Morphius has worked it out. The angel travels through the star stream in Rezta to go to Earth and then returns here."

I frowned. What was the netherworld? Krystith smiled at my puzzled expression and seemed to understand a little of the immense confusion I was feeling. I opened my mouth to speak, but she cut me off.

"The netherworld is a divided planet. That is the worst type of planet. It's separated in two. The angel is from the dormant side of the planet that has only stirred once in the time it has been known to us—and I pray every night it never happens again. Morphius is from the active side of the planet, the side that threatens Rezta and all its inhabitants. Morphius was raised from the ashes of the soldiers in the Great War between the two sides of the planet. He, in his own way, is from both sides. This makes him more dangerous than any other being on his side of the planet. Do not be fooled. Any creature from that planet has in its potential a very powerful capacity for hate and destruction and an ever-growing lust for the death of others."

"How did this gem come to be on Earth away from Rezta?" I tried to look like this wasn't the most confusing thing I had ever tried to comprehend.

"A murderer called Minos. He tried to take the sword, thinking he was a great hero, but he was such a man that even the gems punished him in the worst way a Reztarian could suffer. It sent him away from Rezta and into your world. You see, Minos killed a man in cold blood, making him less than worthy of holding the sword, so the sword did not just kill him. But something went wrong when the sword exploded. Its violent eruption dislodged the stone and sent the gem to Earth as well."

I nodded and looked at this goddess.

"Take the necklace back." I reached for the necklace, but my hand went through the necklace and I touched my throat. Krystith had vanished from my sight.

"Keep the necklace hidden, Shana. If you activate it, then you must be discrete." Her voice echoed around me.

"Wait! What's going on? How do I use the necklace?" Wind ripped around me, tugging at my dress.

"Follow the wind, Shana." I whipped my head around and saw Krystith. She hugged me, and the necklace burnt like fire around my neck. "I am so sorry. Learn the ways yourself; it's the only way."

She wiped the tears away from my face and kissed my forehead. The wind ripped me away from her, and I was hurled away with the wind. All that passed was blackness. I couldn't even see my hands, when I covered my face as I curled up into a ball.

I felt the floor beneath me. It was cold and hard. I opened my eyes, and in front of me I could see feet moving about. I lifted my body and looked around. Everywhere men and women and children were running around. I looked left and right and realised I was sitting in an alley, out of the way of the mob. I grabbed the wall and hoisted myself up. I watched the crowd all running in the same direction.

"Move! Move!" A deep voice sounded above the crowds. No one seemed to care. They just kept running, like pigs about to be slaughtered. I looked to where the voice was coming from and saw that a huge line of men were elbowing their way through. They walked past the crowd in my alley, and I could see that in their hands were swords. Crap and bugger, was all I could think. I had just been put in the middle of a battle.

I looked behind me—damn nothing but a dead end. The crowd was thinning out a bit. The line of men had passed the alley. It was decision time. I could peg it with the rest of the crowd and probably live a little longer, or I could do what I needed to do and follow the men, which would probably lead to death. Hmmm, such a hard choice to make . . .

"Shana, do not cower!"

I jumped backwards and looked around for the person who had spoken. I was panting like a dog, I knew what I was going to do, but I had no sword, and I was wearing a dress, so this seemed likely to end well. I looked at the alley and saw that the men had vanished. I ran out of the alley and followed them. Dodging people was like dodging bullets, except that people were bigger.

I was running down a dirt path with houses and shops on either side. The people were dressed in muddy old clothes, camouflaging them with the dirt road. They all had an expression of resignation and fear on their faces. This did not look good.

I could see the men running in front of me. They were no longer in a line but were just running through the crowd. They all had their swords pointed upward.

At the end of the street was a huge field that stretched out as far as I could see. The field was scattered with bodies of men, lying in muddy pools of blood. The sky seemed instantly darker out on the field. The men I was following scattered out on the field now, running around and trying to get the bodies out the way. They all looked so tired and withdrawn, almost as if they had given up.

"Get the women and children into the houses!" A huge voice drowned out the groans of the men. I looked over to see a huge man dressed in grey, dim chain mail. He had wet black hair and a fuzzy beard that looked like it hadn't been shaved in months. He was coated in blood and had a lazy eye.

There was no way I was going to hide out when these men looked as though they were at death's door. I looked around; no one had noticed me yet. I ran over to a man lying on the ground, looking like he had been dead for a while. It seemed cruel to disturb him, but not to help seemed barbaric. I tried pulling at his chain mail, but instead I just fell backwards and smacked my head. Bugger! I yanked harder at the chain mail, and it started to slowly shift off. It finally fell off the man, and I quickly yanked it on myself. No one was wearing a helmet; I needed to cover my hair. I looked over to a huge mud pool; yes, I was going to regret this. I crawled over to the pool. The grass seemed to smoke a bit, which helped me to remain unnoticed. I looked in and gagged. This stuff made me retch. I grabbed the surface grass, dunked my whole head in, and quickly pulled it out. My eyes were watering, and I knew what was coming next.

"Hey you!" I didn't even need to look up to know it was me they were yelling at. I threw up into the pool and let the tears roll down my cheeks. This stuff was toxic.

Then I felt a hand on my shoulder and looked up. I held my breath.

"Are you one of the new recruits?" He had dark blonde hair that wisped around his face. His dark brown eyes hypnotised my brain into a stupor, and his lips were full and rouged.

What should I say? "Yes, I just needed to sit down and, you know, spit." I deepened my voice, hoping that was a manly response.

"Don't worry. It's a shock for most men when they first see it." He looked around at the dead bodies and sighed. "My name is Nathan Johnson. What's yours?" Bugger! A name . . . a name . . . Why couldn't I think of a name.

"My name is John Smith." John Smith? Did I want to be completely unconvincing? I stood up and looked him in the eyes. My Doctor Who addiction was going to get me caught.

"Well, John, Thetas just asked everyone in the new recruitment to form the front line." Who now, asked what?

"Thanks mate!" Oh my god, I was an idiot. To be fair to myself, I didn't have much real experience of being a man.

Okay, dressing like a man was definitely not my most convincing lie or the most well-informed. Who were we fighting and who was Thetas?

I wondered what I looked like now, considering I had just dunked my head in mud. I pulled my hair up and jumbled it in a pile.

"All of you get in line now!" I looked over at the man I had seen before. He was now wielding a sword and waving it at the men.

"Sir, yes, sir!" I whispered under my breath. I never did take orders well.

"What did you say!?" Everyone turned to face me. Oh crap, did they having the hearing of a bat? "You there, come forward." He pointed at me. I lifted my head up and walked out of line. Everyone was silent and watched him as he walked up to me.

"A newbie, eh? Well, we'll soon see how tough you really are when you come face to face with the enemy. Or maybe you'd like to just go take on Morphius? Or maybe you'd like to take me on?" He brandished his sword in my face.

What an idiot!

"Why would I fight you when there's another army coming over the field?" He swivelled on his heels to look over the field. I grabbed a sword from a man standing next to me, giving him an awkward smile as I turned back to the initial problem; I kicked the obnoxious prat in the buttocks. The men laughed, and I watched as the temperamental twit fumbled for balance. He shot round like a tiger and thrust his sword at me. I dived out the way, and his sword landed on the floor. He brought his sword up again and swung it over my head. I ducked and threw my sword at his feet. He jumped into the air to avoid my blow, so I knocked his legs out from under him, and he toppled over. He landed on his butt and seemed disoriented. I grabbed his sword from his hand and backed away from him. The men were applauding and laughing, I looked at the man on the floor. Why was I so stupid? Why had I just attacked my commanding officer?

I threw the sword hilt down to the man in command. He glared up at me. The phrase "if looks could kill" came to mind. He jumped back on his feet, grabbing his sword on the way.

"I will end you." His face was right next to mine. His breath stunk of garlic and cheese. I didn't back down but just stared at him as he towered over me. He brought his sword up and threw it down, aiming for my head. I slammed my eyes shut and held my breath.

"There will be none of that in this army, Thetas!"

I opened my eyes and backed away. Thetas' sword was inches away from my face. Someone had grabbed his arm and stopped him. I looked at the man who had saved my life and nearly laughed. It was Nathan. I nodded at him in appreciation.

Nathan dropped Thetas' arm and stood squarely up to me. "And if you ever assault your commanding officer again, I will make sure you run by yourself into the enemy's land. Do I make myself clear?"

I pursed my lips and nodded. "Yes, sir!" I forgot to deepen my voice, and he raised his eyebrows.

"Get back in line, Smith." I nodded and walked back in line, smiling to myself.

"We all know why we are here." Nathan stood in front of the crowds with Thetas by his side. "Our village is under attack. Mulbeta has failed to send help. Morphius' forces are strong, but we will defeat them. We will make them rue the day they brought war to our village and to our people."

A roar went up amongst the men. I looked around me. The men were all muddy and tired and were looking at me very strangely. Oh yeah, I'd just dunked my head in mud. I probably look like a loon round about now.

I roared with the men and held my stolen sword in the air. A wave of swords went up behind me, and I could see Nathan smiling at me. I looked at the man next to me and handed him the sword. He shook his head and laughed. "It's okay, I have another one." He reached back and pulled out two curved swords. I weakly nodded at him; he smiled and nodded back.

At that moment I heard a faint rumble in the distance, and I looked around. From the back of the field a black line was slowly making its way across. Everyone was quiet, and Nathan turned to face the army. This was it.

Looking over the field was a surge of men and creatures, some of the creatures I had seen in Morphius' castle, and I didn't wish to be near those things again.

I looked back and forth. We were surely outnumbered twenty to one. Why hadn't Mulbeta sent any reinforcements? We were doomed to lose this fight.

The clouds that rolled by slowed down and became an eerie combination of grey and black. It became instantly colder, and I shuddered in my chain mail. The man next to me patted me on the shoulder. He was so much taller than I was, and he had a beard and was looking lethal with those swords. I really didn't belong here. The only thing I could use was my necklace, if only I knew how to.

This was so frustrating. I looked over the numbers again. "Odds of winning—slim. Odds of living and complaining about odds of winning—even slimmer." A deep chuckle erupted from the man standing next to me. I looked to my left; he was a well-built man with a thin receding hair and a long scar down the right side of his face.

"You'll get through it all right, laddie. Just use your wit, and they'll fall over laughing." He wiped a tear from the corner of his eye. I rolled my eyes and looked in front of me.

Nathan was looking over his shoulder at me. I looked into his eyes and couldn't see an ounce of fear. My mind seemed to melt into mush. It was a shame I was going to die.

A huge scream rang out from the north side of the field. I watched as a huge man with worryingly pale features stepped forward.

"We give you one last chance to let us take your village and all your women and girls. You understand that even if you fight today, you will not stop the bigger plan."

Why specifically the girls? Was Morphius feeling a little rambunctious and getting tired of the company of slime balls? Oh damn—yeah, they were looking for the fallen angel. I needed to find her before they did and get her to safety, even if it meant fighting this crap load of peopley things.

"We give you the same message we give you every time. We will defend them all to our graves and to yours." Nathan stood strong a little in front of us all.

Damn, I was on the front line, on a side with bad odds of winning. I closed my eyes and felt a jolt in my chest. I listened to the noises around me, but everything was still—the silence before a storm. The wind brushed my face so lightly it tickled. The warmth I was longing for was on my neck. I smiled and opened my eyes. The heat grew from my necklace so intense that it hurt. It was a little pain or a lot of death. I clasped my sword, and it glowed bright orange. I pulled the sword to my side so no one would notice. The man beside me, who had given me the sword, looked down at the glow and raised his eyebrows. "Still don't want it back?" I smiled at his weak nod.

"*Charge!!!!*" The pale man screamed and started running with his army flowing along behind him.

"*Charge!!*" Nathan screamed, and I started running with the men. Nothing slowed down like I hoped it would. I watched Nathan slam into the first soldier. I knocked into a man and sliced open his stomach. I felt sick as his guts spilled all over the floor. Oh god, I'd killed someone! I didn't have time to think too long. Another man charged at me, and I swung my sword at him. My glowing orange sword sliced through his flesh like butter. My sword exploded a bright orange, stunning all the enemies around me. I ignored the stunned enemies, feeling sick with guilt for helping to take these men's lives. They were only obeying orders. The other men on my side did not feel the same compassion as they hacked off one man's head and then moved on to the next one.

A man charged at me. I raised my sword over his head and slashed it down; I could hear the cracking of the skull under my sword. My gut lurched as I recognised this man from Morphius' castle. I looked at the man, feeling sick and completely in shock. I heard a vague yelling from behind me. I slowly turned to face a great big beast charging towards me. Its inky black eyes were focused in on me. It had a thin layer of hair covering its cracked pig-like skin.

I had a blank expression on my face, and my eyes widened. The thing jumped up and pounced towards me, and all my feelings rushed back. I dived to my right and jumped up. I turned with my sword ready, and now the creature was standing where I had once stood. My sword tingled in my fingertips. I lowered my sword and let the tip touch the floor; the orange glow fell from my sword. I looked to the sky, and the grey clouds were shifting quickly. I lifted my sword back up and charged the creature. It looked bewildered and confused. It screamed as I slammed my sword into its side. The creature let loose a high-pitched squeal that sounded a lot like a child. It swiped at me with its leg and scraped a chunk out of my arm. I screamed and dropped my sword, which dimmed as it hit the ground. The beast threw me away from my sword, I crashed into the ground. Whimpering loudly, I clambered to my feet and stared at the beast.

Standing my ground and facing the beast, my necklace piqued and started to burn me. A huge rumble echoed in the sky, and the rain poured down like a waterfall. Now the battleground became a haze. I could hardly see anyone, which meant they couldn't see me either. I lifted my hand, and my fingers strained for release as the power of my necklace was being harnessed through my hand. The beast cowered away from the blackness it would now be seeing in front of its eyes. I closed my eyes and clamped my hand into a fist; a bolt of lightning shot out of my hand and hit the creature. It struck so fast it would feel no pain.

I ran to the beast and picked up my sword. It started glowing orange as soon as I touched it. The rain had turned into a drizzle. My arm was dripping with blood; the stupid thing had nearly taken it off! I looked up. Some men were lying on the ground screaming for their lives as a man stood above them holding his sword over them. They were writhing in pain. I looked around for a rock. I scraped a few pebbles up off the ground. "Please work!" I kissed the pebbles and murmured a quick spell. I lobbed them at the man and watched as they soared through the air. They sizzled like a couple of meteors, as I hoped they would. They hit the man all over his head in various places and burnt into his face like molten rock. He pulled his sword away and clenched his face.

"*Yeah!*" I jumped in the air. I had saved lives. I realised I had basically just confessed to screwing with this man and his attack, and he did not look happy about it.

I turned away to fight another man who was attacking someone else.

"You bitch!!" I stopped and hunched my shoulders. Crap.

I turned around and faced the man I had just pelted with molten rock; he had huge bloody holes all over his head. Oh Christ! I recognised this man. He was their leader—the one who talked to Nathan at the beginning of the battle. I had a nice knack of making things worse for myself. My sword glowed brighter orange than before. I quivered as his ultra-red eyes burnt into mine. His white skin seemed transparent against the rain.

"A girl on a battle field? Is that how desperately they seek soldiers?" A girl? How did he know? Damn, the rain must have washed off the mud.

"They didn't know." My voice was weak, but it didn't stop him from hearing.

"Well, no one else will know once I'm done mutilating you, you bitch."

My temper boiled. The only person who ever called me a bitch was my dad, and I didn't like being reminded of him. "You best make sure they all know who you are!" I signalled towards his men. "It looks like I beat you to the mutilation part. You look like pumice!"

He screamed at me, completely beyond words. He pointed his sword at me and charged. I held up my sword. My stomach dropped. The glow had gone and I was completely vulnerable, and my arm stung like hell.

He bashed into me and knocked me to the ground. I gagged and choked for air. He backed away and looked down at me. The blood from his face dripped onto me.

A blazing pain seared through my whole body. I looked down at my stomach. I was coated in my own blood. His sword had cut through my chain mail and had gone right into me. I slowly crawled out of my chain mail, leaning on my good arm.

He dropped his sword and slowly walked over. I tried to crawl away on my one arm, and he laughed loudly. I felt I had done this before in the cellar with my father, except that my father was worse because of what he did after.

The man bent over me and lifted me up by my dress. "I would sincerely like to know your name before I kill you." I fought for air and winced at his stagnant breath.

"John Smith." I whispered the name and smiled at my own joke.

He brought a knife out of his pocket and brought it to my throat. It felt cold and sharp against my throat. But then again, it was not worse than what my father did to me. He just did whatever he liked to me in a soundproof basement and then called me a slut for letting him do it to me.

Adrenaline pumped through my veins. No matter what, this was better than what my father had done to me. I scowled deeply and brought my head forward, letting the knife slice my neck a little. He moved back and let the knife fall slack.

"*Do it then!*" I screamed at him.

He pulled his arm back and grabbed my hair and got ready to stab me. My neck was fully exposed to him.

"*Ahhhhhhhhhh!*" We both looked round, and I saw Nathan charging at us with the two men who had been standing beside me. Nathan looked so much younger than the two men, but they followed him freely.

The man got up and started to run away letting go of my hair, letting my head bash to the ground. They pulled him to the ground and started hacking at him as if nothing else mattered. I watched blood and pieces of his body fly up. I leaned up and swooned, but I stayed up, though. They all turned to face me as I lay on the ground. I looked behind their feet. The enemy leader, who had nearly killed me, was a bloody pile of mush and bones; I could vaguely make out a few fingers and an arm, but that was all that was recognisable. I looked over at the beast I had killed with the lightning bolt. I realised I had done that beast a kindness by killing it so quickly.

I looked at the two men behind Nathan. They were scanning the field.

Nathan nodded to the men. They took out their swords and raised them high above their heads. "*We won!*" They ran into the crowd cheering and laughing with the other survivors. I looked at my arm and sighed. It was going to fall off if it didn't get bandaged soon. I tried to reach for the hem of my dress, and I winced as my stomach overstretched. I pulled my good arm away and held it to my stomach, trying to hold in the blood.

"Bugger!" My voice was so weak. I winced. The blood wouldn't stop gushing. I was so tired, but I knew that if I closed my eyes the fight for my life would start as it had in the ambulance, and look how that ended.

"Lay still." Nathan knelt beside me and placed a cool hand on my head. He pulled off his chain mail and put it underneath my head. I lay back reluctantly. "Close your eyes for a second, this might hurt."

"No, are you having a laugh?" I slapped him away, but flinched when my stomach tore a little wider.

"Fine, don't close your eyes." He touched my stomach, I slammed my eyes shut, the argument seemed fairly pointless now. The pain started to sub-side a little. I opened my eyes, there was still a lot of blood but it wasn't flowing out as quick.

"Thank you for helping save my life again." My voice was so weak it was ridiculous. The rain had lightened but was still heavy.

He ripped shreds off his white shirt and started wrapping them around my arched stomach. "Try not to talk. How could you be so stupid as to come out here?" He seemed to be talking to himself rather than me.

I felt my thank you come back and slap me in the face. "You're right, I should of just sat in the street and waited for the nice army to come and kill me!" I gestured over to the hacked pile of flesh, smiling sweetly at Nathan.

"Maybe you should have. I don't want any more deaths on my conscience, especially—"

"Especially a girl?" I stared at Nathan, waiting for him to try and squirm out of it.

"No! Especially a brave and magical girl, who tried to help defeat a powerful army." He whispered in a very hypnotic voice, almost making me miss the words.

"You saw me then?" It was more of a rhetorical question.

"You're good with the magic but really bad with a sword with no glow." He pressed gently against my stomach with his hand. He tore some more material from his shirt and began to work on my arm.

Save us all the trouble and take your shirt off. Okay, don't judge me. I am still a hormonal teen. But I did have enough sense to know that would be one of the most stupid things I could say.

"Where do you live?"

Crap! Just lie. "Umm, does it really matter where I live?" I felt my face get hot. I needed to actually lie not just avoid the question.

"Yes, it does. How am I going to get you back home if I don't know where you live?" He sat down beside me.

I sat up and looked around. Behind me the men were walking back to their houses, and the women were coming out. I saw the man from whom I had taken the sword run up to a woman. He hugged her and held her head in his heads. They kissed, and a bunch of children ran out to them. I heard the squeals of the father and the mother's own laughter. I smiled and felt tears come to my eyes as the kids tackled their daddy. Was that how it was supposed to be with a family? Nathan was laughing at the sight of his soldier being grounded by a couple of infants.

To my left were some very dense woods I hadn't noticed before. Perhaps I could just crawl into them for a bit.

"I can get home by myself." It came out as slightly defensive.

He seemed amused. "Can you even walk?"

I rolled my eyes. "Of course I can walk!" No, I couldn't. I didn't think I could breathe properly ever again, even with a pacemaker. I pushed myself forward and swallowed a heart-breaking scream. I used both arms to push myself up. I swear I was going to die.

"Can I help?" He had an arm extended in front of me.

"You help, and I swear I will mutilate you." I pushed his hand away and hauled my dead weight up.

Yay! I was standing, and ouch! I don't think I never will again, when he leaves me alone I will probably collapse.

"See, I can stand." My knees were shaking violently under me, luckily covered by the dress.

"That's not what I asked. I asked if you can walk." He was playing with me, the little bugger.

"Is it important to walk right now? The battle is won and I am tired." It was a weak argument.

"Is that permission to walk you home?" Yeah, if you want to walk back to Earth, mate, you can do that without me.

"No, I can walk fine." I lifted my leg and plodded it down a millimetre away, and then I did the same with the other leg.

"There, I walked! You can go now." Hmmm, yes, I will admit freely to weak arguments and poor strength.

I looked at the ground I was standing on. I was standing in a pool of scarlet blood, peering at the body from which the blood oozed from, I immediately felt numb. It was a tragic scene; I hated myself for what I had done.

The man was facing upwards looking at the sky. He had a great big red slash where I had sliced him. The first man I killed. I stumbled over to him, falling to the ground. I crawled over to him through the mud and knelt beside him. Tears pricked my eyes. Nathan knelt beside me and looked at me. I looked over the man and noticed previous scars. "I'm sorry." I closed his eyes, and my tears came out and flowed over him.

Nathan took my hand and squeezed it. "He would have done it to you with no remorse."

I felt numb. "I'm not like him." I couldn't say anything else. My throat was so sore, and I could hardly acknowledge I had any part in this battle. "I have to go." I needed to rest. The woods were no hotel, but they were the only option I had other than the street.

"Please, tell me where you live." He squeezed my hand and I let go. My necklace buzzed around my neck.

"No-where. I live no-where." I stood up, and my knees buckled against each other.

I looked at Nathan, who stood up and faced me. "Can you tell me your real name then?"

I thought that would be a bad idea. The last thing I wanted was my real name going around and reaching certain people's ears. "My name matters as much as where I live." And the fact that I can't walk remains my priority.

Nathan seemed to think about this for a moment. "Well I can't have an injured soldier living on the street."

"So no objection to the woods then?" I waited to see his response.

"I have no objection whatsoever. It's where I am staying anyway." Nathan smiled angelically at me.

Well, wasn't that a slap in the face? I bit the insides of my lip to prevent myself from starting a verbal battering on him.

"Well, we won't be sharing the same tree!" I needed to stop opening my mouth.

"You can't walk, never mind climb a tree." I felt the need to hit the smarmy twit.

"I'll sleep under it." I turned away briskly, but my legs gave way, and I stumbled backwards.

Nathan caught me and put an arm underneath my legs. He was carrying me in his arms in the direction of the woods. Huh? Someone I didn't know asking me my name and where I lived and then carrying me off to the woods? Nothing bad could come of that!

I closed my heavy eyes and fell asleep.

I don't know how long I had been out before I started to hear voices.

"Why did you bring her here?" a deep furious voice hissed.

"She needed somewhere to stay and was heading to sleep under a tree." Nathan's cool voice defended me.

"Please be quiet, okay? She looks completely wiped out. Her arm is so messed up. It looks like it's been broken before." A girl's voice pitched in.

Believe me; it had been broken before, more than once. I heard a grunt, it sounded mocking.

"Shut up, Dunstan. We need her. She's powerful. She just needs help with the sword, that's all. And she isn't a brain-washed killer. She cares. She cried over an enemy she killed. I have never seen anyone do that before, have you?"

"Nathan, what did she do in battle?" The girl's voice chimed in again.

"She turned stone into molten rock and threw it into Karloff. And I know this is going to sound crazy, but I think she took out a Higlom." What a strange name. The girl took in a deep breath, and the deep voice scoffed. Karloff must have been the leader I mutilated.

"Even if she did, she is still undeveloped with her powers and completely dumb. She dipped her head in a pool of mud and fought with a glowing sword and hoped she wouldn't be noticed." I wanted to punch this guy.

"She isn't clumsy. She has heart. Give her some credit. She kicks butt with her powers, and she could wipe you out if she fought you." Excuse me while I die inside, Nathan was trying to be kind to me but I really didn't want anyone to have a misleading image of me.

"Ha, I would like to see her try," Dunstan chuckled.

"Well, you can now, Dunstan. She is awake." The girl patted my head . . . crap.

I felt a cold hand on my own. I opened my eyes and everything was hazed over. I could vaguely make out a male's broad shape, but that was it.

I opened my mouth, but he clamped his hand over it.

My vision cleared, and I saw a young man with ash black hair and dark bronze eyes. "Just think before you talk, I don't want to hear bull." I slapped his hand away and sat up. He remained silent as he backed off towards Nathan.

"I fixed your wounds for you but Nathan did most of it already though. My name is Kim." Her soft eyes drifted to my wounds. "They were pretty bad injuries."

"Thank you" I whispered softly to the girl, afraid too much talking would rip my wounds open. Even though they all looked pretty secure.

"I don't speak bull." My words were quip and sharp as I looked at Dunstan.

"I know enough of your kind—brave, kind hearted, courageous." He turned away, and I glared at him. "But stupid, reckless, careless of consequences, completely dumb in a war." I watched him pace up and down, listing all my faults.

"My kind? I assure there is only one of me, but there are many know-it-all twits like you." I swung my legs off the surface and landed heavily on the forest floor. I looked at what I had been lying on. It was nothing more than a log.

We were in a clearing that was surrounded by densely packed trees, there was little noise entering the area. A campfire had been set up in the middle of the area.

"Nathan told me you were high spirited; he must have forgotten to mention your ill use of wit." Dunstan sat on a log opposite me.

"Look, Dunstan, if I thought you would be as much of a dick to her as this, then to be quite frank, it was a poor use of valuable time. I will not have you berating her after what she did. She was the key reason we won that battle. If she hadn't taken out the Higlom, the rest wouldn't have run off in fear. And you weren't much help sitting here with Kim." Nathan stood beside Kim and looked down on Dunstan.

"I had to stay here. I can't harm anyone, and you know that." Kim defended herself. Nathan nodded at Kim apologetically.

"I didn't mean to imply you were useless. I only meant he would have served better helping to win the battle than sit here." Nathan's face flushed red, embarrassed that he had offended Kim.

Dunstan was glaring at me. "Why did you bring me here?" I looked at Nathan for an answer, avoiding any eye contact with Dunstan. Unfortunately it was him who answered me.

"He was hoping I would train you to use a sword, and I can see why. If you knew what you were doing, you would have known to move out of the way if a man is charging at you ready to stick a sword into your chest." His tone was cutting.

"It's quite obvious I have never used a sword before in my life" or death "and it seems quite evident I will have to know how to use one. So if you would," and, believe me, I am saying this reluctantly, "help me learn how to fight with a sword." Now all my dignity had gone quicker than I died.

Dunstan leant back on his log. "Well, if you want me to teach you, cut back on the snarky crap. And don't ever be sorry with what you do with a sword."

Chapter 10
Campsite

The night drew in quickly in the woods. I spent my evenings talking to Kim, who had a lot to talk about. It turns out she and Dunstan were old friends who had met up a day or two before I arrived, and she and Nathan just travelled together, she assured me, as friends.

"What is a Higlom?" I asked Kim while she patched up my clothes.

"A Higlom is a shape shifter. They are all gone now. That was last one that had been reported to us." It didn't shape shift on me, a shape shifter that doesn't shape shift . . . . How handy.

Dunstan was nineteen and from Rezta but no one knew who his family was or where about in Rezta he came from. Kim informed me he possessed no magic, but when he held a sword he apparently held more power than an angel from the netherworld. I think she was exaggerating.

Maybe it was a different kind of magic he had, rather than a do-it-all power, didn't seem as good though. I was one to talk. They thought I had power, but they didn't know it was only the necklace that enabled me to do this stuff. And I couldn't even use the necklace properly. As far as I was concerned, it was really a part of Krystith, even if she didn't want her powers. The way the necklace had reacted around her was enough to make me believe the necklace was still a part of her in some way.

Kim fixed my black lace dress. I had never worn dresses before, and I was pleasantly pleased to know they could be easily torn.

Nathan was being, as far as I could tell, his usual self. He seemed to get on slightly with Dunstan, but the feelings were only loosely reciprocated. I made no attempt to get on with Dunstan, although he reminded me of Mia. I couldn't seem to shake the feeling that he had secrets in his past that he wasn't sharing.

I hadn't told anyone my name, and they weren't buying "John Smith", so I asked them to refer to me as Doctor Who. But I didn't know who to trust with anything; there was still a lot being hidden from me in this camp.

"Right, doctor." Dunstan rolled his eyes; he personally hated the name. "Today I will show you how to strike a deadly blow with as little strength as possible—perhaps the best way for you." He tilted his head as I tried to swing the sword. I picked it up and tried to swing it, but it was too heavy and I threw it into a tree.

Kim retrieved the sword and handed it to me. "Doctor, watch."

I sighed and sat down. Dunstan signalled for Nathan to get up. Kim shifted to sit next to me. "This is where they both show their complex manliness with a sword." She giggled and rolled her eyes. "Neither of them can hold a 'manly' argument for less than five minutes without resorting to swords. Well, Nathan can a little better than Dunstan, I suppose." I folded my legs and dumped my sword on the ground.

Kim stood up on the log. "Ready?" The two of them nodded at each other. They both looked so incredibly concentrated. I hoped they'd remember this was only to show me how to hold a sword and they weren't going to hack each other to death. "*Go!*"

Dunstan stepped back and swung his sword at Nathan's throat.

I watched as the two dodged and swung their swords at one another and fighting mini duels with each other.

Days passed us by; they fought occasionally when I didn't understand something, which was most of the time. They taught me all kinds of techniques, I didn't understand any of them, but at least they were attempting to show me. Kim had been lecturing me on watching them and telling me I had to be more interactive.

I was tired of always finding the sword wasn't doing as I wanted it to.

I was watching yet another duel, when Kim jumped up beside me. "Doctor!" Her face was pressed close to mine "You really must watch everything they show you. If you miss something, you can't see it again." I burst into fits of laughter, and she left. Oh, if only she knew the irony!

"I'm Doctor Who, I can time travel" I laughed, but I should have realised that was a bad idea, I spent the next couple of hours calming down Kim, who was now under the belief I could time travel.

A cold brush of wind tickled my senses. I looked up to the sky. Golden brown leaves danced in the air, scattering into the tree tops. I swivelled round on the log and jumped off. Branches rustled backwards as if someone was walking through them moving them out the way.

I looked back at Dunstan and Nathan. They hadn't noticed me leaving yet, and neither had Kim. She seemed fixed on the fight.

I smiled to myself, the lightness of the current moment made me feel like a child. I glided slowly forward towards the trees, my dress trailing behind me. The trees looked at first really very dense, but if you looked into the woods from the outskirts, it seemed as if they were all spaced out. I moved the branches out the way and stepped into a quiet peaceful area. Everything swayed with the weight of the trees. The pine bristles moved delicately around on the ground. My heart felt as light as ever. I recognised the familiarity of this place; it was so similar to what my mother had walked me through, she always told me one thing, it was the one thing I remembered about her. I looked up at the tree's stretching up, they were like yawning arms. She always told me the view was beautiful from a treetop if you caught it at the right moment.

I gazed across the woodland floor at the tallest tree. I looked up but couldn't see the top. The tallest tree always has a glowing view worth seeing from the top.

I grabbed the closest branch and pulled myself up to stand on it, I scraped my nails into the bark, finding wedges to put my feet in. My hair tussled around my face as I kept climbing further up. I never looked down or in front of me. The view was to be saved until the top.

The air got warmer the further up I got. The hot breeze amplified the smell of the soil and the freshness of the leaves. Twigs hung from my hair and dress, and the black lace was torn at the bottom. Kim was never going to forgive me for that.

I grabbed a small branch which buckled under the weight of my hand. I looked around for another branch, but there was none. I heaved on the branch and yanked it as hard as I could. When it didn't break, I pulled myself up and hugged the trunk of the tree, standing on the branch. I looked around me; there were no further branches and no further trunk.

I gasped and held my breath. The trees stretched on for ever, and each one seemed as luminescent as a single sun. The golden sunset burnt with the brilliance of an entire galaxy, with flames stretching up into the oncoming dark night that brought with it a thousand glowing stars.

A loud rush of wind swept across the sheet of trees, lifting a tidal wave of glowing specks. They all seemed to dart out of nowhere and move very much independently away from the wind towards me. They made a very mellow quiet buzzing sound as they got closer.

Their glow shone brighter than anything I had ever seen before as they got closer. I squinted at them. I must be going crazy. I swear they had wings. As they got closer, I could see clearly that they did have wings and beaks. They were birds—or whatever a twinkly-eyed beaked thing is called in this world.

I heard a twig snap, and I looked down. The branch I was on was breaking,

Out from the darkness below a hand shot out.

"Quickly!" My heart flipped at Nathan's voice, as if a thousand tiny fireflies had jumped into me and set my heart on fire.

I grabbed his hand and slid down the trunk. He caught me round my waist and balanced me on the branch. The branch I had been standing on snapped and fell out of sight into the darkness, ricocheting off the trunk and catching on twigs, echoing all around.

His eyes sparked so violently even in the dark that it was hard to look at anything else. "Thanks," I panted in the darkness and let him hold my waist closer to him. "You saved my life again."

"Hmmm, it seems you owe me." His hot breath brushed against my face. He smelled so sweet and honeyed.

Nathan's face was just a millimetre away from mine. My ears flared red hot, as they always do when I get embarrassed. His golden hair swayed above his eyes, making him even more illustrious and god-like.

His intense eyes bore into mine, and his breathing got heavier, as did mine. He pulled me closer, and our lips touched. The feeling set me on fire. My blood pounded through my head. It was rough—too rough, it felt—harsh and too intense.

A huge torrent of wind blasted above our heads, I tore away from his lips and looked up. A thousand blue, yellow, green, red, and purple lights were dancing above us.

I looked at the trunk. No twigs in sight. I peeped round the other side of the trunk. A huge branch was sticking out a little above us. How had I not noticed that before? I looked back to Nathan. "Come on," I whispered, because my voice wouldn't speak with the amount of excitement I was feeling right now.

We jumped up and grabbed the branch, using it to pull ourselves up. We stood on the branch, towering over the leaves that were in the magnificent tree. We were standing right in the centre of the dancing birds, and their colours reflected onto us. I lifted my hand, and multiple colours engulfed my hands, making them look like a crystal that had caught the sun.

Nathan lent against the tree and pulled me tightly into him.

"Enjoying the show?" That wasn't his voice. I knew that voice; I hated that voice. I yanked his arms off from around me and turned to him, I stumbled away further on the branch with nothing to support me.

I faced the one thing I knew of that I hated more than my father.

Morphius stood calmly leaning against the trunk, as if this was a planned visit. His wide crusty grin suggested otherwise. "Shana, you disappointed me, separating from your friends, falling for little Nathan, and taking out my little toy soldiers." Flecks of crusty skin fell from the corners of his mouth. I stared at them as they fell; they reminded me of our last visit. Now he looked even worse.

"Why are you here?" I placed my arms a little further out from my waist to claim some balance. The lights still whistled around my head, making a torrent of wind that ripped through me as if I were paper.

"You have been misinformed of me, my dear." His voice was crusty but still dark and heavy.

"How have I been misinformed? Are you telling me you haven't been burning down villages and killing innocent people?" This is where the word "vomit" didn't help me. My voice shook, and I felt all the blood drain out of my face.

Morphius chuckled. "You assume I am the bad one in this war? You barely have the courage to speak a few words without feeling a tight knot in your stomach." He stepped away from the tree and edged slowly towards me. "It wasn't me who left you so unprepared and alone, with no one around you except an enemy. It wasn't me who brought you to Rezta to meet the killer who ended your mother's life." He spat the words at me as if I were nothing more to him except a little adolescent girl with a temper.

He was right about one thing: I had a temper. "What are you trying to accomplish here? You stand in front of me telling me you are not the bad guy, when you freely admit to killing my mother and being here as my enemy. The one thing you don't know is that I am never alone."

My necklace shattered light in front me; orange tendrils wound in front of me swerving to Morphius. He stretched out his arms, and black smoke burst from his cloak. The black smoke slapped into my magic and sent him stumbling into the back of the tree. I grabbed the trunk slipped down the tree and landed on the branch I had been standing on with Nathan. I stopped moving.

In front me stood a faint image. It was watching me. I had my hands wrapped around Morphius' waist. He was an inch away from me with his hands around my waist, and he was so much taller than me. He moved his mouth. No sound came out, but I knew what he was saying.

"Hmmm, it seems you owe me."

I watched in horror as the two of us came closer and were locked in a fierce kiss.

Chapter 11

Nathan

I opened my mouth in disbelief. Morphius opened his mouth and looked at directly at me. The corner of his mouth curled up in a bitter smile. I felt myself shaking on the branch.

A bitter laugh echoed around me. I looked up at the branch above. Morphius had disappeared.

A gush of wind slapped into me; shattering me like glass and pressing me to the trunk. I heard a loud scream and recognised it as Kim's.

I pushed myself away from the tree. I looked at the tree and had an idea—a very painful idea.

I scrambled back down the tree, ignoring all safety precautions, every single painful touch of the tree's limbs against my skin were intensified by the speed.

The tree ripped my entire body to shreds. Blood trickled from every part of me; I slipped on a branch and a twig slapped me in the face. I swallowed the scream, I looked down, and it was only a small jump to the ground. I jumped and landed on the floor, painful vibrations were sent throughout my body. I must have been looking rather feral by that point.

Blood dripped from my legs, and twigs hung from my hair and dress. I felt my head and winced. The twig had gashed my head. I pulled a leaf out of the cut and whimpered. I looked at the leaf. It was dripping with my blood. More of that was bound to be on the way.

I heard a huge clang and someone shouting. I started to walk forward and fell down on one knee; I looked up, but my blood-soaked hair frazzled my vision. I got up and limped forward. I bit my lip against the pain my battered body was going through. I felt my neck getting hotter but decided to ignore it. The necklace was getting slowly warmer, and the warmth travelled down to my leg and dulled the pain.

I reached the end of the trees and pulled the branches apart. I found myself standing to the right of a soldier's back.

In the clearing where I had been practising fighting, Morphius' soldiers had surrounded Nathan, Kim, and Dunstan and had bound them together.

"Never thought I would see you being tied up, Dunstan." Kim smiled and shuffled her legs.

"Never thought anyone wouldn't gag you as soon as they bound you." Kim frowned and blew her hair out of her eyes and gave a sarcastic laugh.

Nathan was facing me, but he didn't notice me, which was good. Nobody should notice me right now. I looked at the soldiers. They had all put their swords away and were watching the hostages. I looked at the soldier in front of me and noticed his sword was poking out of its scabbard and pointing towards me, almost beckoning me to pull it out.

I knelt down so I was level with the sword and very slowly reached out my hand. I looked around. No one seemed to have noticed me yet. I gently touched the sword hilt and pulled it away. The sword was going to be heavy. I needed a distraction.

My necklace was now glowing a flaming hot red. I peeped round. All the soldiers were dressed in heavy metal. Listening in the few science lessons I had had was finally about to pay off. I lifted the palm of my hand to a soldier standing directly opposite the one I was trying to steal from.

I was not feeling anything except determination, so I had no regret for what I was about to do. I slowly pulled my fingers together. The power I was using strained against my fingers, and the blood on my hand oozed out more violently as I stretched the knuckle.

I saw the effects immediately. The metal at his feet started to glow orange. The soldier started to shift, trying to not draw attention to himself. Not what I wanted.

I closed my hand and set the flames on him. The screams followed, but I didn't care. Everyone was looking at the soldier. The other soldiers started to run over to help him. The soldier in front of me moved forward, and I held on to the sword's hilt and let him move forward, allowing the sword to fall out of the scabbard.

The sword's tip touched the ground and I pulled it back into the woods.

The soldier's screamed echoed around the woods. No one was watching Nathan, Kim, and Dunstan, but they were now all looking at me. Kim had a blank expression on her face, which broke my heart. Nathan's eyes were wide with admiration, and Dunstan had a pinched smile on his face. I quickly dived out of the trees and landed in front of Nathan. I put the sword down and started to tackle the ropes around his wrists.

"Hey you!" I looked up. The soldier, who I set fire to, lay face down on the ground not moving. The others had all turned around and were looking directly at me. I picked up my sword and stood up.

"Shana Hale, I thought you'd turn up sooner or later." A soldier stepped forward and removed his slit helmet made mostly of leather. It was the soldier who had held me when I was at Morphius' castle, Nistal. "I see Diran didn't kill you. The master will be so disappointed."

I choked. "Diran betrayed you; he is loyal to us now." I can't believe I am defending someone I had known less than a day.

Nistal laughed. "He's doing the jobs and getting the perks then. He's already won Mia over. I saw them together only a few short hours ago holding hands."

My heart felt shredded. "Where are they?" I lowered my sword.

"They are not that far away actually."

"I don't want them to come and find me. That was the idea of me leaving." I stood firm and raised my sword.

Nistal smirked and raised his sword. I looked down at Nathan. He had a panicked look in his eyes and was thrashing his hands against the ground.

"Don't!" He had turned his entire torso towards me. "Please!" His dark eyes turned liquid. I didn't have another option; I had to fight. My eyes started to sting, and my nose was tingling. I pulled my gaze away from him and looked back at Nistal.

"Now, now, children, play nicely with one another!" I spun on my heels.

Morphius was standing a metre away from me, and his gaze wavered between me and Nathan.

He gave a dark laugh. "I see I chose correctly there." He glided forward, pulling his dark gown behind him, not even disturbing any leaves.

My necklace buckled and started vibrating down by my neck, but it was weak.

"No, no, there shall be no more of that nonsense." He waved a hand at me, and black cloudy smoke shot out towards me.

It hit me in the neck like thunder, and I slammed my eyes shut.

I toppled backward and smacked the back of my head on the ground, and air burst from my lips. My stomach lurched, my entire body lapsed, and fire ran through my neck. I could faintly hear people yelling, but the dulling drone of the beating fire ran louder through my ears.

The fire in my neck burst violently out of me, ripping and burning my skin. Everything was quiet and dim. I opened my eyes. Above me Kim was fiddling with my arm and trying to stop the bleeding. I looked past Kim. Behind her I could see Nistal thrashing his sword at Nathan.

Adrenalin shot through my veins like an instant dose of heroin. I shot up, ignoring the fire that was still faintly burning me. I grabbed my sword and turned to see what was happening. Dunstan was taking on the rest of the soldiers; Kim had run to go and join him.

"Are you going to let them die?" A rusty metallic voice came from behind me.

"Why are you doing this?" I turned to come face to face with Morphius. "Is this a game for you?"

"You know my course." He walked behind me and started circling me. "No one knows the suffering of my planet. We need to thrive and feast and kill. We are joined at the hip with such creatures who can give us that. As I am sure you have heard, I was born from the ashes of the two great leaders from either side of the netherworld. I will have this planet as a world for my creatures. They will thrive on this pitiful life here. They will be free, away from the angels and free to kill as they please. My children will be slaves to them no more."

I turned to face him. His stagnant breath reeked and made me want to retch all over him. "Your people are slaves to their own instincts and you feed them. The angels would be doing everyone a favour if they woke and destroyed you."

His thin bottom lip curled up. He leaned further in so his lips were close to my ear. "The angels are waking, and when they come, you and your friends will be the first to die a most painful death, and I will be strong." He stepped back. "I will be seeing you again, Shana Hale."

I held my breath and pulled my stomach in. He lifted his arms. Black smoke shot through the ground and ripped the dirt up. With it a screeching ripped round the woods. The black smoke shot around the camp, dragging away the remaining soldiers. Then the smoke vanished, leaving everything as if nothing had been disturbed, like robbers in the night.

I stood still, letting the knowledge that worse was to come consume me completely. I let it overwhelm me. My friends were going to die, and Morphius was about to wake the angels to do it.

"Shana, well, at least you have a decent name now."

I dumped my sword on the ground and brushed the hair out of my face.

I was not going to let my friends die.

I felt a tap on my shoulder, and I flinched away.

"Sorry." The honeyed voice sliced through me. "I need to stop the bleeding." I turned to face Nathan.

He had a deep look in his eye. He took my face in his hand and wiped some tears away from my face. I didn't remember starting to cry.

I pulled away, the stinging memory of Morphius plaguing my memory. "Is there a watering hole nearby?"

Nathan stared at me and put out his hand. I gently touched his hand. He slowly intertwined his fingers in mine, scraping the blood onto his own hand. "This way," he said. His voice was almost a whisper, too intense to resist.

He pulled me through a maze of trees to a clearing with a huge pool. I let go of his hand and walked over to the pool. I sat down and took my black boots off.

Nathan walked over and slowly sat down beside me. I sat and stared out at the pool. It was an amazing sapphire blue, twinkling with purple from the night sky. Stars reflected into the pool, making it glisten that much more.

"Shana!" I looked up at Nathan. "So it is your name?" He gently laughed. He took a strand of my hair and moved it out of my eyes.

"Yeah, well, some people shouldn't know where I am or who I'm with." Nathan lightly touched my hand. I curled my fingers through his and placed my head on his shoulder.

"I will never let anyone hurt you again for as long as live." He put his head on mine, and we sat just sat there listening to the water.

I laughed. "Most of this wasn't Morphius. It was me trying to get down a tree in top speed" Speaking of which, my cuts were hurting. My necklace had taken some of the pain away but they all still bled.

"We need to clean those cuts. I don't want them to get infected." He moved his head off mine and stood up, pulling me up with him.

We walked hand in hand into the pool, leaving our boots on the bank.

We stood in the middle of the pool, letting the water gentle ripple around us.

Nathan lifted my arm out the water. The water dripped off my arm. Nathan looked at my arm and stared intently at the scrapes.

His eyes started to glow bright blue. My arm started to tingle, and the cuts faded from my skin, leaving not a single scar. His eyes were stunning. They resembled the moon and all its glory, making him look like a god.

The glow in his eyes faded; he looked up at me smiling. "It's not much, but it helps."

I looked up to him. "Beautiful!" The word came out, almost as a one-word passionate clarification of my opinion of him.

We lent towards each other and kissed. His lips were perfect, firm yet soft. I wrapped my arms around his waist and let the feeling of pleasure lavish me.

Nathan and I walked hand in hand back to the campsite. We spent the night talking. We were up most of the night until I drifted asleep cuddling in his arms. The whole night was incredible.

When I woke up the following morning, he was already awake and getting my boots for me. We sat a little longer on the bank, and Nathan told me about his life in Rezta. Nathan was born in Rezta. His parents lived in Mulbeta. He ran away to join the army—a childish dream of his which he regretted. He never saw his parents again, and he said that he regretted not telling them he loved them and was sorry for leaving them.

I told him I was on the way to Mulbeta to find a friend and that if he wanted, he could come with me and see his family and tell them. But I didn't know the way to Mulbeta, as I had lost my companions. This led to me telling him the story of how I ended up in the great big mansion belonging to Grint.

Nathan hadn't heard of Grint, but he had heard of an island that had been separated from the rest of Rezta. The island was supposed to belong to an old sorcerer who had nearly brought about the destruction of a city.

"About ten years ago on a particularly cold night, the veil of stars had only just appeared. There was a huge festival down in the city's centre. It was a festival to celebrate the star stream that only happens once every six months. The one that night was supposed to be the biggest one ever known to come to Rezta. Everyone had come into the town square for a night they would never forget.

Sprays of light dashed into the air from the young practising their magic, not that you'd find many Reztarians openly using magic any more. They would laugh, just like children should. I used to love bursting colours in the air, especially the blue and silver colours. They danced vividly in the shapes of birds, and they seemed to laugh with me. Music would be playing, and great singers and dancers would line up to perform in front of everybody.

I was very young then and had no idea what the following events meant. An explosion was set off just a little north of the city square. Everyone was panicking and running around, but I remembered that my mother often wandered down there to get some magical supplies that she later gave to me. I ran against the crowd towards the road from which the explosion came. Being seven years old, this was hard. When I got to the road, I was consumed by the heat, but it didn't bother me enough to stop me. I ran down the road and turned left. The entire shop where my mother had bought me my stuff had been blown up. From the shop emerged a figure. He was old and withered and looked very tired. He resembled the master of sorcery, who trained members in the imperial guard, which I thought was odd—him being in a magical book shop when he was a master.

I hid in the shadows and watched him slip round the corner into the night. I was getting ready to leave when another figure started to emerge. He wasn't as old as the other man, and he wasn't as run down as the training master but his injuries were greater. He limped away in the same direction as the other man. I stayed where I was, too afraid to move in case someone else came out. That was my first mistake. Soldiers swarmed the place like mosquitos to heat. They found me hiding and took me. He asked me what I had seen. That was my second mistake. I told him what I saw and whom I thought I saw.

The sorcerer was taken to the king. The King explained my account of what happened, to the sorcerer. The King's court confronted him about starting the fire, but the court did not believe him. As he was a great friend of the king, he wasn't killed. Instead, he was banished to a happy retirement on an island which he was allowed to keep as long as he never stirred off it.

The fire was big enough to wipe out the whole of Mulbeta had it not been for another sorcerer. This sorcerer was proclaimed a public hero and was awarded the shop when it was rebuilt. He invited everyone in the square to see the opening. My mother took me and my family. I saw his face announcing the opening of his shop, Sincos. When I saw the man, I recognised him as the second man who had come out of the shop."

I looked at Nathan in shock. I opened my mouth, but nothing came out.

Nathan laughed. "I never told anyone, not even my mother, about my involvement in the incident."

I looked down; my cheeks were slightly inflamed, I was embarrassed that he trusted me so much.

"Would you recognise the master if you saw him now?" I asked, trying so save myself some dignity.

"Yes, I suppose so, though it never crossed my mind that I would see him again. He wasn't allowed to leave his island." This sounded incredibly familiar.

Nathan and I got up from the bank, the wind picked up some leaves and scattered them around us. We shared another kiss before we wondered back to the camp.

Nathan pushed some branches out the way, and we entered the campsite hand in hand, smiling like there was no tomorrow. But our smiles were wiped from our faces.

Kim was leaning over her bag throwing things in it. A man was standing next to her talking quickly; I had never seen him before. On the other side of the camp Dunstan was hauling his weapons onto his back and ran to Kim. The man next to Kim looked up and nudged Kim.

"Nathan this is Murray" Kim pointed absently at the strange man. "Keep packing!" I saw it was mine and Nathan's things that she was hurling into the bag; Kim stepped in front of us.

"It's Nistal. He was decommissioned by Morphius because of what he said to you about someone called Diran. He's gone mad, completely rogue. He's attacking a village nearby. He's killing everyone, every way possible. He's acting with his own army. He's still looking for the angel to try and redeem himself." Kim turned to Nathan, tears streaming from her eyes. "He is killing them like cows in a knacker's yard; he's killed nearly all of them."

We were running through the woods. Our bags seemed to be deliberately trying to slow us down. Nathan had taken my bag on his own back. I tried to protest, but he was having none of it.

The twigs scraped our legs and faces as we ran past them. Leaves scattered in all directions as we ran desperately after the man called Murray. Dunstan was asking about the positions of the soldiers and how many there were.

I looked at Kim, who was running next to me. "Do you think we are going to get there in time?"

Kim nodded, wiping tears from her already swollen eyes.

CHAPTER 12

GOODBYE

We broke out of the forest. It ended abruptly, allowing us the full view of hell.

A small village packed tight with houses was completely ablaze. The fire roared high; the smoke clouded the sun, bringing further darkness to this land.

Our bags were dropped on the ground. Kim yanked her sword cleanly out of its scabbard. Screams rang out all over the village. Kim ran behind me and dashed for the west end of this small village.

"Kim!" I yelled after her. I was hoping she would stop, but she didn't. She had drawn her sword and was running for the fire-consumed village.

"Murray, go after her. Help her with whatever she does." Dunstan ordered. I watched Murray run after her, trying to keep up with her. Tears stung my eyes; this could be the last time I'd see her; for the second time I was losing a sister, I had lost Mia just as quickly.

Heat blasted my face from the village.

"Shana." I slowly turned to face Nathan and Dunstan.

Nathan walked forward and took my hand. He placed it on my sword's hilt. "Use this when nothing else works." I swallowed a lump in my throat.

"Okay." The only word I could muster to the person I loved was "okay". He took my hand and clenched it.

"In your boot!" I frowned and looked at Nathan. I opened my mouth to speak, but he lightly kissed me and turned to Dunstan. What a nice way to say shut up.

"How many men are we against, and how many do we have to stop them?" Nathan was looking intensely at Dunstan. I looked across the village; the majority were probably dead and gone.

Dunstan looked across. "About a dozen men wait for us on the east side of the village. The western side is completely taken. The village is occupied by at least fifty men." Dunstan watched my reaction. "No fewer."

"Then why are we here and not there?" Nathan smiled.

"My thought exactly." Dunstan lifted two swords from his back and started to run for the eastern end of the village.

Nathan ran ahead of me. The wind whipped around his face as he ran to catch up with Dunstan. I wasn't a fast runner, and my legs became more reluctant to run to the battle.

I stopped running and closed my eyes. Everything around me slowed down as if nothing but wind was around me. My heart slowed, but my head felt compressed within itself. I focused in on the pressure in my head. It slowly started to become more intense, and the darkness rippled around in my eyes. The pressure was building, it started to hurt, but I focused in on it still. The pain burst from my head, and I knew it was there.

I opened my eyes and looked around. Nathan and Dunstan were nowhere to be seen, but I knew where they had gone.

A dirt path led into the village. The scattered dust was settling. I ran through the settling dust and down the road. All these houses had not yet been burnt, but they were vacant like a ghost town.

At the end of the road I made a sharp right and ran into a small crowd of a dozen standing in a cobbled courtyard. They all whipped their swords out but kept their distance. My necklace was a dim scarlet—the most powerful it had ever felt. It oozed magic that I had never tapped into before.

But I didn't feel like I was in control, which made it all the more dangerous.

I smiled at the crowd and gave a two-finger salute. "Shana!" I looked at the front of the crowd. Dunstan was standing above the crowd and was staring at me with incredibly sharp eyes.

I walked past the crowd, who moved easily out of the way. "Shana, you stay at the back with some of the younger fighters. They'll need you." Dunstan was standing next to me and moving through the crowd.

"Nathan and I shall stay at the front with the more advanced." I stopped walking; Nathan turned reluctantly to face me.

"I am not staying at the back." I stood still and folded my arms.

"Yes, you are." I opened my mouth to protest. "All that needs to happen is for you to falter once and you're dead Shana." I severely wanted to kick him. "I am trying to keep as many people alive here as possible, so do as I say." He whispered the words with harsh venom injected into every word.

"Fine!" I spat the words and turned away.

"Shana! Use what I taught you and you'll be fine." Dunstan hadn't moved from the spot where I'd left him. He was looking at me as if he was concerned for my safety.

I turned away. Now that wasn't likely. I walked to the back of the crowd and faced youths of my own age. "Right, are you ready?" (Are you ready to die?) Their faces were coated in blood and dust; they looked as if they were already resigned. "This is not the end. If you fight hard and trust yourself, nothing can stop you. Let yourself go, but be aware and don't think with your sword." This was the only help I could give them, but I hoped it would work a little.

"Don't be afraid!" I looked into each and every one of their eyes; I might have been mistaken, but I think I saw hope twinkle there.

I faced away from the youths and faced the rest of the men. To my horror and pride, they were all staring at me as if I had just given them all the hopeful words, looking into their eyes. I hoped it would work for them as much as it could.

"Couldn't have said it better myself!" I looked at the front of the crowd. Nathan was staring at me, admiration flickering in his eyes.

It all went quiet and I looked around. Something wasn't right.

"*Now!*"

I turned around. Charging from the shadows came an overwhelming army, and leading them was Nistal. The dust on the ground rose up in the air as Nistal charged in. I pointed my arm at the ground and watched it explode as if a bomb had been set off.

The army rushed into the explosion and were thrown off the ground. "Get the girl!" I ripped my sword out of my scabbard. As soon as I touched it, an eye-shattering red glow burst from it. I had done what I was meant to do—buy my friends enough time to think.

A rush of men sprinted out from behind me as they charged the shocked ambushers. I charged in with them, and I completely lost myself. My sword sliced through the men as if they were made of butter. I was thinking clearly, but this time killing these savages didn't seem the unholy evil it had before.

"You bitch!!" A knock in my back sent me hurtling to the ground. I spun over to see who had pushed me. When I looked up I saw Nathan swinging his sword at Nistal. They were both dodging each other's swings and blows that could kill each other. I got up to run to Nathan.

"I'm getting tired of you interfering, boy!" Nistal spat the words out at Nathan.

"You're tired of me interfering? Then give up!" Nathan swung his sword violently at Nistal, who jumped back.

I swept my sword across into an enemy, and he fell like a lump of rock to the ground.

"Retreat to the western side!" I shot a gaze round to see who was calling the retreat. One of Nistal's men was yelling blindly at his fellow remaining soldiers.

I knocked the man down with my sword as he skidded past me, running for the exit from which they had attacked.

Men were starting to run to the exit, but many were still fighting. I looked round for Nistal and Nathan; they were on the far side of the courtyard. Nathan looked up at me.

It was Nathan's words I heard. "Shana, duck!" I pulled my head down; a sword trimmed my hair. As I ducked, it swept through the air. I swung my sword round and sliced the man's legs. He fell to the ground and stared at me. No emotion of regret or hope was in his eyes, just pure hate.

"Do it!" I stared coldly at him. I brought my sword up and brought the hilt down on his head. He fell unconscious to the ground.

I slowly turned around to thank Nathan; he was leaning against a wall coughing. He seemed choked of air. Both his hands were clutching his stomach; blood streamed from his hands and down to the ground, pooling underneath him. Nathan dropped down against the wall and lay on the floor, spluttering blood and air.

Nistal looked at me. "He told your friends he would die," he chuckled darkly as he slipped into the darkness with the remainder of his men. Dunstan yelled and ran after him with some men.

I dropped my sword and sprinted over to Nathan. My feet carried me like air across to Nathan. I fell to my knees beside him. He looked into my eyes and smiled. Tears streamed down my face. I moved his hands away from his wound to look at it. The tears poured over my face uncontrollably when I saw it. The blood gushed out freely, pouring down him like water out of a dam.

"Nathan!" My lips quivered; I touched his face. "Can you hear me?"

Nathan reached his hand to mine and held it to his heart. "Shana!" Blood gushed from his mouth as he spluttered my name. "Tell my family, please. Let them know everything I told you."

I grasped his hands. "You're not going to die. Please, you can't!" My hands tightened on his.

"Shana, my love will always be with you." His eyes were no longer a deep brown; they were misty and distant, but the words cut through me like a machete.

I heaved in my breath and cried "I love you!" He brought our hands to my face and brushed my tears. I closed my eyes at his touch.

Then his hand became a dead weight in mine. I opened my eyes; I was gasping for air. Nathan's eyes were closed, and his peaceful face lay in my lap as if he was sleeping. I put his hand on his heart. I leaned forward and kissed him, his lips were blood stained and warm but they were still and unmoving. "My love will always be with you." I repeated his last words slowly. I gently took his head out of my lap and placed it on the ground.

I heard footsteps coming towards me, but they were distant—almost a dim noise that I didn't care about. I felt a hand on mine, but it felt like a light breeze against a rock.

"Shana, we have to move him." I recognised the voice. I frowned and looked up. The face was familiar, but no name came to mind. "Shana, can you hear me?" He stared at me, firmly grasping my hand.

"Dunstan, I think she's in shock." A whispered voice came from behind me.

"Shana, Shana!" The names whispered around me like a taunting ghost. My sight curled in around me as black corners folded in around the man. "We have to bury him, Shana."

"I know." I whispered the words. Everything became clear, but I wished it didn't. Fires roared from the other end of the village; cries were swept to the wind; bodies lined the street, but no one moved them.

Dunstan helped me to my feet. The floor spiralled around me, and my legs buckled. Dunstan lifted me up off the floor. "You're okay, Shana."

My head pressed against Dunstan's chest. Tears flooded over my face and onto his shirt. Nathan was dead.

I started to hear voices but I didn't want to hear anything.

"The bodies are being moved to the field, sir. Each pyre has been made."

My eyes fluttered open; I was lying on the ground staring at a lot of moist gravel and dirt. Dunstan was sitting next to me holding my hand.

"How many are there?" I took my hand away. "How many?" I looked at Dunstan.

"Seventy-six. Those are the ones we found." The other man spoke; his tone was mournful and distant.

I pushed myself off the ground. "Take me to him." Dunstan helped me to my feet.

Dunstan held my gaze. His eyes were deep and wet, and he looked as sad as I felt. "Are you sure?"

I held my breath and nodded.

Dunstan nodded. "Okay." He walked down some stairs.

I was looking over the entire courtyard, on some elevated ground. The cobbled floor was blood-stained, and weapons were spewed all over the ground as if they were toys. I avoided looking at the wall where he had died. I followed Dunstan down the small steps off the little podium. We walked slowly off the courtyard where the battle took place; I was overcome with grief but couldn't show it.

We walked to the field and stopped. Pyres were lined up all around the field. I choked back tears.

"This way!" Dunstan walked slowly through the pyres to their centre. He stopped dead in front of a pyre. A sleek breeze wavered past me.

I glided in front of Dunstan and stopped. The pyre was built of tall bundles of golden and copper straw all folded together tightly. Lying on top of them was Nathan. He looked asleep still, as if nothing had happened, except that his face was drained of colour. His golden brown hair didn't catch the sun as it did normally. His lips were parted as if in the middle of a sentence or a kiss.

No tears pricked my eyes. I only felt the wind and a crushing sense of loss and love.

Night fell as I stood by his pyre. Still the stars seemed to give Nathan some life, marking his lifeless skin with their radiance in the dark.

Many people had gathered around his pyre now. Dunstan stood opposite me holding the torch. Kim stood next to him, crying her eyes out.

Dunstan moved forward. "You will be missed, my friend." He tossed the torch onto the pyre.

The flames quickly curled up the straw, and the wave of heat danced off the top. Nathan's face was illuminated by the fire. He lay there so peacefully that the burning fire seemed to soothe him.

I stepped forward, my head completely filled with sorrow and pain, but amongst them were memories. I raised my hand to the pyre and fought back tears. I clenched my fingers until my knuckles went white. Silver and blue sparks shot up from the pyre. They danced around him like laughter gliding through the air. Silver birds sung in the smoke, gliding and singing, like they had done when he was child.

I stepped away from the pyre and melted into the crowd. Looking across the pyre, I could see Kim crying against

Dunstan's shoulder. Dunstan was staring across at me, as if he could read my thoughts. I had to leave.

I looked across the pyre, but Dunstan was gone. "I know what you're thinking." I didn't jump or flinch. Instead I nodded. "You're not going anywhere. I promised him." I gazed up at Dunstan.

"I promised him too. I need to get to Mulbeta." Dunstan frowned at me. "Don't ask why, but I need to leave. More innocent people are going to die, but before I do, I need a favour." Dunstan nodded. "I need you to look out for someone. I have a group of friends travelling, and they have with them a possible traitor. I need you to find him. He's called Diran. If he is a traitor, then you must stop him—I don't care how." I turned to face Dunstan. "I won't lose any more friends! I need to leave now." My voice rasped and stung, and as I turned away Dunstan grabbed my shoulder.

"Do you know the way?" His eyes were pained and cold. Nathan's death had hurt him more than he was showing.

I shook my head at his question. "No."

Dunstan looked at the sky. "Tonight it will be easy to find the way. Follow the stars." He dropped his hand from my shoulder and walked away.

I walked past the burning pyres. Not many of them had mourners. That was probably because anyone who cared or loved them were burning in some part of the same field with no one to cry for them or miss them—no one to remember them.

A deafening silence cracked through the night sky. A white light spread wide across the night like a blanket. The light shrank rapidly in size, and the silence was broken by a deep rumble. The white light was the same one that had taken me to this place, the same one that took Krystith to the stars to give up her powers.

The stars light shattered through the Rezta sky and smacked onto the land. The stars streamed one after the other, all landing in the same place, over the trees and far away. I looked over at Dunstan. He nodded at me. I sighed; I was off on my own again with more pain and strength in my heart than ever before.

I got into the woods and broke down. All around the wind ripped at my mangled dress and hair. I didn't try to contain my loud sobs as they drenched the land around me. He was dead, and I had to tell his family. Nothing was going to take the pain away. The star stream was going to continue through the night. If I was going to do anything, it was to get to his family, but I am not well known for the sympathy thing.

That night I dreamt I was standing by the sea with no one around me. My cares seemed to get heavier as the tide came in.

Nothing was able to take the pain away from me; not even my dreams could hide my broken heart's cries. Around me the sand seemed to be lighter than the air, it wisped around my feet and blew into the sea. It hovered over it as if it was waiting.

I walked gently forward. My legs seemed a little independent of me, and walked slower than I wanted into the sea. The damp sand was moulded by my toes. As soon as the sea touched me, I was consumed by grief.

"Don't be sad. My love will always be with you."

I looked up. The sand had risen up into a vertical shape. A face had appeared through the sand. Nathan's eyes were heavy and drawn. "I'll never leave you, Shana." The sand fell into the sea and drifted away.

I crumpled into the sea, and the tide washed around me. "I love you," I whispered. "*Nathan!*" I screamed, *"please come back!"*

Six Months Later

Chapter 13

Mulbeta

The woods were clear, and the fresh smell of the leaves clung to my damp clothes. I sat there again crying. I had cried so much lately it hurt.

His death had hurt me. I had gone away from any friends to put his dying wish to rest and to find Grint. But instead I had wound up getting lost in my nightmares.

My nightmares had intensified from seeing this world to being in this world. Now I was watching Nathan's death; I was reliving the helplessness of not being able to save him, to keep him with me forever.

Tears hadn't stop cascading from the eyes since the second I turned away from Dunstan. There were so many things I had to do—and before the angels awoke to kill us all.

First, I had to get to Mulbeta and find Nathan's family. Second, I had to find this angel and the sword with the rest of the gems. The full power of the gems must be unleashed; it was the only sure way to destroy Morphius. One thing I worried about continuously was Mia. Nistal had told me that she and Diran were a thing. It was dangerous to annoy her. It was gonna be even more dangerous to tell her that her boyfriend was a traitor.

That name rang in my head so many times. Nistal! He murdered Nathan and was going to kill the rest of my friends. He and his men had butchered the whole of that village, except one boy that Kim had rescued. But he was near dead when she dragged him out of the burning flames. Only five men of our army lived, but they had valiantly taken out over half of Nistal's army. Nistal was alone now. Morphius decommissioned him after he told us about Diran, and now he's rogue looking for redemption, and he would stop at nothing to get it. He planned to do this by finding the angel. I was going to have to find her first.

These thoughts had been plaguing my mind relentlessly for six months; I had walked aimlessly through my tears into the woods, following the star stream only to get lost.

I stood up against the tree and tried to walk, but the floor rushed back to my face. "Ooof!" The air was pressed from my lungs.

I had only eaten small amounts of food these past six months and was virtually starving. I had seen no one in that time, and I am pretty sure I was going stark raving mad.

Something heavy was in my boot, but I couldn't be bothered to look. Every time I took it off and shook it, leaves and mud just tumbled out; I would put my boot back on and it would still be there.

A deafening silence cut through the woods. The leaves stopped rusting and dropped dead on the ground. It could not be. A white light spread wide across the night sky and rumbled and then darted across the sky. The white light streamed in a desperate flurry in lumps—one after the other quicker and quicker—until it resembled nothing more than liquid light. I picked myself up; the stars were so close. I had come that far in the past six months, and not known it.

I moved twigs out of the way. Leaves crunched under my feet, but no wind disturbed this early night yet. The light was so blinding, but the light was what I needed to follow. The trees suddenly stopped, and I was standing in a mix of mossy roots tangled in with the earth. Beyond this stood a large number of little houses; they were all clustered together, stretching out further than I could see. A sign stood at the opening to a road. Reading the sign was like hugging a puppy or drinking a bowl of melted chocolate. The huge wooden sign was hanging from a pole that was pinned into the ground with ivy growing up it; the sign read "Welcome to Mulbeta". It made me laugh: it looked as though it had been written by a child. However, when I looked closer, it was chilling. The sign was rotten, with huge cracks running through it.

I walked through the paved area, but not a single voice was to be heard. It was if everyone in this part of Mulbeta had disappeared, but warmth rolled pleasantly out of the houses. Distant yelling broke the silence. I jogged forward, lightly scattering dust around my boots. I turned right and stopped. A huge shop loomed in front of me. I looked at the sign and saw that it was called Sincos. I darted into a dark alley. Living in the woods had taught me not to be timid and shy but to be everything that you fear. That way nothing could harm you. I looked into the shop and caught my breath. Sitting on the couch nearest to the window were Diran with Mia on his lap. Next to them sat Joshua, and standing beside them was Kim. She looked different—a lot more tired and angry. I blinked twice. No way! Oh my god, Jamie! Jamie had been my childhood friend on Earth, and we had gone together out for a bit. That was before I never stirred outside my house.

"Because no one can be trusted to know who the magical beings are in Rezta, and we are all magical, so until we know who to trust, no one can know who we are." Joshua was glaring at Jamie, as if talking to a child.

"Oh, how silly of me to not know that on my first day here!" Jamie gave Joshua his special version of a death stare. He whisked around and headed for the front door; I backed into the shadows, he pranced out through the door and glided right past me.

I needed information about what was going on. Jamie was a bit of sap to get around, so weeding information out of him would be easy enough. I darted quickly out of the alley, taking speed as a precaution not to be seen. I slowly jogged after Jamie. I needed to get his sympathy; luckily for me, Jamie had a weakness.

I silently walked behind him, and gently prodded him on the back.

Jamie flung his arm round; I let it take me on the face and fell over. I knew I looked a mess. After all, how great can anyone look after six months with only the rain for a soak?

Jamie knelt down beside me. "Oh my god, I'm so sorry, I panicked and—"

"It's okay, I'm fine. I was just wondering if you had any food." I looked into his eyes and felt that the tears from earlier were still there on my face.

"No, but if you want, you can come back with me and we can find you some." Jamie extended his arm; he pulled me to my feet, but this helped only slightly.

"No, that's okay, I can manage." Jamie fished in his pockets and pulled out a pound coin. He obviously hadn't been here long. I laughed weakly and took the coin.

"I haven't seen one of these for ages." I looked up from the coin. "You're from Earth. Whereabouts are you from?" I smiled. He had always been full of himself, and maybe he still was. Ready to spill his guts to someone he'd forgotten.

"I'm from Crowthorne. You probably haven't heard of it." I laughed. Jamie winced; he recognised my laugh.

"I know you." I smiled up at him.

Jamie took a step back from me. I had to keep anyone who knew me as far away as possible.

"No, no, it can't be . . . you died and . . . !" he fumbled for words "Shana" he whispered.

I forced a smile. I heard faint footsteps from behind me. It looked like I'd been wasting my time. Then again maybe not. A quick warning should keep him on his toes and safe.

"I know I should have told you what was going on but . . ." I looked down. "I was so afraid of him." I looked up. The memories were painful, but the truth is I wasn't afraid of him anymore. "I'm not any more though. Tell no one you saw me, especially the people in the shop. One of them cannot be trusted."

Jamie nodded. He was always such a drama queen. Hopefully he was going to heed my warning and find out who it was.

The trees rustled, and a strong wind gusted past me. Jamie closed his eyes. I ran back into the darkness and looked back. Jamie stood there, looking at where I had played my part. Now he had to play his. I still needed to find Nathan's house; he said he lived near the shop that was renamed Sincos.

I wandered down a dirt track, taking different turns, not knowing where I was going. I didn't want to do this—to tell his mother and father that there son was dead and that I was the last person he spoke to. I wouldn't tell them how I knew him, only what he had asked me to tell them.

The rattling in my boot set my teeth on edge. I was this close to ripping the boot off and lobbing it down the street.

A rustling interrupted my contemplations. I put my hand on my sword. I looked slowly to my left, but nothing was there. I looked down. A small child was huddled against the wall. She was shivering and crying. I took my hand off my sword, took a step forward, and stopped. Yes, she was crying now, but if I tried to befriend her she would probably die.

I took a step back. "Do you know where a family by the name of Johnson lives?" I sounded cold and unkind, but it was for her own good.

"It's the house at the end of the street on the right." Her voice trembled and shook like paper in the wind.

"Thank you." My voice was cold and unyielding; I walked away hurriedly down the path.

My destroyed dress had been worn down and cut up but still fluttered behind me, disturbing the dust off the ground. The houses all slanted towards each other as if they needed to be comforted as much as the people inside them.

I wandered to the end of the street and stopped. The house on the right was the same as any other, yet my heart beat against my chest, aching to be near it but yearning to run away as fast as possible.

My heard turned over. What I was going to say? How could I say it? I already knew there was going to be no easy way to do this.

I walked to the door. Light shone through the cracks. I hated the thought that my knocking was going to set the scene for the worst night of their life.

I knocked on the door gently. I heard a woman's laughter and light footsteps head to the door. The door opened back into the house. The woman standing in front of me had long flowing golden brown hair, the same colour as Nathan's. Her eyes shone like cascading water in the sun. "Mrs Johnson?" My voice was heavy. It rang like a death march.

Her eyes fell and lost their shine. "Yes, what is it? Come in." I slowly stepped into the house; I was quickly hit by the warmth of a fire.

I stopped walking and turned to her. My eyes had run dry of tears, but I'm sure they looked ready to burst. "Mrs Johnson, it's about your son." Everything went quiet. It was as if my words had sucked the life out of the house. "He's dead." Her face went pale, and I stepped forward to help her stand. She started to shake violently.

"Nathan, oh no!" Her knees buckled and she fell lightly to her knees. A man came round out of a doorway and ran to her.

She looked up at me. Her eyes were puffed and red. "How?"

I dropped my eyes. He had died warning me, saving my life again. "He died in a battle, saving a village against an attack from Morphius." She cried noisily against the man, clinging to his shirt. "He told me to tell you he loves you and he is sorry for leaving you the way he did." I choked on the words; the woman trembled and shook. "I'm sorry." My voice was hoarse, I scratched my throat.

She looked up and took my hand. "Thank you for coming." Her hand dropped, and she flopped back into the man, her limbs turning to jelly.

"Mrs Johnson!" I looked at the man; his face was a canvas that held no picture or emotion.

"Don't worry, she's been waiting too long to hear that news. We both have." His lip quivered.

"I'm so sorry to be the one to tell you. I wouldn't have come, but he asked me to when he was . . ." I choked back the tears. "Sorry!"

The man's eyes grew wide and slits seemed to form instead of pupils. "You were with him when he died?"

I nodded and looked away. "I need to go. I need to go now." I leaned back to leave, but his hand shot out and grabbed my wrist. I swear I could hear someone else in the house.

"You must stay. You look like you need food. There is some in the next room." I pulled my wrist away and held his hand. "You were the last person he ever spoke to; I want to know how my son died."

Tears ran off my cheeks. "I need to go now." My voice was rough and distant. "You don't understand I owe Nathan enough not to stay." They weren't going to die like their son. They had the rest of their lives to live; their son's life was over because of me.

He dropped my hand. "Take the food, please."

I sniffed and nodded. I left the house without the food and walked down the street. Memories of Nathan rang round my head like a drug.

My boot rattled again. 'In your boot!' His voice sounded in my head as clear as if he was beside me. I walked to the side of the path and sat against a wall. I wiped the tears away from my face. I pulled the shredded ends of my dress up and grasped my boot. I pulled hard at it, and it slid off my foot easily enough, but the rattling continued as I moved the boot. I plunged my hand into my boot. Nothing was there except leaves and soot. I pulled my hand slowly out.

I stopped. There *was* something in my boot, but it seemed to be actually inside the fabric. I took my hand out and scanned the rim of my boot. A little slit had been made at the front of the rim. I forced my fingers down in the crevice and felt something cold, made of stone. It had a hole in it. I pulled it out of my boot and inspected it.

It was a solid grey stone, roughly rounded with a hole in the middle. The hole had lots of spikes coming out of it. Intricate vines had been carved around the edge of the stone, but other than that it was plain and rough. I looked around. Why did he give this to me? I ripped some material off my dress and wrapped it round the stone. Something else I had to find out! I stuck the stone back into my boot; it was cushioned next to my foot and didn't rattle.

The night passed in a hurry. I only caught a couple of hours sleep, but against a stone wall it did more harm than good.

Dawn was just peeking over the city of Mulbeta. The dust was damp, and the streets reeked with heavy air. The castle stood out big and clear, looming above all of the little houses as if they were nothing but dolls houses. The sun beams streamed into the city, but their warmth passed straight through me, leaving me shivering in the cold. I felt as if this world had turned its back on me and left me to fend off the evil by myself. I didn't mind, though. Why should I? I needed as much distance from civilisation as I could to kill Morphius and stop the angels from waking.

I walked down a maze of paths and into a huge open area. The ground was paved in huge chunks of stone that had been stood on and flattened into the ground. Several stalls lined the outskirts of the area. A few people wondered around looking at things.

"Psst!"

I looked over at one of the stalls. A tall slender woman behind the stall was trying to get my attention. She waved her hand at me. I looked round the area; no one had noticed her. I walked casually over to the stall. The woman was bouncing up and down, extremely excited.

"Hello, how are you? Never mind. Can I have your dress?"

This woman was trying to be bubbly, but she was fidgeting with her fingers and mulling over my dress. That made me more uncomfortable than I was showing.

"What can you give me for my dress?" I asked.

The woman giggled. "Here!" She reached under her stall and pulled out a bundle of clothes. "You can take two items in exchange for the dress."

I reached into the bundle. The only two pairs of trousers she had were one made of a dull brown material that looked tight and another that were ripped with blood stains on them. The tops were plain and simple. I yanked out the brown trousers and pulled a large loose white top off the pile as well.

"Oh, I love that top! It goes well with this." She yanked out a black cape and threw it at me. "Free of charge." I nodded—perfect! I didn't want to think too much about the other pair of bloody trousers.

I walked behind her stall and pulled my dress off. I didn't care for modesty, not any more. I pulled on the trousers and the top, and I wrapped the cape around me and tied the string around my shoulders.

When I came out from behind the stall and said thank you, the woman was laughing and hugging the dress.

"No, thank you! This dress can be made up nice for my family's funeral." She laughed hysterically.

I slowly backed away from the stall. Damn, what a weird lady! I turned away from the stall, but kept looking back at the lady. I watched a man wander from stall to stall, not looking at any of them. He threw quick glances up at me; I looked away from him and back to the other stalls. My necklace was tingling, as if it knew when to automatically get ready for use.

A hand grabbed my arm. I grabbed the hand and got ready, but I let go of the man's hand when I saw that he was old and bent over, with his bald head facing the ground. He moved his head up and winced slightly.

"You have to get out of here. They're coming all around for you—look!" I backed away from the man. "And you're perfect!" I turned and walked away. "They'll get you!" I heard his voice tremble behind me.

"Let them try!" I stomped away and walked out of the area and away from prying eyes. The streets were now swarming with people buzzing around. For some reason everybody kept staring. It was becoming harder to fit in. I threw my hood up and looked around.

Yelling from up ahead silenced everybody. "And who do I pick today?" A swarm of men dressed in dusty bright clothes were moving through the crowd ahead of me. A woman beside me pushed her young daughter behind her. I stepped closer to the woman.

"What's going on?"

She looked terrified. "You don't know?" Her face was pale and covered in grime and soot. "They have begun searching here for the angel. They want her help in the coming war with Morphius. But the girls they take are never seen again. They take one every day off the streets. She hasn't been out the house in so long I felt I must bring her out, they never tell you where they collect the girls; otherwise I would never have brought my child out today."

She looked behind her. I heard her gasp and turned round. The woman grabbed my hand. "Where is she? Where's my baby?" Her voice was shrill.

"How about you? Would you like to go and see the king?" I turned round. A man was bending over, giving a girl a toothy grin.

"I want my mummy."

The man laughed. "Well, you really have no choice now; besides it's better at the castle." He kicked a basket over. "No more filthy living from now on!" The basket rolled towards me.

The woman turned round. "No, No! You can't take her." She ran forward. I caught her waist and pulled her back. The men had drawn their swords. She was writhing in my arms.

"Stop or they are going to kill you. Is that something you want your daughter to see?" I whispered in her ear.

She stopped writhing and faced me. "I can't let them take her." Tears flashed through her eyes.

The men put their swords away and chuckled darkly. "Well, at least one of you parasites has a brain." He was looking directly at me.

My head snapped up. "What did you say?" The man stopped laughing.

"Are you deaf? Well, you have half a brain then." The men around him snorted at me.

My necklace started to burn violently. I held my breath and it cooled down. "Let the child go."

The man laughed mockingly at me. "Why would I do that?"

I threw down my hood and faced them. "I'll go!" The men stopped laughing. "I will go instead of her." The girl was wiping the tears from her face.

"Hmmm, we have a volunteer, lads!" They chuckled. "Take her!" Two of the men took my arms in a grip as tight a vice. "Let her go." He pointed to the snivelling girl. The child went running back to her mother crying.

"Thank you! Oh my god, thank you!" The woman squeezed her child tightly, the way a mother should—the way my mother couldn't. "I will never forget this." the woman picked up her child and smiled at me.

I smiled back. I bet she forgot almost immediately. Everyone had their own problems here.

"Move it!" A soldier pushed me from behind.

"Is this how you treat all your volunteers?" I laughed lightly. "No wonder you don't have many."

The men looked at each other. "Let go of her!" The men let go of my arms and moved away slightly. Their leader moved next to me. "Make one move and you will greet the king unconscious." My necklace gleamed on my neck. It was a wonder they hadn't noticed the scarlet glow yet. Maybe the necklace had an ability to stay hidden when it wanted to.

I had no intention of leaving these "charming" men. The castle was exactly where I wanted to be.

Outside the castle a huge drawbridge was being pulled down for us to enter. We were out of view of any passers-by, so the soldiers had closed in on me again.

"May I ask you something?" I looked at the man who seemed to be the leader.

"No, you may not." He prodded my cheek.

"I assume that means yes. Are you in charge of gathering possible angels off the streets? Or do you just love the dirty work?" The man grabbed my hair and pulled my head back.

"I am second in charge and more than entitled to slit your throat and gut you like a pig."

I pulled my head up, and his hand followed, not bothering to pull away. I stared defiantly up at him. "Do it then." I spat the words at him.

He laughed and let my head go. "I will, but first you meet the first in command and the king." He turned his head slowly towards me. The leather neck of his top pinched his skin. "And then I will!" I squinted up at him.

"Set me a date and I'll show up" I replied.

The drawbridge landed, and the soldiers pushed me forward into the castle. We entered a huge courtyard, where stone crunched under our feet. A small grey well stood in the middle of the courtyard. It seemed so out of place, like it should have been in a shadowy corner rather than in the middle of a courtyard.

The walls all held many windows, but none of them showed that there was any activity inside the castle. This place seemed deader than the market place. The huge wooden doors at the top of some wide dull stairs were closed firmly shut.

"This way!" The soldiers pushed me forward.

Screams echoed and shook the courtyard. "Help! Help us please." My head darted round to locate the screams, but they were gone to soon for me to follow.

What was going on here?

The doors were swung back, and a man stood in the doorway. There was something wrong, very wrong. I tried to look at his face, but my eyes kept pulling away. It was as if he was masked by a veil of darkness.

"Latsin, we have a girl." My eyes pricked up. Did he say Latsin?

He stepped out of the doorway and walked soundlessly down the stairs. His toes gently crushed the pebbles. He stood at the foot of the stairs and beckoned me forward with his finger. The guards hadn't bothered to look under my cloak, so I was still armed.

My necklace happily provided a warm feeling against my neck, which I sorely wanted to use against him to see his face, because his name set my all my senses on fire.

I walked wearily to Latsin. Not one inch of me was afraid of him, but every inch of me wanted to draw my sword and ram it through him. I stood looking up to him scowling.

"Hmmm, what a lovely specimen! New clothes." He walked around me as if I were prey. "I think this carcass could stand the test." He stood in front of me on the step. "Be afraid!"

I wasn't afraid. My necklace was glowing scarlet. If the necklace got any hotter, I was pretty sure flames would spark out. I had become used to the burning; it gave more comfort than pain now.

"Latsin, bring her!" A voice boomed out of the doors. Latsin spun round, and his black cape brushed against my face. He tottered up the steps and went inside. I bounced up the stairs after him. Inside was just as dim and lifeless as outside. Guards stood posted around the corridors. They stood as still as death. None of them leaned against the walls, although they must have been so fatigued by now.

Latsin stopped in front of a tall wide door and faced me. He pushed the door open with one hand. "Get in!"

I glowered at Latsin. That definitely wasn't his name. He knew me, and I knew exactly who he was. I shoved past him and walked into the room. But it was hard to look at his face; every time I tried I wanted to look away.

People were moving freely all around the court, but the buzzing of their voices dulled down as I entered. All the people moved silently to the side of the room behind the wooden pillars that stood tall against the side of the room.

"His Majesty King Artimos and Princess Etrina!"

At the top of the room sat an old weary-looking man. His face was pale and his wrinkles looked like someone had started digging trenches in his face with a pin. He was so old he resembled a decrepit corpse more than he did a living being. He was wrapped in huge brown fur coat, and a heavy looking crown was placed upon his head. It was a small crown, as if it represented the little city he had to look after, even though this was supposed to be the biggest city in Rezta.

The person standing on his right stopped me in my tracks. A tall beautiful girl stood there in a white flowing dress; I knew her as the girl I saw in the pool that day I ran away. She saw me looking at her, but right now my focus was not on her but on the old man standing behind her. He was just as I remembered him. Grint stood tall behind the girl, looking at me. His eyes were dim and drawn. He sighed.

CHAPTER 14
LATSIN IS THAT REALLY YOU?

There was something else wrong. I couldn't quite put my finger on it, but there was someone else in the room. Someone I couldn't see. I looked into the corner of the room behind Grint. It was there that my vision went blind and my necklace pricked up. It looked like someone had broken into the castle.

"What is your name, girl?" I looked away from the corner to stare at the king.

"My name doesn't matter; neither does where I come from or why I volunteered." The king lifted his chin and leaned forward. Grint smiled at me and looked at the corner. He knew who was in the corner; they weren't a threat. "Don't bother wasting my time. Ask decent questions."

The court gasped, and Grint chuckled. "My, you are bad-tempered, aren't you?" The king sat back in his chair. "Very well, I do not want to 'waste' your time." His voice sounded scratchy to me; you might as well have been ramming a wooden stake into my ears. The chair creaked and the court hushed.

"Do you know why you are here?" The king gestured to the court with his hands.

"Yes, I do." I stepped forward. "Do you?" The soldiers fidgeted closer to the king, but I continued to walk slowly forward.

The king looked behind him and smiled. He looked back into my eyes. "It appears I do not know why you are here, Miss Hale."

I laughed at the king. The entire crowd shuffled and mumbled. "You know my name. So you know why I'm here." I walked up to the throne and placed both my hands on the arm rests. "I am here because you have some questions to answer." The king shuffled uncomfortably in his seat.

"Questions?" The king spat the words in my face.

I leaned closer into him. "About your loyalties."

The king pushed himself forward, but I didn't budge. "Clear the court!" The king peered round the room. "Clear the court!" He screamed the order. At once a loud mumbling came from around the room; I pushed myself away from the king and his throne.

This had not been my intention in coming here in this manner. My intention was to find Grint, but the king knew my name. The angel hunt was not for the city's sake. I had rattled him enough to know that. I had no reason to stay other than Grint, but he wasn't going to walk out with me today. To the king's right side stood a very powerful girl.

I turned to leave. The king jumped forward and grabbed my wrist. "You are staying!" I yanked my wrist from his grip and turned to the door. Fine, I'd stay, but first . . .

Latsin was standing against the door. "Oh, Nistal!" Latsin's head darted up. His eyes were extremely alert. "You can stay too, keep me company maybe." Latsin's eyes shot to the king.

"Don't be a fool, Nistal, close the door." I smirked at Nistal. The doors were slammed shut and the murmurings died. The king was on his feet panting like a dog, "How do you know? How did she know?" He screamed the words across the hall. "You knew his name. Only I know his real name." The king looked at Nistal. "How does she know?"

I smirked. This crapper had murdered the person I loved the most in this godforsaken world.

The king panted back into his seat. "It's not what you think." He whispered the words to himself more than to me. "I am not a traitor to my people." I spun my head round at the king. My necklace was pelting a scarlet glow around me. Grint looked at my necklace and back at me. My nostrils flared. A movement behind me sent my head spinning round.

I yanked my sword out of my scabbard. "Then why do you have a traitor here?!" I screamed the words at the king.

I lobbed the sword at Nistal. The sword glided quickly through the air and pinned Nistal's side to the wall. His screams flooded the hall. I can quite honestly say that this gave me an intense amount of joy.

My eyes were completely ablaze. The magic veil had been lifted from his face; I could see clearly the face that had smirked at me when Nathan lay dying.

"Wait!" A girl's voice came from the corner of the room. I looked at the corner; a boy was running out of the corner swinging his sword. He had a completely feral look in his eyes. He was running straight for Nistal. I stepped into the boy's path and knocked the sword of out his hands and sent him plummeting to the floor. Stupid child, get a grip! Many more people wanted Nistal dead, it seemed. What a surprise that was!

"Stop this!" She looked directly at me. "No more!" Etrina moved out from beside her father. She waved her hand in the direction of the corner. A ring landed in her hand, and she smiled at the figures standing in the darkness. I had nearly set them all on fire. What the hell were they doing here? Bloody people were going to get themselves killed.

"Shana!" I couldn't help but smile at the voice. A girl stepped forward, and the darkness peeled away from her face as she entered the bright hall.

I nodded at the girl. "Mia!" She walked hastily forward but was pulled back.

I looked at the figure behind her. "Wait until it stops." Diran had his arm wrapped around her waist.

Mia pulled away from him. "It's not going to stop. It's been going on too long." Mia ran to me and threw her arms around me.

"Thank god you're safe." I pulled her arms down from me quickly. I looked at Nistal. He was trying to tear himself from the sword without success; all he did was rip his flesh.

I looked back at Mia. She had grown since I last saw her. "Not here," I whispered slowly to her.

"It's too late. He will come, and he will end her life, like I ended Nathan's." I stepped towards him, and he chuckled. "You should have seen him look up at you and yell your name. It was easy to simply plunge my sword into him, the whimpering fool." I ripped the sword out of his side. He stumbled forward laughing. "He sliced as easily as butter."

I dropped the sword and plunged two of my fingers into his cut. His screams shrilled around the room. "You will feel his pain before you die." The fire burnt from my neck. I felt my fingertips simmer, and I rammed them further in his cut. His screams chorused loud through the hall. I tugged my fingers out of his wound. Nistal tumbled to the floor, panting and whimpering. His cut was smoking and blackened. I bent down to him and held his face. I brought my blood-soaked hand to his face and wiped the blood off.

"I don't want your filthy blood on my hands." I stood up and turned my back to him.

Mia held no look of disgust, only sorrow. She walked up to me, she hugged me again, and this time I hugged back.

Kim hugged me after Mia. I stared at Joshua. I didn't want to see him again.

"Shana, how are you?" I bit my lip to stop myself from screaming at him.

"Fine!" The words came out blunter than I thought they would.

Jamie stepped forward smiling, "Hi, Shana." He took another step forward. I looked away.

"Is someone going to tell me what's going on?" I faced the king. "Do you bring the potential angels to him?" King Artimos was slouched over his throne, far too apprehensive and jittery to sit down.

"No, no, he thinks I help him, but I don't I give him the girls that I think could be the angels." He smiled a toothless grin. "It seems I may have to pick another girl to go to him today." Kim moved next to me.

"Try it!" I folded my arms and I looked behind me. Nistal was foaming at the mouth; the boy I had flattened was being helped up by Etrina.

"Who are you?"

The boy looked savagely up at me. "My name is Spencer, and I will not let you kill him. That's my pleasure."

I looked away. "Is he the boy from that village?" I whispered the question to Kim, and she nodded at me. "You made more than one enemy that day, Nistal." Nistal glared at me in pure hatred. "So did I." I looked at Diran, Diran frowned at me in confusion.

"Where are Hendric and Anna?" Grint had stepped away from the throne. "Are they safe?"

"We left them at a shop called Sincos." Grint's face turned grave. "Who did you say that man killed?" He pointed an anorexic finger at Nistal.

"Nathan Johnson."

Nistal laughed at the name. "He died like a pig on a skewer."

I stepped towards Nistal, but Kim caught my waist.

"No, Shana, no more." She looked into my eyes. They seemed like they were about to spill over. Nistal chuckled and my anger flared. "You're no better than him if you do."

I looked away from Nistal and back at Grint, feeling a little hurt. "Why do you ask?" Grint looked close to collapse.

"My lady Etrina, is there a room where Shana and I can talk in private?"

Etrina backed away from Spencer. "This way." She walked to the back of the room; in the corner some spiral stairs were practically invisible. Grint followed Etrina up the stairs.

"You've shaken my father, Shana."

I pursed my lips. "I'm sorry for that, but what he is doing is vile."

Etrina groaned in agreement. "I can't say a visit from you wasn't expected. My father has been burdened with guilt for a long time now." She entered a corridor. "I will see to it that the he stops giving Morphius girls, now that I know he is." She stopped outside a door. "But it won't be easy. Morphius will assume we have the angel and will try to come and get you."

"You do understand I am not the angel?"

Etrina pushed the door open.

"Even if that's so, my father is certain that you are, and he plans to keep you safe behind these walls."

"What of my friends and Nistal?" I raised an eyebrow at her.

"I believe the dungeons will do well for Latsin." She stopped. "Nistal." She smiled a little, and a shot of darkness crept through her brown eyes. "As for your friends, call for me when you want them to be brought up." She looked at Grint.

"Come in. Thank you, Etrina." Grint was breathing extraordinarily hard.

Etrina walked back down the corridor. Her tiny intricate little footsteps bounced along the floor.

Grint shut the door and faced me; he looked incredibly pale and washed out. Then he strode right past me, blowing my hair across my face. "Did Nathan give you something?" Grint looked back at me and then looked away. I stared blankly at Grint. "Anything?" Grint paced up and down the room. "Would you tell me?" Grint stared at me.

I folded my arms. "I think my questions have been prolonged long enough, don't you?"

Grint smirked a little and snorted. "What are your questions, Shana?" He walked away from me towards the window.

"Where are the other parts of the necklace? Why did the necklace choose me? How is Morphius going to wake the angels?"

"He isn't going to wake the angels." Grint looked out of the window, not even bothering to give me a decent answer.

"And you know that?" I stepped forward. "How?" I shrugged my shoulders at him.

He turned to face me. "Because in order to wake the angels, he would have to give himself completely over to his other side, the side that belongs to the angels. Morphius would have to give up some of his other half, the side you know.

To do this, he would have to harvest enough strength from an angel to become strong enough to wake them."

Wrong! "He's going to try and fully wake them, whether you know it or not."

Grint shrugged. "Now, to answer your other questions, I will have to relate to you how I came to be banished to the island with my mansion and not placed in a dungeon."

"The night the shop went into flames?" Grint tightly smiled at me.

"Exactly."

Chapter 15
History of Sincos

"It was ten years ago—in exactly six months to be precise—we were holding the festival to celebrate the star stream, every decade the star stream gets brighter so it's a big thing. And this one was to be the biggest one yet. You can always tell how big it is. The stars shine brighter the closer it gets to the star stream, and the stars were glowing, getting ready to burst to Rezta. That night I was in my shop, the shop today known as Sincos. I was re-organising some books. One in particular was key to the events of that night. A magic book, the diary of Krystith, keeps the lost secret of Rezta; it holds the sword of Krystith. The book I speak of has revealed secrets to me that would make the angels weep—the sadness and loss Krystith faced, she was too young. On a hidden page a short scripture blares unreadable words at you. I had this book for many years and noticed an occurrence. Whenever a star stream was close the writing became clearer, almost readable, but I was not able to see it clearly enough until the night before the festival. The writing was the clearest I had ever seen it. It read, 'Whisper to the magic. Whisper to blood. Whisper to the name lost in the Earth.'

I lifted the book.

On the night of the festival I was arranging some more books I had acquired that day, and the book started to glow on the shelf. I opened the book, and the pages zoomed to the last page, but instead of the usual writing a keystone was set in place and the writing had changed. "Insert the stone. If you're of the blood, then you will be given a sword." So it was obvious to me that the book also shed light on one more way to kill Morphius, but this person had to come face to face with Morphius and come to no harm. This is something you proved you could do.

If you are what it has been searching for, then you will be granted entrance to the sword, and the greatest power ever known to Rezta will be in your hands. This information was only known to me and one other person. His name was Detrix. We studied the art of magic together when were young. Morphius' attacks were already hard on the city's heels; this was just before he took it over, and we looked hard for ways to defeat him. The only foreseeable way was to locate the sword. I had heard a rumour the sword was somewhere in the city; so Detrix and I began our long search for the sword. Then I remembered that Krystith herself used to have a residence in the city. After a few enquires, I found her old residence, but by this time Detrix had become warped with the idea of becoming as powerful as Krystith. Inside her residence was a single table, rotten and browned. On top of the table was a pile of wilting pages. Reading these pages, I found them to be missing pages from her diary, containing all her thoughts, battles, and longing for her escape from Rezta. In her last entry she noted the existence of the secret page in her diary. Also of how she was pulled back to Rezta, but she was without her powers. When she went to retrieve the sword, she found the gem was gone, so until the sword was full again she was not able to have her powers to fight Morphius. I learned several things that would be of use to you. The gems once separated lay dormant until they are all together again. This was one of her final entries, after she returned and found the gem missing from the sword. She was entirely without her magic, your gem was the activator and without it the sword could not be used, but your gem could be used, even though it would be weak.

And so she hid the sword, more specifically she hid it in the back page of the first part of her diary, the keystone could open the secret page and you would have the sword.

This, of course, was what I wanted to know. I bound the decomposing pages into her diary for fear of losing them.

Now I had located the sword, I had to get to work searching for the answers to get inside. On the night of the star stream, I continued to sit through the books, putting them away as I went. To be honest, Detrix and I had not seen each other since I got the job at the castle as magic trainer of the imperial guard, about three years before that night. Then we met again that night. He had been spying on me whenever I was with the book and had learnt everything. He wanted to try to get in the diary's secret page but I told him, "You won't get in. The riddle speaks of blood. You have magic, but I don't know if the diary will harm you if you don't get in." But he wouldn't have it. He wanted to take it to Morphius and see if he could get in. Detrix had become warped, completely maddened with the idea of the being the most powerful being in Rezta. He screamed at me, and set the shelves on fire. The smoke took hold of the store at once. I couldn't see where the book was, and I couldn't see where the entrance was. I fumbled under the smoke, choking and spluttering as I ran out of the store.

I felt the breeze on my face, but I couldn't leave yet, I turned round and could make out the faint shape of the table. On top of it was the book. I ran forward. The keystone was lying next to the book. I reached forward. A bolt of red magic hit me in the back. I was thrown forward into the table. I couldn't see anything. Now I ran my hands along the floor, searching for the book. My hand rammed against a rounded rock, and I knew it was the keystone. I grabbed it and decided it was better than nothing. I stood up and walked to the breeze. I walked outside; the shop was now completely engulfed in fire and smoke. No sign of Detrix led me to believe he was alive.

Once outside I was very much aware I was being watched from the shadows, by none other than Nathan Johnson. He was very afraid, and he had every right to be. I asked his name, and his voice quivered in reply. I gave him the keystone and told him to keep it until the day he died. I knew it wouldn't be long. His mother had told me he wanted to join the army and fight Morphius. I told him to send it back to me when it was most probable he would die and to give it to the person he trusted the most.

The next day I was in hell. The boy had been questioned, and he had told them he saw me. I, of course, denied it, but Detrix was also at my hearing, saying I set the store on fire to kill him. I had been a faithful servant and friend to the king during my service, so instead of killing me he sent me to my island to live in a palace. But he warned me that if I returned, I would do so as a prisoner. But when I explained that Morphius had taken my castle, he welcomed me back as a hero.

And here's something else. Mary was his sister. She had followed him into this world with the rest of his family and had a child here, so she didn't want to go back to Earth. Therefore, she accompanied me to the island. The child was very brave and powerful, and his links to the royal family led me to believe that he was the chosen one to kill Morphius, but it all went very wrong. I bet you can guess who he is?"

"Joshua—he's the king's nephew?" I raised my voice in shock.

"Yes, Shana." Grint had a tight smile on his face. "Now I have told you everything I can, I hope it helps you with whatever it is you plan to do." Grint sighed. "So tell me, did Nathan give you the keystone?"

I shook my head. "No, he didn't, but in his last moments both Nistal and another friend of mine were with him. Either one of them could have it."

Grint smiled. "Of course, and who is your friend?"

I stood there, silently fuming. "His name is Dunstan, and I left him the day Nathan was burnt at his funeral. I haven't seen him since."

"Ah, well, then." Grint walked to the door. "We will have to get to work on finding him." He opened the door and yelled, "Etrina, send them up!"

They all funnelled into the room. I moved out of the way and sat on the window chair and looked out across the yard, and the well seemed a little bleaker and darker than when I had arrived. I was so mucked up that even a well was seeming dark to me now. I couldn't help but smile to myself. Kim sat down opposite me on the seat. She didn't say anything; she just looked out of the window. The night was drawing in, but I wasn't going to sleep tonight. I was going to find someone first.

"Kim, what happened after I left?" Kim bit her lip and looked around her. No one was looking over.

She leaned over towards me and spoke in a whisper. "To be honest, I was a wreck. The death of that village was the worst I had seen in a while. Dunstan stayed with me for a while, but he said he wanted to go and see if a promise was being fulfilled. I can only assume he meant one that you were doing, because he said before he left, 'I'll tell Shana you said hi.' He also told me about Diran before he left as well. Did Dunstan never meet you?"

"I got lost in the woods almost as soon as I entered them." The tears blocked out anything for a long time.

Kim acknowledged my comment before continuing. "The rest of the time I spent with Spencer, trying to get him to health. I didn't know if he would make it. Thankfully he did, but I know he is hell bent on killing Nistal, Morphius, and the angel." Kim nearly choked on the last one.

"Kim, what happened that day? I know it was a horrible day, but you never before seemed willing to go into battle. That day it was as if something had possessed you, as though you were obligated to save anybody you could, even if it meant you dying." Kim swallowed a lump in her throat. It looked like I wasn't the only one with a secret here.

"I just felt like it was my fault." Kim looked at me with wet eyes. "It felt like those people dying was my responsibility and I have stayed too quiet for too long." She leaned forward. "Shana, I told everyone I was going to Earth to look for the gem but . . ."

The doors were swung open and in burst the king.

"You!" He pointed at me. "You need to take the test. You need to prove yourself to be the angel."

"I can promise you she is not the angel. She was born and raised on Earth." Grint stood in front of King Artimos, and the king's crazy eyes darted from me to Grint. "I can prove it. That boy there" —he pointed to Jamie—"he was with her on Earth. He aged with her through the years and knows her father."

My eyes darted to Jamie. He didn't know the other half of what my dad did to me. No one could prove what vile things he did to me. The only witness to what he did to me was me, and I was dead in that world. He had no idea about my mother.

"I need to send someone, otherwise he'll get suspicious. He will try to get into the castle through the well, where the girls are put." He pointed outside the window. "He'll come and kill us all." I looked out of the window and stood up. The well going darker wasn't my imagination.

"Are you telling me you put girls down the well *for him*?!" I strode towards the king.

"*Don't talk to me like that!*" The king flung his hand back. "You bitch!"

I squinted. "Go on then!" I whispered the words quickly, not flinching as he brought his hand down. I waited for the slap, waiting for the chance to pummel this man. When the blow didn't come, I looked at his hand. It had stopped in mid-air, and it was shaking violently. His hand was getting redder and redder and slowly went purple. I looked round the room. Mia was holding her hand up and clenching her fist shut. Her finger tips slowly edged to her palm.

"Apologise to her!" The words sizzled through her teeth. The king spat at her. White mist shot across her eyes. "Fine!" She shut her hand. His hand went quickly purple and exploded across the room. Blood splattered the walls and carpet and caught my clothes a little.

The screaming quickly followed. Blood gushed from his hand. Mia smiled, and black veins ran around her mouth. "I gave you a chance." The king was cradling his hands crying violently and screaming.

"Mia! What have you done?" Grint ran to the king's aid. He cradled the king and looked at Mia. He gave her a quick wink and went back to cradling the king.

"Dear god!" Grint ran the king out of the room, yelling for Etrina. A fumble of voices arose outside and faded away.

Joshua, as the king's nephew, I expected to react but he did not seem to care at all.

"Nicely done!" I smiled at Mia. "Saved me the trouble."

She was beside me now, looking at the mess the splattered hand had left. "Well, I thought you might appreciate a little help." Bitter sarcasm clung to every word.

I stepped over the hand, closed the doors, and turned to face the rest of the faces in the room.

"Tell me everything."

Everyone told me their stories. Not much had happened to them really. Mia, Joshua, Diran, Hendric, and Anna had all been trying to locate me and had been visiting Grint frequently until six months ago when the search for the angel began. The king had started summoning a large number of girls to the palace. None of them came back. He started asking for only one a day in his search for the angel, but even they did not return. So for safety my friends kept hidden. I found out that they had only met up yesterday with Kim and Spencer and Jamie and made a plan to break into the castle with a magic ring—the one Etrina took off them in the hall. I couldn't help but laugh at the uselessness of the plan.

Spencer didn't say a word. Neither did Joshua or Jamie. Only Mia and Diran seemed eager to convey the story. They told me how they had ended up together. It was when Mia nearly took his head off with a sword when she was going mad with Anna. It turned out they hadn't gotten on well since I left. Diran found Mia after the feud and consoled her. From then on they were inseparable. They said they were in love; I caught a lump in my throat. Images of Nathan and me in the pool ran through my head.

"So that's how that happened, but the question is what's going to happen now?" Kim shot a quick look at me as I became distant from the conversation. I passed her a grateful look.

"Well, I've got to go to a lot of places tonight. But first things first. I'm off to go shopping."

I told them the tale that Grint had told me, and they were all eager to help. I told them they couldn't, but they wouldn't listen. "You don't even know where the shop is." Diran seemed eager to join in, discomforting Kim quite a bit.

"I know where the shop is." They all looked confused, except Jamie. "I saw you all last night. I didn't come in because I've already lost someone I loved, and I wasn't about to lose any more."

Sympathy was rank in the air, making me uncomfortable.

"Hendric and Anna are there. You are going to need someone to distract them. That'll be easy for us. They are easily swept up into arguments." Mia grinned enthusiastically.

"A tactic you use to get your own way all the time!" It was the first time Joshua had spoken.

"Wait! Why are we so sure the book even exists anymore?" Spencer chirped up. "You said there was a fire. The book

207

might not have survived, and even if it did, then Detrix would have taken it to Morphius. "

I hadn't thought about that, and the truth was that I had become so attached to the necklace that the answer was clear. "The book is there. The pull of magic that led me to Sincos last night—the magic was familiar. The sword is there. I know it is."

"Shana, have you lost it.? I can't see it on you." Diran was squinting at my neck, and so was Joshua. I looked down. What were they on about? It was right there, as clear as day.

I quickly looked at Kim. She didn't know about my necklace yet. "I need to make a stop first, Kim." I looked across at her confused face.

She was quickly apprehensive. "You should come with me." She nodded.

"Meet me at Sincos. I'll be there as soon as I can." I hugged Mia quickly and walked out of the room with Kim.

I hurried through the courtyard and out of the castle. Kim and I drifted down different paths until I came to a familiar one. I stopped at the end of the path and turned right. "This was his house." She stared blankly at the house.

"Why are we here?" Kim looked at me inquisitively.

"Last night I told his parents he was dead. It was the promise I made to Nathan, the promise Dunstan was checking up on." I stepped up to the door and knocked gently. The door opened, and the man I had seen the previous night answered.

"Why are you here?" His tone had changed quite a bit since last night.

"I came to see Dunstan." The man frowned at me, as if I was going crazy. I heard footsteps from inside the house.

"Who are you?" The footsteps stopped.

"You can call me doctor." A figure came round the corner. He walked out of the darkness. Kim bounced on the spot.

"Hi!" His deep voice rocked me; it was the last voice I had heard before I was alone for six months.

"Dunstan!" Dunstan walked out of the house and hugged Kim. She squealed and hugged him back.

"It's so good to see you both." I felt incredibly cold in seeing him again; it brought back fire-spitting memories.

Dunstan let go of Kim and turned to me. "How have you been?" It was the first time anyone had sounded as if they understood the pain I was in.

"I've tried." It was the only answer that wouldn't reduce me to tears.

Dunstan wrapped his arms around me. "I know." He rocked me gently, and I hugged him back. I didn't realise I was hugging him quite so intensely till I realised my face was basically being smothered in his black top.

I let go and looked at him. "I missed you." He hugged me again. This time I hugged him back more tenderly.

His dark voice made my heart bleed. It brought back so many memories of the four of us, just sitting round discussing what we were going to do for our next sparring lesson.

I told Dunstan and Kim everything that had happened. I also told them about the necklace. They didn't take to it very well.

"Wait a minute! Are you telling me you have some of the power Krystith did, and that's how you know the book is in Sincos?" I nodded as we walked down the street.

"Another thing—when we get this sword, I am going down the well."

Dunstan grabbed my arm. "No, you're not."

I tried to yank my arm from his grip, but he was like a bear. "Why not? Those girls need help, if they are still alive."

Dunstan moved closer to me. "Nathan gave his life to save you. I won't let you waste your life." His breath was ice cold on my face.

"He gave his life because he knew I could help Rezta, and that is exactly what I am going to do."

Dunstan dropped my arm and stared at me. "He gave his life because he loved you." His words stung me like poison.

"No, I don't want to believe it was just that. I can't." I brushed passed Dunstan, not looking back to see if he was following.

"Shana!" He slammed me against the wall. A huge jet of fire whistled past me, Kim, and Dunstan. We pulled our swords out and I got ready to fight.

"Are, you going to hide there or fight me?" I recognised the voice—Nistal.

We all rounded the corner and faced Nistal. He had a dozen men standing behind him. One of them I recognised. He was the man I didn't kill, the one I knocked out. The rest of them must have been the survivors from that day.

"Leftovers!" Dunstan sneered. There were a dozen of them. It was going to be hard enough as it was with no help.

Nistal raised his hand. Figures moved out of the shadows. They had us surrounded. Two men came out of an alley closest to me. We had hidden down there. Why hadn't they killed us then?

"You cost me my life." He lifted his sword; the edge glowed in the moon light. "Your life is mine."

"Wrong!" A deep familiar voice sounded from behind us. "We owe her ours, so it looks like you will just have to make do trying to kill us instead." Soldiers moved past us and backed to our sides, but they looked very weary.

I turned round to face them. Hendric and Anna both had their swords ready.

"Long time, no see." Hendric smiled a little at me.

"For the most part, it's not something I regret." My eyes flicked to Anna.

She looked uncomfortable and shifted at being paid attention to. All the soldiers edged towards the two of them.

"Is this the great rescue of Shana?" Nistal said. "Well, I can tell you now you two will be easier to mow down than her friend was."

I swivelled back round to Nistal. "How did you get out of the dungeon?"

"Do you not realise by now that no one gives a damn about right or wrong? They want to survive and are willing to co-operate with Morphius to do so." Nistal smiled sweetly.

"Morphius won't spare their lives. So for once I hope the traitor will be the first to die if Morphius regains his strength and lets the angels in."

"Why wait till then? You have my blessing if you want to kill princess Etrina." He laughed, as did his army.

"Etrina?" I snickered "I have a lot of problems right now. She is not a big problem to me."

"You'll be a fool to overlook her." Nistal laughed. "Checked up on Diran yet?"

I shot a quick look to Hendric and Anna. They were clueless on any of the past events.

"It appears not." He stepped forward. "I wouldn't worry too much. He's probably gutting Mia right now."

I swung my sword at Nistal, but he quickly dodged it. All the other men moved forward behind me and started the attack on my friends.

A large burst of lightning shot through my hand at Nistal. It smacked right down his side. He writhed and squealed in pain. I lurched forward and drove my sword into his side. I yanked the sword out and stepped away.

He stumbled away from me and pointed his sword to me. "He said you wouldn't take revenge." I swung blindly at him.

"Shut up!" I swung again and sliced his legs.

"He said you didn't have the heart." I kicked him in the shin, and he toppled over. "I guess he was wrong about you; the person you loved knew nothing about you."

I stared down at Nistal. "You took that chance away from me." I dropped my sword and punched him square in the jaw.

Blood dripped from his face. "Go on!" Blood gushed out of his mouth. "End me!"

"I don't kill for mercy. Besides, your life isn't mine to take." I picked up my sword. "I have a friend who wants a word with you."

"A word?" Nistal sneered "Are you saying he won't kill me?" I turned my sword round.

"No, he'll probably kill you, but honestly I am hoping he won't." I raised my sword

I slammed by sword's hilt down onto Nistal's head. I knew it wouldn't kill him. Spencer needed to learn a lesson about who he was. He needed to decide now if he was a murderer like Nistal or my friend I could rely on.

I ran from Nistal's seemingly lifeless body. Kim was backed into a corner. The soldier brought his sword down quickly on her. I slammed into the soldier, knocking him onto the floor. I threw my sword down on him, the last wisps of air peeled out his body. The fight was nearly over. Anna was locked in a battle with a rather weedy-looking soldier, and everyone else was killing them as if they were simply using their swords to get rid of an irritating itch.

I turned to Kim. Her eyes were wide and panicked. I looked over her for a wound, but the sword had left none. I looked at her arm; it was covered in white liquid. The white liquid dripped off her and down on the floor, pooling at her feet.

"What is that?"

Kim looked at her arm and back at me. "Help me!" She slumped forward.

I dropped my sword and caught her. I set her down on the ground and kneeled beside her. The position stung me; it was the same one I was in when Nathan died in my arms.

"Kim?" I shook her "Kim!" Her eyes fluttered.

"Shana, don't talk. Just listen. Dunstan knows what to do. Just get the book. Detrix isn't to know why you are there." She clutched her stomach, and more of the white liquid pooled there. "I have been travelling to Earth frequently. Detrix thinks I went there to try to find the gem stone, but I went there because—" She writhed and screamed.

"Dunstan!" I screamed over my shoulder. "Dunstan, help me!" Fear ran through every inch of me. The situation was too similar. I couldn't let it happen. She said Dunstan knew what to do.

Dunstan slashed the stomach of the soldier he was fighting and looked over. Three soldiers remained now. "Hendric, take them." Dunstan threw him a second sword and ran to me and Kim.

"No, Shana, listen. This is important" Dunstan rolled up beside me. He looked desperately at Kim.

"Bloody hell!" He looked at the liquid on her.

"What is it?" The liquid scared me. It resembled blood, but no one has white blood. Dunstan looked at Kim.

"Shana, go to the library." I stared at Dunstan hopelessly. "Shana, listen to me." He cupped my face in his hands. "I can save her, but you need to get to the library, find the book, and get the sword."

I looked back at Kim. "Save her!" I got to my feet. "Please!" I wiped the white liquid off my hands and onto the wall as I ran past it. "Take Nistal to the library" I yelled behind me as I ran round the corner.

I ran down the path and round the corner. The magic in the atmosphere got stronger the closer I got to Sincos. My fuel was no longer my blood; it was my desperation and my hope to find the sword and any other secrets in that book. I rounded the corner as I had the night before. The building was quiet. I quietly walked into the entrance of the shop. It was a wide arch made of stone, and it was more like an entrance to a castle fort than a shop.

The bookshelves towered high. Books, boxes, and ornaments cluttered the shelves. The couch and table were to the right of the room, where I had seen them all the previous night. Mia, Diran, and Joshua still weren't here.

The magic was so strong it was like a drug to me. The calling of magic pulled me into the shop. No one was around the shop, so I freely started rummaging through the shelves.

"Can I help you?" The voice made me jump. A man was standing by the shelf. Behind him stood Joshua, but there was no sign of anyone else.

"No thanks, I'm just looking." I shot a warning glance at Joshua. Why didn't he keep away from me?

"I'm Detrix, the shopkeeper. Perhaps there is something I can help you find?"

I shook my head. "No thanks, I'm not really looking for anything specific. I'm just browsing."

Joshua shot a smile over to me, but it wasn't a smile that was comforting. It was more of a tight-lipped smile.

"Okay, well I will be at the desk if you need me." Detrix walked away with Joshua obediently following behind him like a faithful lap dog. I went round the bookshelf, out of sight of Joshua and Detrix.

Where was everyone else? A strong calling of magic made my necklace glow feverishly red. I closed my eyes and let the necklace's power consume me. I willingly let my feet float me through the shelves. The darkness rippled in my eyelids, and deep orange light shot across my eyelids. I opened my eyes. I was standing at the farther end of the shop. In front of me was a mess of boxes and books, all piled high above me. I ducked to the lowest shelves.

A whispering voice sounded in my head. "I can't take it anymore! I am so tired. I want a life outside war." The voice got louder and louder, saying more words into my head.

"I know of a way to get rid of my powers, but it's tricky." I pulled out a book from the shelf and the voices ceased.

I looked at the book. It was made of brown leather with tiny silver intricate writing on the cover—"Diary of Krystith". Underneath was some more writing in a different hand—"Hero and Legend of Rezta".

I smiled to myself. I opened the diary and flicked through the pages straight to the back. The back page was made completely out of stone. In the middle was a circle with a chunk of stone missing in the middle. I looked round quickly; no one was anywhere to be seen.

I lifted my trouser leg to reveal my boot. I found the rip in the seam, and the gap seemed smaller than last time. Instead of putting my fingers in and pulling it out, I began to tease the tiny parcel out of my boot. When the black material showed itself above the boot, I yanked it out quickly. I held the package in my hand. I wondered what I was about to do—to hold the sword in my hand to wield the power of Krystith.

I unwrapped the black material to reveal the stone and gently lifted it to the book. I held it above the slot that I knew it should fit into and let go of the stone. It dropped into the gap. I sat and waited for something to happen, but nothing did. I turned the stone but nothing happened. I lifted the keystone out and looked closely at it. I thought back to what Grint had said. "Whisper to the magic. Whisper to blood. Whisper to the name lost in the Earth." I said the words out loud, hoping it would shed some light on the situation. What did that mean? Defective piece of crud.

"I told you she wasn't the right one." I dropped the stone and book and looked up. Joshua was standing beside Detrix looking down at me.

"I know, son, but you also said she had the necklace." He pointed a hand at me. "Can you see it?"

"No, but then again she's become stronger. She could me masking it." Joshua looked apologetically at Detrix.

"What? Did you just call him son?"

Detrix looked amused. "Has my brother told you nothing?"

I looked desperately at Joshua. "Who's your brother?"

Detrix chuckled. "My, he has kept you in the dark." He turned to face Joshua. "Would you like to tell her?"

Joshua sneered. "My pleasure! Detrix is my father, the best father. You see I was never held prisoner by Morphius. That was just what we wanted you to see. My father found out I was going to find Morphius and fight him, but instead he told me Morphius had no ill will against me and promised me that if I co-operated with Morphius, he would free me from the island. My mother is Mary. She died by Morphius' hand as a reward to me for helping him." I fumed at Joshua. "My uncle is the traitor. The traitor is Grint; he was the one who sent you here, wasn't he?" Wait! What! Grint is his uncle . . . Detrix's brother?

I ignored the question, Joshua smiled. "The king is your uncle and you let him have his hand blown up by Mia? You did nothing?"

"Why should I have done anything? He had me banished with my drip of a mother on that godforsaken island."

I tried to keep relaxed, but he was making it very difficult.

"Why weren't you banished?" I turned to Detrix. He was a slimy oily creature I would never trust.

"I blackmailed the king of course. I threatened to tell everybody the truth about how his wife died." Detrix smiled cruelly at me. "How he had an affair with young Anna, the dead queen's sister." My eyes widened in horror. "He killed his wife to keep her from finding out the truth and then banished Anna with Grint, Mary, and my son." So that's the kind of love this family generates, and probably why I had a bad vibe from Joshua when he tried flirting with me by the lake. So Mary was the king's sister and Anna was the dead queen's sister . . . to all sisters out there *please be careful with this family.*

A flicker of realisation crossed my eyes. That was why she didn't want to come to Mulbeta and why she looked so admirable when she spoke King Artimos' name.

"You bastard!"

All our heads spun round. Behind me stood both Anna and Grint.

"Oh, look here, a family reunion!" I scoffed at them.

A bolt of red magic zapped at me. I ducked to the ground, and I grabbed the book and stone. Magic, fire, light and dark mist shot to and fro. I crawled out of the magic feud. It looked like I wasn't the only one with family issues.

I crawled through the bookshelf, throwing books out my way. Once through the gap, I ran down the aisles past the bookshelves.

"Don't let her get away!" Detrix' voice boomed after me.

Black mist shot beside me, narrowly missing my waist. I ran into the main entrance and turned. Standing there blocking my way was Joshua. "You think you can have it that easy?" He pulled a dagger out. "Wasn't the scripture clear? '*Whisper to the magic. Whisper to blood. Whisper to the name lost in the Earth.*' Blood, Shana. It needs blood to work. And I don't mean to skimp on the amount of blood used to make it work."

I whipped out my sword. "Bring it on, daddy's boy!"

Joshua threw dark mist at me. I ducked out of the way, and it whistled sweetly through my loose hair. I dropped the book and stone on the floor.

Joshua ran forward swinging his sword. He rammed the sword at me. I blocked his blow and threw a punch into his chin, and he stumbled backward.

"So the carvings I saw in the mansion?" I enquired, I was so confused.

"All fake, made by my mother after my father spread the lie." He swung the sword at my side. I rolled out of the way.

"Nistal said Diran was a traitor, but it wasn't him, it was you." I screamed at him lividly.

Joshua sneered. "You bought that one better than Morphius thought you would."

A loud scream sounded out through the store. My head snapped up, and I looked down the aisles of bookshelves. I didn't see it, but I was suddenly consumed by black clouded mist. I waved my hands to clear the mist. The wind was blasted out of me, and a searing pain shot threw my stomach.

I dropped my head to look at my stomach. Through the mist I could see a shining dagger poking out of my stomach. It was coated in my blood. I looked up. Joshua's face was inches away from mine.

"Looks like I did bring it!" His lips curled up. "Daddy's girl!"

I crumpled to the floor. I ripped the dagger out of my stomach and stared disbelievingly at Joshua. I backed away from him on my hands and knees. Memories flashed through my head. *My father strode after me as I backed myself against the wall. There was no one to help me, but I knew more was to happen to me.*

I did it again. This time I was backing away from Joshua. I backed into wall that was filled with books; my back was pressed right into the shelf.

"Nothing you do is going to hurt me more than what has already happened to me." The words gave me a little strength but no hope.

Joshua sneered. "We'll see."

Dunstan raised his hand slowly up to me. A dazed look passed over him.

Joshua swayed back and forth, and blood began to drip from his mouth. He looked down, and I followed his gaze. The thick point of a blade protruded from his stomach.

"You're not going anywhere near her." My heart lifted at the sound of Dunstan's voice. Red lightning shot into Joshua from the entrance. I looked over. Diran stood alone in the entrance, holding the book and keystone. I must have dropped them.

My head swayed against the bookshelf. I lifted my hand towards Diran. I tried to open my mouth, but all that came out was a rush of air. Diran ran over to me, and Dunstan held me to his chest; he held me tight as Diran came over.

Diran passed the book over to me. I flicked to the back page. Diran gave me the stone. I looked at the stone. This was going to hurt. I shoved the stone into my stab wound; I writhed and pulled the stone out.

"Shana!" Dunstan's voice whispered into my ear. My gaze was completely fogged over. I dropped the stone onto the page. My hand was spread over the page, and I closed my eyes. The only things I knew that were going on around me as I lay in Dunstan's arms were the growing heat around my neck and Dunstan's voice shouting my name.

CHAPTER 16

MOTHER OF MINE

The ground was cold underneath me. I felt no pain and no noises sounded near me. The only sensation was the mind-piercing heat of the necklace. My eyes shot open and I sat up. I tried pulling at the necklace, but my hand went through it. Tears pierced my eyes. I looked around the room, if you could call it that. The walls were made out of solid grey rock that matched the floor. An open arch was pressed solidly against the wall, but in the middle of the room was a glowing orange light.

I tried to get up, but the necklace scorched every muscle in my body; the glow was calling me. It was like trying to follow a missing piece of my heart.

I crawled on my hands and knees to the glow. My necklace started spitting sparks of fire into the air, but I was completely oblivious. The sword was clear to see in the orange glow. My senses were completely dulled as I reached to the sword. I gently touched the swords hilt. A huge bolt of blue light spread across the entire room, completely blinding me. I covered my eyes and let go of the sword.

The heat from my neck vanished and the light dimmed with a hum. I uncovered my eyes and looked at the sword; five gems sat neatly in the middle of the hilt, but they were clear. Two of the gems had formed a cross, two more of the gems had also crossed through each other, the crosses were joined from one crosses top to the others bottom, and there in the middle of the two crosses sat my gem. It didn't really resemble a star; maybe it was a star that I didn't know of, it was pretty enough though.

I sat there confused. Were they meant to be clear? I touched the gems. Clear blue liquid were moving in the gems. I watched as the liquid moved to the five points of the gems. Then the liquid rose into the air, and a thin line of liquid puffed lights out into the room. The lights travelled through the air and towards the arch.

The arch was filled with the light. The lights stopped, and liquid blasted into the arch. A white light shot through the room. I looked away. The light faded, and a sweet singing voice gently took its place.

I looked back into the arch and nearly stopped breathing. A picture had formed almost like a film recording. I was looking at a man and a woman cradling a child. The woman was singing a soft lullaby to the baby. The words were both dark and enchanting to listen to. I recognised both the man and the woman. The beautiful woman with long flowing Dark hair was Krystith, and the man was my father.

Krystith stopped singing and spoke words to the baby, hugging her closely to her chest. "My darling Shana, I'll always love you."

My father laughed. "So will I, little one."

The baby laughed and hugged Krystith. The happy picture faded, and standing in the arch in its place was Krystith.

"Shana, if you are listening to this message, then I have failed in my mission to destroy Morphius and your life has ended on Earth. I don't know how, but I hope you will not be too upset about leaving Earth. The recording you just saw was taken of you when you were two weeks old. I loved you so much. That's why I left you. I had a visit from an old friend who lived in Rezta. She told me a gem had gone missing from the sword and that I needed to return to fight Morphius. They said that only I or someone related to me would be strong enough to defeat him, but I knew where the gem was."

"I married your father for that simple reason. My magic called me to him, and it was he who tried to take the sword and it was he who was banished to Earth. But he never knew he had the gem—that is, not until he lost it to you. When you were born, the necklace latched onto the next in my bloodline—you!"

"I used the name Tania, to protect you from the truth as long as I could." Her eyes were solemn and withered.

"You are my daughter, Shana, and I know that if you are reading this, then I have failed to return to you and that you have touched the sword. The power was meant to be in the sword and to be wielded by a hero, but you are a descendant of its original owner. So instead of the power staying in the sword, you and you alone have absorbed my full power. You have the power to defeat Morphius."

"But hurry, Shana. I have learnt he plans to awaken the angel. He needs the fallen angel to do the ceremony, only she can do it for only she has the power. Morphius has been getting weaker every star stream, for he is feeding the angels his own power, the resontvie, to help them to wake up. And every ten years they get closer to waking up. And now the time has come for them to fully awaken and enter this world. This will bring about the destruction and ultimate finality to Rezta."

The archway shimmered, and the light blasted out of it. It shot at me and completely consumed me.

I opened my eyes. I was lying on a couch staring up at a very high ceiling. I heard faint weeping and turned my head. At the end of the couch Kim was slouched over my feet crying. On the adjacent couch Mia was crying into Diran's shirt. Dunstan sat on the floor by the bookshelves. Blood covered his knees, and he had a distant look in his eyes. It broke my heart to see him like that. What had happened?

Completely hacked to death, Joshua was strewn across the floor; I recognised Mia's work.

"Dunstan, what's wrong?" The crying ceased. Kim's head popped up, and Mia jumped to her feet. Diran wiped his eyes and looked at me as if I was an idiot. But my eyes were locked on Dunstan's.

"She's dead." He whispered the words.

I sat up free of pain. "Who?"

Dunstan frowned and looked up. He stared at me as if I were a ghost. He looked at Mia, Kim, and Diran and then back at me.

"Shana?" I notched my head round to Mia. "Is it really you?"

I frowned. "Of course it's me! Who else could be this dumb about why you look so sad?"

Mia smiled a little and stepped forward. "What happened to you? You died. Over there, you died." She pointed to Dunstan, who was still on the floor.

I looked at the object I held in my hand. No one had seemed to notice it yet. I held the sword up for all to see the clear gems.

"I took the power out the gems. As Krystith's daughter I now have her power and I am going to kill Morphius."

I told them all what happened and most of what Krystith told me. I left out the bit that the angels were coming to Rezta with the next star stream. I hoped I could stop him before it happened.

But Dunstan was still in shock. "You're alive?" He got to his feet.

I walked over to him and looked into his eyes. "I'm alive."

His arms wrapped around me. He was cold and shivering; his black hair was damp with blood.

"I'm sorry." His words were whispered into my hair. I hugged him tighter.

"You thought I'd betrayed you?" I let go of Dunstan. Diran looked like he'd been punched.

Kim looked guilty. "It was the only way it made any sense."

I mulled the information over in my head. "Nistal was sent away by Morphius because he told us you were a traitor to us, but if you're not . . ." I stopped talking and turned to Kim. "If you're not, then Nistal hasn't been shunned by Morphius. He's still very much in commission."

Dunstan walked me down the aisles of bookshelves to where they had left Nistal. They had tied him up to a bookshelf after finding me. Anna, Grint, and Detrix had gone missing. They'd probably blown themselves up. I strode over to Nistal and ripped the gag off his mouth. As soon as I did so, he spat at me.

I punched him in the mouth. "Why were you at the castle, pretending to work for the king? What were you after?"

He snickered. "The angel." Blood ran down the side of his mouth. "I bled the girls to see if their blood was white. Only an angel has white blood."

"What else is down that well?" He laughed. I plunged my hand into the cut I had created back in the castle. "What else is down that well?"

"In the well." He writhed. "His pet. The well leads to an underground city. It's where the girls were to stay, so the king would keep bringing Morphius potential angels, and if a day went by that a girl wasn't brought to him, then they were all to die and be fed to Morphius' pet." He looked at Dunstan and back at me. "Are you gonna kill me now?"

"I told you." I stood up. "Your life isn't mine to take." I kicked him in the face, and his head dropped onto his shoulder.

I turned to my friends "Where is Jamie?" I noticed he wasn't with them.

"He is back at the castle with Grint," Kim sniffed. She still had tears down her face.

"I'm going to go see him, alone." I smiled at them before strolling out of the store. As soon as I was out the store I sprinted down the street.

"You aren't going down that well by yourself?" Mia was running behind me down the path. "You may have managed to convince them all you're not going to the well but I know you better."

I stopped running and turned to Mia. "I won't risk your life," I yelled at Mia. "The reason I stayed away from you for so long was to keep you as far away from danger as possible."

"I was always in danger. I can take care of myself as much as you can. I know you've lost friends, and I know you're hurting, but I am not about to leave you to face danger alone again." She had said all she needed to say to get through to me.

"There's no way I can stop you, is there?"

Mia shook her head. "Nope!" She ran ahead of me. I ran after her. "So what's the plan?"

"Get the girls and whoever else is down there out of the underground city and get rid of the pet."

We ran quickly through the streets silently, leaving our friends behind us.

CHAPTER 17

WELL, WELL, WELL

The castle bridge was still down. It seemed more like a ghost house than it did before. We ran into the courtyard and straight to the well. There was no bucket or rope, no way down.

Mia got up onto the well. "Mia, stop!" I threw my arms round her to stop her, but instead I grabbed the air.

"Damn!" I climbed up onto the well and jumped down. The walls whistled past me, and I landed with a thud on the ground.

I looked back up. The well was only about five metres above my head; no wonder my ankle hurt.

"Mia!" The name I whispered echoed around me.

"Over here!" I felt a tap on my shoulder, and a cold breeze flicked through my hair. "I think there's a tunnel behind us." I heard her move. "Follow me!"

I crawled after Mia as the walls brushed against either side of me. Light flickered ahead of us. I could make out Mia crawling quickly in front of me. She stopped moving.

"Shana, something's wrong." Mia crawled out of the tunnel and I followed her, drawing my sword. We were standing in the middle of a street, an empty street.

"Where is every one? There's supposed to be nearly every girl who used to be in Mulbeta."

Mia took out her sword in response to my question.

Screaming made us turn our heads to the right. We ran as fast as we could, following the screams. My heart sank deeper and deeper as the screams got louder. We hurried past blankets strewn across the streets. They had all been tossed and ripped up.

We turned the corner and stopped running and moved in against the wall. Two guards were standing out in front of a metal bar gate. They were standing facing us.

"Looks like we missed some!" They drew their swords and strode forward, but the other guard halted their movement.

"They're armed!"

"Damn right!" Mia charged forward and slashed her sword across the guards. They didn't even have time to take a step back.

"Not so good against armed girls now, are you?" She taunted the dead bodies.

"Mia, the keys!" The gate had a huge lock on it. Mia lifted a silver loop with about a two dozen keys on it.

"You've got to be kidding." Mia dropped the keys.

I raised my hand and exploded the gates off their hinges. "Why bother using keys?" I smiled; I had Krystith's power. I still couldn't think of her as my mother.

The screams interrupted our brief victory. We ran through the gate and up some steep steps that lay shortly behind it. At the top of the stairs was another gate. Girls pushed against the gate. Some were as young as the girl I had saved in Mulbeta.

"Help us! Help us, please!" They were all pressed against the gate.

"What are you waiting for? Explode it!" Mia waved her arms frantically at me.

"I can't. I could hurt them." They were all crammed against the gate.

"Move, move back!" Mia yelled at them.

They all pushed back. It was going to have to do. I waved my hand at the gate, and it exploded inward. The girls flooded out like I had just exploded a dam holding back an ocean. Mia ran with them.

"Follow me!" She shouted the orders as if they were soldiers. The girls eagerly followed her.

I elbowed my way past the girls. I ran through them and into a huge room. At the back of the room were some more stairs that led high above the ceiling. No one was running down those stairs though.

I walked to the stairs. What did I have to lose? The girls were safe; Mia could get them out of here safely. Hopefully, she would take them all the way and get herself out of here too.

I jogged up the stairs as fast as my legs could take me. A blast of hot air shot from the room above. I stopped at the top of the stairs and slowly turned around. Bodies of girls lay decapitated all over the floor. Arms and legs lay all over the floor. It was if they had been chewed off and spat out.

I walked cautiously into the room. The sword of Krystith fit my hand perfectly, but it didn't glow. I didn't need it to glow now; I had the power the sword had. The strange thing was that I didn't want it.

At the end of the room was a huge pit that stretched wide. At the end of the pit was a cave. A rocky stone wall stretched to a high ceiling, and an arch was carved into the wall. It was a strange thing to be there. The wall looked climbable: maybe I should go and see what was in the pit and investigate the arch? Something told me that would be a bad idea.

White light and fire shot out of the pit. I slammed myself against the wall back into the shadows. A huge claw stretched out of the pit and onto the floor I was standing on. A tail flicked out of the pit, and a shrieking flooded the room.

A black scaled foot landed on the ledge, and then another one slapped heavily next to it. Horns rose out of the pit. Slowly a head rose higher and higher until its whole neck was on show. Its body was wide and smooth with a few deep crevices lining its body. I would have said it was a dragon, but it had no wings. Its inky black eyes were like beads pressed into his head. They scanned and roamed around the room, looking for something to eat. It nudged a lifeless body in front of itself. I looked at the body; it was the girl who had told me where the Johnsons lived. But how could she have got down here? I was the only one who was supposed to come to the king that day. The king must have found someone new to give to Morphius after all.

The beast blasted the body with white light and fire. I stepped out of the shadows and whacked the beast in the head with lightning.

"Get away from her!" I yelled at the beast.

The beast jerked its head up and shrieked at me. Fire raged across the room; I lifted my hand and deflected the fire. The energy it took was almost like brushing away a minor inconvenience. My power was phenomenal to me; it seethed and writhed within me. It felt like using it in a fight, even once, made the magic in me react violently.

My eyes misted over, and I let myself go. I shot magic bolts of lightning, dark mist at the beast. It writhed uselessly against my magic. I shot a sheet of pure fire and pure water across the room, creating pure deadly light. It slammed into the beast. Its head was thrown back, and its shriek was like that of a banshee. Fire and puffs of white light pumped out of its mouth. Its claws scratched at the stone floor. It fell backwards and slammed into the wall. The room rocked violently, and huge chunks of rock fell from the ceiling. The entire place was going to collapse on top of me.

I skidded to the stairs and stopped briefly at the top. The beast writhed and struggled. The girl it had been about to eat lay on the floor. Her neck was bent backwards, almost to the point where the bone was sticking out and piercing the skin.

I sent a final bolt of red lightning spiralling towards the beast. I dashed down the stairs and through the room where the girls were kept. The entire place was rocking. No one was left in the room. I jogged down the second staircase, the gate was lying broken, and I wobbled out through the gateway. Everywhere pieces of the ceiling fell heavily to the ground, and I dodged and dived out of the way of the chunks.

Debris was scattered in front of me. I sprinted down the paths and streets. The little tunnel was tucked away, almost invisible to someone who wasn't looking. I dived into the tunnel and crawled through. This tunnel seemed smaller than before. It was pitch black at the end of the tunnel. I stuck a hand out of the tunnel and put my weight on my hand, expecting to touch solid ground.

Instead I toppled forward and down a hole. My entire body dropped further down with no sign of stopping. I scraped the sides, ripping my hands to shreds.

I heard the faint noise of water. Spits of water splashed off the wall and into my face. The noise got louder and louder. I looked down and held my breath. A long path of water was tumbling along a narrow tunnel.

I hit the water hard. I may as well have fallen onto concrete. I went straight under. I remembered something someone told me: "Hold your breath and you'll float to the top." I had no idea if this was true, but it was worth a try.

I broke the surface and dragged the air into my lungs. I floated down the water, the water carried me down to what looked like a dead end, but the current didn't break. I jumped up a little and stuck my head up and looked over.

There was a drop. I stopped letting myself get pulled by the water and started the battle of swimming against the current. The current dragged me closer to the edge; my swimming was only prolonging the inevitable. A huge chunk of debris chugged towards me at breakneck speed. It slammed into me and knocked me back and over the edge.

The water gushed past me. I looked down. A huge lake awaited me at the bottom. I held my breath, but it was smacked out of me when I hit the surface.

Chapter 18
Preparation for the inevitable

I woke on the bank of a lake. Everywhere around me trees were dotted thinly about in the distance. I couldn't hear anything but the constant hammering in my head and the droning of the water.

I was completely lost again, but I knew I couldn't be far from Mulbeta. I lay on my back as I drifted closer to unconsciousness. I lifted my arms into the air and drained power into my hand until it glowed the familiar orange that used to hang around my neck. I shot the magic into the air. A gust of orange light shot into the morning sky. My eyes darkened. I slowly closed my eyes, trying to keep the magic going longer. I dropped my arm and let the blackness of my eyelids drift me to sleep.

I saw him when I closed my eyes. Nathan. He was smiling at me. "My love will always be with you, Shana." I reached my hand out to him. "Always." His face melted in front of me, and his entire body warped and shifted. Instead of staring at Nathan, I was running away from Morphius. I didn't want to run, but I couldn't make myself face him. I reminded myself how he had pretended to be Nathan and what I had done.

When I opened my eyes, the rising sun was faintly lighting the sky. I sat up but fell back and smacked my head. "Bugger!" I spat the words as I shifted my leg. Hot pain shot up and down my leg. It was broken.

I heard a few mumbled voices and yelling.

"Over there!"

I looked round and behind me. Distant figures ran through the field towards me. I looked closely at the figures. They were moving around like ants. I looked back at the waterfall. I couldn't see where I had fallen out. There was only a flat top on the waterfall, and rocks bordered high on either side of the cascading waterfall.

A man knelt down beside me. "Are you okay?"

I stared at the man. "My leg, it's broken!"

He looked at my leg and nodded. "Are you Shana?" He looked concerned.

"Who are you?" I eyed the swords on his back.

"My name is Fredrick Artimos. I was instructed by a friend of mine to find a girl named Shana. I saw the orange light and brought some of my army out to look for her."

"Would you help me if I wasn't her?"

He nodded. "Of course, but I would want to know if I had found her or not so that I could get my men back to camp."

I thought about this. "Who's your friend that told a prince to come look for me?"

He smiled. "So you are Shana." He picked me up. "Your friends have the entire camp out looking for you." I jumped out of his arms. He stared at me.

"I don't want to be carried. My bum's numb!"

Fredrick laughed. "Can I at least help you walk?"

I nodded. "How else can I walk with a broken leg?"

He put a hand around my waist. "They definitely did not exaggerate their description of you," he laughed. "Boys!" All the men ran to us. "Spread the word. We found her."

The men smiled and sighed. They ran away and disappeared into the woods.

"So you're the prince? I really do not like your dad."

He bit his lip, but the corners of his mouth pulled upward. "Was it you that exploded his hand off?"

"No, that was a very good friend." I stopped walking. "Did Mia get out of the well?"

Fredrick nodded slowly. "They all did. What happened to you down there is what we need to know."

I told him what had happened as we walked through the woods. The sun was full blaze in the sky; no clouds blocked the harsh rays.

"How far away is this camp?" I stopped against a tree.

"Not far, but it would be easier if you let me carry you."

I scowled. "No, I hate being carried when I can walk."

He laughed. "They said you were stubborn. I was also recommended to do this." He stepped forward and slung me over his shoulder.

"Let go!" I kicked him in the stomach with my good leg and punched his back. Both of the blows hurt.

"They told me to wear armour if I did!" He sounded like he was smirking.

"Put me down!" I screamed at him; I hated being lame. I was thinking of putting a lightning bolt through him, but I think it could be interpreted as mean.

He walked me through the woods for ages.

"I thought you said it wasn't far."

"It isn't. We're here." He put me down onto the ground, where I was immediately tackled by Kim. She gave me a ferocious hug.

"You idiot, you should have let us come with you." Kim stepped away from me quickly. She slapped me lightly on the arm.

I shrugged. "Maybe, but all is well—only a broken leg!" and mental images that I will never be able to get out of my mind.

"Where's Mia?" I looked at Kim. Trying not to get too annoyed at her, she never told me her secret . . . when it was something I needed to know.

"I'm here." I looked past Kim. Mia was lying on a log, and Diran was holding her hand.

I walked over to her, leaning on Kim. As I got closer I saw that Mia was pale, extremely pale. "What happened?"

"The tunnel collapsed on top of me. One of the girls dug me out and cleared the tunnel." She smiled. "I was coming back for you."

"She nearly suffocated. We were forced to bring her out here." Diran looked petrified and clung to her.

I felt tears prick at my eyes, but none came out. "You shouldn't have come with me." I sat on the floor beside Diran.

"Someone needed to. I got the girls out while you were fighting." She leaned up slightly, and Diran got up to sit behind her. Mia put her head on his lap. "Judging by the shrieks that echoed in the streets, I take it you killed it?"

I passed the thought. Killing that thing out of pure rage didn't make me feel a little guilty. Instead I felt nothing; I felt like a stone after killing it. To be honest, I had been feeling empty for a long time now—except for the pain in my leg. I winced and looked down at my leg. My magic wasn't helping it, like it had when I fell out of the tree.

Mia looked at my leg and gently pressed her fingertips to it. I winced as the heat travelled up my leg. Mia's eyes closed and her hand fell. The sound of her breathing kept me and Diran from having a heart attack. "I'll let her sleep."

"She has been saving her energy to heal you, instead of helping herself." Diran held her close, a little part of me thought he was hating me for Mia's suffering.

I got up and looked around the camp. It was set up in a field. Tents had been pitched, and a huge fire raged near me and Mia. Fredrick was talking with his men. Nistal had been tied to a tree, and he was glowering at me. I waved petulantly over. Kim was walking away from me. She looked as bad as I felt.

"Kim! Wait!" She turned around, and I jogged over to meet her. No one was around us. "Do you have something to tell me?" I nodded my head in the direction of her arm.

"You already know, don't you?" Kim's eyes were sad.

"You're the angel?" She nodded. "How are you the angel? I thought the angel that brought down the destruction of her kind was a fierce and great destroyer."

Black veins shot across her eyes "I hid that part of me; I never want to see it again. And believe me, neither do you!" She hissed the words.

"Spencer, he said he wanted to . . ." I drifted away. The pain in her eyes hurt me.

"I know. I was the reason the village burnt. It's my fault people die every day. It should have been me down that well freeing those girls that were taken because of me. It was my fault that Nathan died." She whispered the last sentence.

"No, unless you put the sword in their stomach, you are not to be blamed. You ran into a village where everyone was dying and saved Spencer's life. He was left with terrible mental scars, but whether he decides to kill Nistal or spare him will make him who he will be for the rest of his life."

Kim frowned. "That's why he's here." She shifted to look at Nistal and back to me. "For Spencer's sake."

I nodded. "I need to know who he is and if I can rely on him."

Kim nodded. "I understand, but surely, so soon after it happened—"

I held up my hand. "We don't have any more time. If I'm right, we have we have till the next star stream."

Kim's eyes widened. "How did you work that out?"

"Krystith said the magician she found in the sky told her that the angels will get stronger, and when they do, the stars will brighten every decade. Well, ten years ago Grint said the stars shone brighter than he had ever seen them. Ten years ago was the last star stream."

"What? You missed that bit of information out."

I frowned. "I thought I could stop him, but I can't—not without your help." My stomach sank. "Will you help me kill him?"

Kim was already shaking her head. "No, I can't. If I kill anyone, I will change. I'll wake the sleeping angel inside me. It took me long enough to let my human side take over."

"I understand. I won't make you." I frowned. "You were going to let that soldier kill you, rather than kill him."

She looked down. "If I lose myself for one second, I will destroy everything."

"You stopped the angels before. Wasn't that your human side shining through?"

She laughed a little. "I killed the angel leader out of rage and hatred. That was how the war ended. It's technically my fault Morphius is even alive. The angels burnt their dead leader and mixed the ashes in with the ashes of the netherworlds' leader. That was how Morphius was made, and it was my fault." She opened her eyes; they were bloodshot. "Nathan knew this, and so does Dunstan. That's how he saved me. By closing an angels wound, the blood will seal it and repair any damage."

I looked at the woods past Kim. Dunstan and a whole mass of men came out of the trees. "Why did he not tell me?" I felt hurt.

"I told Dunstan not to."

I turned away from Kim, but I spoke my words loud enough for Kim to hear. "It wasn't him I was talking about." Kim fell silent. I walked briskly past Mia.

"Shana, what's wrong?" I ignored her and walked straight to Fredrick.

Fredrick looked briefly at Kim. "What's wrong?"

"Are your men ready to fight?" I looked over the camp. Many men were standing around or sitting down.

"They still need much training. Why?" He frowned and looked at Kim, who was talking urgently to Dunstan.

"They need to be ready by the next star stream."

Fredrick looked back to me. "Why then?" He looked worried—rightly so.

"Because the angels are waking up, and they're coming to Rezta." Fredrick looked blank. "Next star stream."

Fredrick got his men all moving in different directions. They lined up in groups. Each group was assigned to be trained by Fredrick, Dunstan, Diran, Mia, and me. Fredrick's brother Otius was going to join us in a few days and bring many more men with him.

Only a few men here were magical, and none were exceptionally powerful. Mia was set aside to teach them, mainly because I was not used to their small-fry powers any more.

Dunstan and I hadn't spoken since he got back. I was furious with him. He should have told me something. But something still confused me. If Kim was the angel and she knew I had the gem, then why did she lie to Detrix and tell him she was looking for the gem? Why go to Earth at all?

Spencer, Jamie, and Hendric were with Otius's men in a different campsite. They had been sent to look for me and were coming over in the next couple of days with the rest of the men.

I hadn't spoken to anyone except Fredrick after my talk with Kim, but I wasn't ignoring them because I was angry. I was ignoring them because I was upset with myself. Nathan had kept the secret from me; even when he lay dying he didn't tell me.

I loved him so much, but he didn't trust me enough to tell me that. Maybe I was looking at it wrong. Nathan had kept Kim's secret and it did him credit, but it still hurt.

I trained my group hard for long hours with only short intervals until late at night. They were improving quickly, but I felt like I was punishing them because I was upset.

"Shana!" Dunstan slid in front of me. His dark eyes were big and rounded. "Please talk to me."

"I have nothing to say to you." I brushed past him and back to my men.

"Shana, we need to talk. You may not want to, but we have to." I adjusted one of my men's arm positions. I noticed Nistal smiling at me from across the field. A guard had been set to stand by him at all times.

"Shana, if the angels are coming, we all have to discuss a plan!" I stared at Nistal, trying to ignore Dunstan.

"Tell it to Kim." I walked away from Dunstan. The hurt on his face gave me little joy. Why did he feel pain? I was the one betrayed.

"Take a break!" I yelled at the men, but the words were loosely meant for Dunstan as well.

Nistal was smiling like an oily fish. I bent down to Nistal and ripped the gag down to his neck and sat down opposite him.

"Come to kill me at last then?"

I looked at the guard. "Go!" The guard walked away. Dunstan started quickly conversing with him whilst looking at me.

"Don't worry. The person who decides your fate arrives today."

"Then why are you here?" He squinted up at me through the sun.

"I need to know something." Nistal smiled. "I need to know when Morphius will be at his weakest."

Nistal laughed loudly. "Why would I ever give *you* that information?" He laughed hysterically.

"Because I can influence the outcome of how your day will end." Nistal stopped laughing. "You're no use to Morphius dead. Everything you have given up, everything you have ever done will have been wasted. Everything you were promised will be lost."

Nistal swallowed and began fidgeting with the ropes that bound him. "When will he be here, the person who decides my fate?"

"Could be any minute." I lay back and tilted my head towards the sun. "Are you going to tell me?"

He bit his lip and sighed. "I thought it would have been obvious." I set my head straight to look eye level with him. "Morphius is going to be at his weakest when the angels are ready to give him their blood."

I smiled. "Just before the next star stream." Nistal nodded. I got up. "Let's see how your day pans out then, shall we?"

"Shana, you said—"

I turned away. "I said can influence, not that I will." I strode away from Nistal and waved at the guard to go back on duty.

"Shana! You can't do that!" He screamed after me, and I whirled around.

"Yes I can! Did you give Nathan a chance to live?"

Nistal was seething around the mouth. "He squealed your name before I killed him, and I would do it again in a heartbeat."

I looked up. Men were pouring out of the woods, and Fredrick ran over and hugged one of them.

I turned back to Nistal. "Your heartbeats are numbered. I gave you more of a chance than you did Nathan. I gave you hope, but only to watch it shatter and break as the scorned boy's sword is rammed into you."

The guard pulled the gag back over Nistal's mouth.

I turned back to my men. They were already on their feet. Dunstan had put his group and mine together.

"No, wrong! You have to turn your sword the other way to actually inflict damage." He adjusted a man's sword and helped him angle it.

"Spencer!" Kim's voice shrilled high above the crowd. She flung her arms around Spencer. I wondered if he would hug her like that if he knew who she was. I looked at Nistal and pointed to Spencer. Nistal yelled muffled words.

"Shana!"

I turned around. Jamie stood in front of me smiling.

"I missed you." He hugged me tightly. His hug wasn't warm; it wasn't the hug I wanted.

I pulled myself out of his arms. "How have you been? How was your mother when you last saw her?" The last time I had seen his mother she was attached to a drip in his living room, waiting for a call from the hospital to say they had a kidney for her.

"She was still in bad shape," he sighed and dropped his head. "I left her with Ella."

"I'm sure someone would have been round by now and seen you weren't there." I held his shoulder.

"Jamie!"

I turned around. Dunstan was standing behind me with his arms folded.

"Oh, hi, Dunstan!" Jamie stood beside me. "How are you?"

Dunstan frowned at Jamie. "I've been better." Dunstan looked at me. "We need to get back to training."

I nodded and started to walk away from Jamie, but his hands gripped at my waist. "What's the rush? We have plenty of time."

Dunstan knocked Jamie's hands away from my waist and stood squarely in front of him. "The rush is that in the next star stream the angels are going to awaken and destroy Rezta, torture everyone on this planet to the brink of death, but keep you ever so slightly alive and continue to torture you."

Jamie laughed nervously. "That sounds like it was aimed specifically at me."

I butted in between Jamie and Dunstan. "Jamie, why don't you come with us and join in with the training?"

Jamie thickened and bulged out his chest. "Yeah, why not? I've had quite a lot of practice these past few days. Maybe Dunstan here would like to help train me?" I turned away from Jamie to give a frantic look to Dunstan. "One on one!" Jamie extended his hand and stepped beside me.

"It'll be my pleasure!" Dunstan shook his hand and smiled in a sickly sweet way to Jamie.

This wasn't going to end well for Jamie. "I'm going to go see Spencer." I quickly moved out of the way of the two of them. I could already hear them drawing their swords.

"Hi, Shana." Spencer spoke timidly. The voice masked the hatred I saw in his eyes when we were in the king's courtroom well enough.

"Spencer, there is someone I want you to meet"—I paused and looked at Kim—"again."

Kim's eyes were alarmed. Was she really thinking I would expose her? She was like my sister that I always wanted.

Spencer looked confused. I moved out the way and extended my arm to present Nistal. Spencer immediately looked wild but fought to contain himself.

"What is he doing here?"

"His life was in my hands, but he wronged you a lot more than he wronged me." I sighed. "I lost one person I loved, but you lost everyone you loved that day." I stepped out his way. "You need to decide whether you want to take his life the way he took your family's or to let him live."

Spencer ripped his sword out of his sheath.

"Spencer, don't!" Kim grasped his arm. "He's not worth becoming a murderer for."

Spencer strode forward, and Kim and I followed him over to Nistal. Spencer slashed the sword down Nistal's face, tearing away the gag. Nistal screamed as blood dripped down his face.

"You killed all of my family!" Spencer was panting heavily.

"I did." Nistal glared at Spencer.

"Fine!" Spencer slashed his sword, and Nistal closed his eyes. The sword cut through the ropes that tied him to the tree. Nistal opened his eyes and looked baffled. "Get up!" Spencer stuck the sword under Nistal's chin and forced him up.

"I don't want any blood on my hands, and having your life on my conscience would never allow me to sleep again." Spencer backed away from Nistal and pointed his sword to the woods. "Go!" Nistal stood there in shock. "*Go!*" Spencer's voice boomed around the camp, and Nistal ran into the woods.

Spencer put his sword away. "Thank you, Shana." Spencer was calm and his face seemed peaceful. "I needed that chance to see him cower, to see him for what he is. I can try and move on, and so can you."

Spencer hugged me and walked away. I smiled after him.

"Looks like you can rely on him," Kim happily chirped in.

"Looks like it."

Kim stood in front of me. "He's right. You can start to move on. I know you loved him, and he loved you too. But he's gone, and he went in peace knowing you loved him."

I hugged Kim fiercely, and she hugged me back.

"I told Detrix I went to Earth to try and find the gem, but I really went to help the people." I stepped out of the hug. "Jamie's mother, I helped her, the day he left she got a phone call. She will be healthy when he returns to Earth, ready to hug him and for him to hug her back. The people of Earth are why I go to Earth—to help them. I painted the view of the good angel, but the rest of me paints the demons that people fear in death. Shana, I never found you, though, when I went. I am sorry."

I smiled the most honest smile I could possibly have given to anyone. "Kim, you are the solely the best person, angel, or Reztarian I will ever know." I hugged her. "You are like the sister I never had."

Kim hugged me back. "Um, Shana, you may want to look behind you." I turned, wondering what was so important.

"Crap!" Jamie was hurtling at Dunstan. Dunstan swung his sword at Jamie's arm and sliced it open. Jamie screamed but still slammed his sword at Dunstan. Dunstan had a scrape on his head, but he didn't even seem to be trying too hard to try and do the damage he was doing.

"Shana, stop them!" Kim was way behind my line of thinking. I was already running to them. Dunstan was getting ready to land another blow on Jamie. I pulled my sword out and caught the blow on my sword. I was face to face with Dunstan. Kim grabbed Jamie and pulled him out of harm's way.

"What the hell are you doing?" I spat the words in Dunstan's face.

257

"Training him." Dunstan took his sword off mine.

"That was not training, that was you senselessly beating the life out of him."

Dunstan shrugged. "It was training."

I scoffed. "Fine, if that was training"—Dunstan looked confused—"then train me!"

Dunstan smiled. "No, I already trained you once." He turned his back.

"Not like this!"

I swung my sword at his back. Dunstan spun round and blocked my sword just above his head, and we were head to head under the swords scowling at each other.

"I said no." His warm breath soaked my face.

"Why do you change the training rules for different people?" I swung my sword at him, and he blocked it at his side. I stepped away.

"You have a group to train."

We were circling each other.

"How can I teach my group if I haven't been trained properly?" I countered his moves and lunged.

His sword blocked my blow. Dunstan swung back this time. I blocked his blow, and Dunstan rolled to my side and swung to my legs. I dived forward and spun round in time to block another blow.

I pushed him away and swung my sword. Dunstan swung a series of blows, all of which I ducked, dodged, or countered. We both swung our swords at the same time and lunged forward. Our swords slammed together above our heads. Our faces were a millimetre away from touching.

"I win!" I smiled and looked down. I had drawn a dagger out of my boot and had wedged it nicely against Dunstan's stomach.

He smiled, pulled away, and bowed. "So it seems."

I turned away and faced Mia, with a triumphant smile.

"Duck!" she screamed.

I slammed my head down. A flash of memory stopped me breathing. I did the exact same thing the day Nathan died. I kicked my leg out from behind me and knocked Dunstan to the ground.

"Never turn away from an enemy." I faced Dunstan. Instead of seeing him, I saw the man that Nathan warned me about. I put my hand up, and dark red lightning sizzled in my palm.

The man looked confused. Mia, who was standing behind him, looked alarmed.

I let the lightning zoom out of my hand and at the man. How was he alive? I killed him.

"Shana, stop it!" Mia was yelling at me as the man ducked. Diran dragged Mia out of the way of the speeding bolt. This man was the man who distracted Nathan. He was the reason Nathan died.

I spun round and shot another bolt at him. He rolled forward to me, dodging the bolt. I waved my sword across his chest, narrowly missing. I swung again, and this time he blocked the sword and slid forward, grabbing it out of my hand. I lifted the dagger that was still in my hand and held it to the man's chest. He dropped the swords and looked me in the eye.

The man was gone. The only person looking at me now was Dunstan. I looked at the dagger I had held to his chest and dropped it, and it clattered to the floor. I was panting like crazy.

"It was my fault." The tears ran down my face. I had spent my timing blaming everyone else, but it was I who didn't see the man who was going to kill me. It was I who distracted Nathan. It was my fault he was dead. "I'm sorry." Tears poured down my face. Dunstan took a step towards me, but I backed away. I clenched my stomach, feeling ill. "I'm so sorry!" I turned and ran to the woods. I had nearly killed Dunstan. I could have done so easily, and it was because I was blinded by hate.

I sprinted into the woods. My tears blurred my vision, but they didn't stop me. I slowed down and slammed into a tree. I slapped my hands against the tree and hurled my head around the tree.

I sank to the ground and let my misery consume me. I stared out into the leaves and let the tears run down my cheeks. What had I become? I thought about how many people I had killed and how I had never even thought about how easy it was.

"I've lost who I am." I spoke the truth expecting no reply.

"You'll never lose yourself." Nathan's voice whispered in my head.

"I killed a beast, Morphius' pet. It was so easy to simply watch and listen to it die."

"You've adapted, Shana. You had to." His honeyed voice cradled my troubled mind.

I shook my head. "This isn't who I want to be, a murderer with no regret or regard to whom or what I kill." I sighed. "When did I change?"

No reply came, no comforting voice in my head, just the silence of the woods and my tears.

I decided it would be a good idea to read some of the diary; I wiped my tears away; sat down and started to read. I felt cold and distant as I read the pages, my mother was so miserable, with so many ideas. I flicked to the end pages, they were written about when she had returned to Rezta. They were frantically scribbled, as if she was on a timer.

She was so scared, I couldn't understand most of it, she had written of the danger of the magic she was inside fighting in herself. And of Morphius; how she knew she wouldn't win the battle unless she gave in to her magic and lost herself forever. I couldn't read anymore, it was too disturbing.

A twig snapped behind me, and I shot to my feet.

"Who's there?"

A dark chuckle deepened the darkness of the atmosphere around me.

"You've become a lot like me." He stepped out of the darkness, and I ripped my sword out. "A murderer, careless, free? Or so my friend informs me." Morphius' white shrivelled skin had picked up a sickly green shimmer which flaked onto the ground with every word he uttered. "You're weak. And when all your ghouls come out to play, you will lose."

I smiled. "Then why did you come to find me? Why bother?" I faced Morphius. My civility was straining.

"Your turning, Shana. Slowly, you are turning away from what makes you weak." He stepped closer to me. Nistal walked up beside Morphius. "You know what I plan to do." He sneered at Nistal. "No thanks to him." He waved his hand, and Nistal was writhing on the floor, "and when you turn, you will join me." I shrivelled; the memory of what happened in the tree scorched my soul.

"Have you not learnt to trust anyone yet? I thought you would have learnt to after Diran betrayed you." I stared darkly at Morphius. "Are you here to kill me?" I looked from Nistal's grizzly face to the weakened structure of Morphius.

"Why would I do that? I always find you straying away from a fight. You pose no threat."

I screamed at him. I waved my hand and shot dark magic at him. I felt pressure along my eyes.

I ran back through the woods ignoring the laughter of Morphius. I stumbled over into the field. I looked at what I had fallen over. It was a body, not one I knew. I scrambled to my feet, and a man charged towards me. I slashed my sword down on his head and ripped it out. The bone cracked unpleasantly under my sword.

"Kim!" I screamed across the field. She couldn't kill anyone, only defend. I yelled her name again.

"Shana, help!" I heard her voice and shot across the field. I didn't even think as I slashed men down. Blood splattered over my face.

Kim was dodging swords and ducking out of the way. I grabbed her hand, and she yelped, "It's me!" I chucked Kim to the floor and thrust my sword forward. The man fell heavily to the ground, and I heard his skull crack as he smacked his head.

Kim scrambled to her feet. "Go to the woods!" I pushed her in front of me and mowed down the men. Kim ran into the woods. "Kim, don't let go!" She nodded at me and turned to run away.

I stared over the battlefield. Men's screams filled my ears, and it pleased me. I felt power ooze from my pores. Flecks of red and black magic surrounded me, snapping and crackling around me. The men stopped fighting to look at me. I pinpointed all the enemies in the field. This was going to be easy. "You are all going to die." I spoke quietly, but the words reached the ears of all the enemy soldiers. I saw the fear in their eyes and smiled pleasantly.

They all started to run quickly away from the fights they were in and into the woods. I blasted the magic into the air and watched them all scamper in different directions. I smiled happily at the fear I struck into their souls.

I heard faint clapping and looked to the other side of the field. Morphius stepped forward. His men ran behind and disappeared into the woods.

"Well done, Shana!" His voice boomed around the field. "I didn't think you would be consumed so quickly, but once again you surprised me." I walked forward and stopped half way across the field. "Do you want to know what made your mother want to give her powers up? It wasn't to go away and have a child or to start a family. It was because of the things she did, the people she killed, the millions of people she killed in her struggle not to be taken over by the powers she had, and now you have become what your mother struggled against. You have become a demon."

I screamed at him. "You're the demon! You're the reason all of this happened! You!" I felt pressure building all around my face, but it wasn't painful. I enjoyed it. I slammed my hand at the ground and let it explode at his feet.

Morphius sent bright white lightning crackling towards me. I stood my ground and opened my arms. His magic poured into me. I smiled at Morphius as I harnessed his magic, the resontvie.

"I will never let you take Rezta!"

I flung the magic at him. A deafening stillness moved at lightning speed towards Morphius. Nistal dived in front of Morphius, knocking his master over as the magic hit. A huge torrent of black mist shot up from Nistal. His screaming tore around the field. Morphius was on his feet staring at what should have been him.

"Shana, stop." A timid little voice sounded behind me. Kim was shaking violently on the floor, hugging someone. Spencer had a sword shoved through his stomach. Kim was shaking as though an earthquake was going on inside her.

"Kim? Kim!" She writhed and jolted around. Her eyes were shot with white, and her pupils had vanished. Black ink washed along her hair. Dunstan stepped out from behind her. "Kim, stop!" I stepped forward to her. Her head shot up, and I went flying across the air and slammed into the ground.

"My people wait. They need a leader, and they need to play with all of this pathetic life!" She pointed past me at Morphius. "You will get them here."

Morphius laughed. "It will be my pleasure."

Kim slammed a spiral of dust at me, the dust was razor sharp, and was sparkling blood red.

"Kim, stop it! This isn't what he would have wanted." I caught the magic and tossed it to the sky. She pelted another load at me, and this time a few scraps of the magic touched my skin. It melted my flesh, and blood poured from my arm.

I tossed black and white lightning spiralling to Kim. Another load of magic shot from behind me, narrowly missing my hip as I rolled to the side.

Mia shot to me as fast as wind. "I'll take Morphius!"

We divided up. I turned quickly. Kim was already shoving magic at me. I caught all her magic and slammed it back at her.

Dunstan ran behind her. My eyes widened. Kim turned to him and lifted her magic. She harnessed the energy and lifted her arms and pelted it at Dunstan.

"*No!*" I screamed at Kim and slammed white and black magic at her. I caught her off guard. She dived out of the way, and it slammed into the ground. Dunstan lay still, staring blankly at the sky. The ground ripped out around

Kim, and she sent a whirlwind of soil and earth around Morphius. The whirlwinds around Morphius and Kim shot into the sky taking them away from the field, carrying the few men that were still alive with them.

It was silent. I walked numbly over to Dunstan. Dunstan's eyes were open and staring up into the sky. I fell to my knees.

"Dunstan!" I whispered his name. "Please, don't leave me." I stared at his face.

"Shana, look!" Mia pointed to Dunstan's chest. "He's breathing." I looked at his chest. It was rising and falling ever so slightly.

"Dunstan, can you hear me?" I shouted frantically. Mia and Diran ran up beside me.

"His eyes are open. What did she do?" Mia stared at me.

"I don't know." I shook my head.

"His breathing is slowing." Diran shook Dunstan's arm. "We need to do something."

"What?" Mia looked at Diran for help.

"He's not hurt. I don't understand what's happening." Diran was confused. He looked to Hendric, but he just shook his head baffled at what had happened.

Something snapped inside me. I slammed my palm onto Dunstan's chest. I lifted my hand away, and electricity shot out of my hand and down through to his chest.

"You're not dying!" I slammed my hand back down onto his chest. His torso pulled up. I slammed my hand on him again, and he coughed and spluttered.

I got ready to slap his chest again, but as I brought my hand down on him, Dunstan's hand shot up and caught my wrist.

"Not again!" He smiled and sat up on his elbows.

"Looks like he's here to stay." Hendric was standing behind us. I smiled at him.

"Hope so." Dunstan panted.

Hendric told me to leave and help the other injured men so Dunstan could rest. I let go of Dunstan and walked away. Dunstan grabbed my hand and squeezed it. He smiled weakly. "You need rest as well."

"I didn't nearly die." I let go of his hand and Hendric and some more men lifted Dunstan out of the middle of the field.

Fredrick, Jamie, and Otius were lifting Spencer out of the field.

"Wait!"

They stopped and looked at me. "He's dead, Shana."

I looked up to Jamie. "I know." I stood up. "I'm taking him home to be buried." The men lifted him again. "We are taking him back to his family, Kim got to Mulbeta quickly from the village so I see no reason we can't make it to the village."

They nodded and walked away. Many men were pulled off the field either injured or dead.

"Shana, what happened?" Mia walked next to me, and an army of men marched behind me. Spencer's body was being carried past me.

"I felt it, the power. I let it in." I felt weary.

"Shana, your eyes went black, completely black." She shivered. "It's taking over you, Shana."

I whipped round to her. "It needs to! It's the only reason this wasn't worse." I yelled and pointed at Spencer.

"Shana, you're not yourself" Mia put her hand on my shoulder "What's happened to you?"

"Everything! Spencer is dead, I am technically dead and as it turns out I have a lot of power that I cannot use unless I am willing to completely register myself to an asylum. I just lost my friend to my enemy, and to top it off," I sighed, "the angels are coming, and unless Kim leaves Morphius, I can't stop them."

Chapter 19
The Past is the Past

I marched away from Mia through the woods. The army followed me dutifully. Dunstan was being helped to walk by Diran and Fredrick. Otius walked at the front with me, but I didn't converse with him.

"You know you shouldn't s—speak t-to her like that. She r—r—risked her life f—for you." Otius stammered; he had a very strong stutter.

"When I want a second dim opinion, I'll ask you." I barked at him and Otius lifted his chin.

"Y—you know I'm r—right." He didn't seem the least bit insulted by my remark.

My head pounded. A loud drumming noise was knocking around my head. "Shana, what's wrong?" Otius grabbed my arms.

"Nothing, sorry." The pounding continued in my head. "Take them to the village. Dunstan will lead the way if you get lost."

"S-S-Shana, what's w-w-wrong?" The pounding intensified.

"Nothing!" I rasped the words. "Just get Spencer home. I need to go."

Otius nodded. He fished in his pocket and brought out my mother's diary and the keystone.

"I-I-I was t-t-told to g-g-g-give you t-t-these." I took them quickly.

"Thank you." I stumbled away from Otius.

I took off into the woods. The pounding had ceased and had become a screaming drone in my head. I fell to the ground clutching my head.

"Shana, open the book. Find the secrets hidden that are for only you." It was Krystith's voice.

I opened the diary at the middle page. The noise stopped in my head, and the wind spun the pages over to the very front of the diary.

She said she had hidden something on the first page. I flicked a corner of the page and found that it was loose. I pulled the page down and unveiled a folded piece of paper. I took the paper out of the diary and unfolded it.

On the page was a single sentence:

"The stars will illuminate everything the sun cannot"

On the back of the paper was a map. It was a map of Rezta, but it was confusing. Everything was constantly changing. The map zoomed in on a forest, and through the trees I was looking at a girl sitting on the floor. She was looking down at something. I moved the map to see if I could what she was looking at, and the map appeared on the map I was looking at, and I was looking at me. The map zoomed back out. The map had changed, centring my position to the middle of the map. A tiny light shone in the corner of the map. It was in the middle of a lake. I frowned. Was I supposed to go there? What was even there? I folded the map over, and stuck it in my diary.

"Shana? Are you there?" Dunstan's voice whispered through the woods.

"I'm here."

Dunstan limped out of the trees. He was alone.

"Where are Diran and Fredrick?" I wrapped my arm around his waist and turned him around.

"I don't like being carried when I can walk?" I smiled to myself, him mimicking me was tragic, I was able to realize he was as much of a girl as I was. Nathan must have told him the story of how we met.

"Come on, let's go join the ranks." I helped Dunstan walk back through the woods.

"Why did you go? Otius said you looked in pain." He caught his breath and gasped.

"You should have stayed behind with the other injured men." I let him lean against a tree.

"No, going to the village was a bad idea," he sighed. "We buried Nathan there, Shana."

I put my arm back round Dunstan's waist and walked him to a path.

"I'm not here for Nathan; I'm here for Spencer."

Dunstan stopped walking and held my face. "Shana, you're vulnerable. I see it in your eyes." I stared at him, and my anger sparked. "Every time his name is mentioned, you're ready to pounce, or you flinch at the slightest thing that sparks a memory."

I took his hands away from my face. "Spencer said I can move on. It's not going to be easy, but I'm going to try."

Dunstan looked unhappy. "Good." We stopped walking. "Then this should help you."

My body froze. Figures moved in front of me. I saw myself sitting on a log talking with Nathan. Kim and Spencer were sitting on the floor. They all turned to look at me and vanished.

I turned around to walk away, but Dunstan grabbed me and turned me around. "He's gone, Shana. He's not coming back."

I struggled against Dunstan. I felt weak and drained. "Let me go. I don't want this."

Dunstan held me against him and turned me around to face the campsite.

"You need to." He whispered the words. "You can't hold on to him forever."

I stopped struggling and melted into Dunstan. His broze eyes were sympathetic.

I turned slowly round to face the camp. I saw the figures of me, Kim, Dunstan, and Nathan. I watched how Dunstan and I trained. Kim and Nathan sat next to each other watching us. I stared at Nathan as if he was real. I reached forward to him and touched his hand on a log. The other figures shuddered and vanished, but Nathan turned around to face me. His face was pale; mud, blood, and black ash coated his face. I pulled my hand off his in shock. He smiled at me, his jaw unhinged like a snake. Blood dripped out of the corners of his mouth. I turned away and covered my eyes, and then I turned back. The log was empty. The figures were gone, and the camp was empty, dark, and cold.

"I want to go now." My voice was dull and emotionless.

"Shana, I'm sorry, but—"

I cut him off. "No, don't apologise. If people were to apologise, then they must think what they did was wrong on some level." I turned back to Dunstan and wrapped my arm around him. I walked him forward. "I needed to see him. I wish to remember him as he was."

I walked Dunstan through the woods. We exited the forest and stood looking over a field. Much of the soil had been turned up, and past the field were the remains of a village. It was where Spencer was to rest.

When he was growing up, I doubt very much if he thought that he would be the one to wake the sleeping angel. In the middle of the field was a grave, but it stood out to me because it had a sword jammed into it.

"Is that his grave?"

"Yes." Dunstan shook my shoulder. "Come on, they're about to bury Spencer."

In the corner of the field was a close-knit group of graves.

"We buried his mother there; we couldn't locate the rest of his family."

I nodded. Diran and Fredrick walked over and took Dunstan's weight on them.

Spencer was lying peacefully in his grave. They were already throwing the soil on him. I watched unnerved as each chunk of soil was showered on Spencer. No tears stung my eyes, and no whimper escaped my lips; instead I felt numb, completely emotionless as Spencer's body vanished under the soil. The soil was piled high above Spencer.

Everyone slowly peeled away from the grave except me, and I was left standing there completely by myself. The stars spun on his grave. I took out his sword that I had managed to take when no one was looking and slammed it into his grave.

"Goodbye, Spencer!" I cried into the air silently.

Chapter 20

Training

My legs shook and waved my body about. I turned around. The field was bare. No one moved around; no one even seemed to be in the village. But that didn't bother me. I shook and tripped over to the middle of the field until I was standing in front of his grave.

I stared at the grave. He was buried under here, where Nathan was to be for the rest of eternity. "I miss you."

My legs gave way and I fell to the floor. I sat there all night staring at his grave. The field had been transferred by its nature into a graveyard. It must have taken forever to get the graves made.

I didn't cry as I stared at his grave, I had cried all my tears for him now.

"Shana, we have to go." Dunstan was standing alone in front of me behind the grave. I stared at Dunstan, too exhausted to speak; I had been up all night. I hadn't even thought about getting up or leaving, as I sat staring at his grave.

Dunstan stepped around the grave and sat next to me. "I miss him too, Shana." He put his arms around my shoulder.

I hugged him. "I know."

We stood up and walked away from his grave. I swayed on my feet. Dunstan swept me off the ground and hugged me close to his chest.

"I don't care if you moan. You can't walk."

I closed my eyes, knowing I hadn't moved on from Nathan. I was never going to let him go.

"Shana, wake up!" Someone was shaking my shoulder. My eyes fluttered open to find Mia leaning over me.

"Why? I want to sleep." I rolled over.

Mia grabbed my wrist and yanked me up. "You need to be awake if want to save your ex's arse." I frowned. "Jamie told everyone that you two used to go out and how he was going to ask you again, and Dunstan, well . . ." I was feeling drowsy. "Shana, focus! You need to go out there."

"Mia, the angels are about to wake, Kim has turned barking flipping mad, and you want me to stop two idiots from killing each other? If they're fighting over me with all of that's going on, well, they can go ahead and kill each other." Mia looked like I'd hit her in the face.

I stepped outside the tent. A huge mob of people were crowded round each other to look at something, but they all dispersed when they saw me. I looked at what they were all staring at: Dunstan and Jamie were punching each other as if there was no tomorrow and they were lifelong enemies.

Diran jumped in front of me. "Shana, don't!" I looked confused.

"You don't even know when you're about to snap." Mia framed Diran's stance.

"You, go." Mia pushed Diran towards Dunstan and Jamie. "I need to talk to you." Mia grabbed my arm and dragged me into the woods. We hadn't got very far when she exploded the ground. It quickly filled with water.

"Look, look at the refection!"

I was confused. What was this going to prove—that I had a pimple or something? I bent down and looked at my reflection. My face was pale and almost transparent, my pupils had dissolved the whites in my eyes, and black veins were shooting around my eyes. I pushed myself away from the ghost in the water.

"That's not me." I was shaking all over.

"Shana, you've got to fight it." Mia sat beside me "Kim is lost, and now she is going to try and bring her people to Rezta and kill us."

"It's strong, so powerful. When I let it in even a little bit, I lose it."

Mia nodded as if she understood. "Shana, control it! You are its master, not the other way around."

I closed my eyes. The pressure in my head was phenomenal. I pushed my eyes tighter. The pressure lightened but fought back. I pushed it further back and opened my eyes. I looked back into the water. The veins had gone from around my eyes, and bright whites shone in them. My skin was still chalky pale and translucent. I looked at Mia, who was nodding in approval.

"Thank you," I said.

Mia smiled. "I'm always here for you." She stuck her chin up and smiled proudly. "I am the best sister anyone could ask for."

I laughed and hugged her. "Boy, will I say!" She hugged me back. Then she pulled away and stood up.

"Are you coming?"

I shook my head, and nodded my head at the tiny pool. "It's been a while. I think I can shed a layer of skin just by getting in the water."

Mia smiled. "Okay, I'll go see if they have killed each other yet."

I rolled my eyes at her as she walked away. I took the diary out of my pocket and set it down beside me. I stuck my foot in the water, and it plunged straight through it. My entire body was pricked by the cold water. Damn! How deep was this thing? It was like a mini-lake. I started to read the diary; some of this stuff was crazy. I turned back to the piece of paper.

I floated in the water and looked at the stars. They shone brighter than I had ever seen. I knew that wasn't a good thing, but they were still beautiful.

"The stars will illuminate everything the sun cannot."

The stars! I grabbed the bank and pulled myself out. I looked at the book and took out the map. Nothing had changed on the map. I turned it over. The entire page was covered in writing, my mother's writing.

> *Dear Shana,*
>
> *It is every mother's wish that her child remain safe and happy, but what I ask of you warps my wish and will have me turning in my grave. By now you will have seen the silver dot on the map. You must travel to that location if you fail to defeat Morphius and the angels run free on Rezta. There you will find my life's work, and my work will help you to win the battle against the angels, which will come. A drop of your blood is the key. I hope you don't have to use your blood for this. I love you, my darling. Remember my lullaby for you.*

I put the letter back into the diary. I did remember the lullaby. Back on Earth, when I had the nightmares about Rezta. I would hum the lullaby. I stood up and walked back to camp, Mia should see the letter. She would know if we should go straight to the location now and get whatever my mother had left or if we should wait, train what was left of our army, and see if we could take Morphius before he let the creatures loose on Rezta.

The only problem was, even though I had the power, every time I used it I could feel it draining a huge part of me. My power was destroying me, little my little.

I heard the noise before I saw the camp.

"Stop it!" It was Diran's voice shouting out.

"Mia!" Mia walked towards me. "You need to look at this." I gave her the diary's front page. She opened it, and I peeled back the cover. She lifted her eyebrows.

She pulled out the letter and read it. "You've got one hell of mother." Mia smiled a toothy grin, just like a child. She flipped it over and saw the map.

"Should we go there?"

Mia frowned at the map. "There is no silver dot."

I frowned and looked at the map. I pointed to where it should have been. "It was there."

Mia looked confused.

"The stars will illuminate everything the sun cannot." I whispered the words. "We have to wait till sunrise."

"I hope you're right." She handed me back the map. "Thank you for showing me." Her voice reeked of sarcasm. I rolled my eyes. "The sun can show us the way but the stars cannot"

I turned to Dunstan. His eyes were intense, not focused on me but glaring at Jamie. Jamie returned the glare. They were both heavily coated in blood. Their swords were dumped on the ground behind them, and Diran was standing between them.

Diran raised his eyebrows at me and Mia. Dunstan and Jamie shot a look at us. They both looked at me.

"What am I supposed to say?" My voice was lifeless and blunt. Jamie had a black eye that was so swollen it was practically a plum. Dunstan's arm was bent backwards, broken. They both stepped forward, they opened their mouths to speak, but I shook my head. "No, just . . . no"

I walked away from them, away from the crowd and to the campfire. Mia walked with me.

I sat on the log with Mia and waited for the sun to rise. Diran sat beside Mia, hugging her as she rested her head on his shoulder. Dunstan and Jamie were sitting opposite each other on two logs to the side of the one we were sitting on.

No one had uttered a word. Only Mia and I knew why we were sitting here. Everyone else either just felt obligated to or felt guilty. Take a guess at who felt what!

The sun peeked just of the trees, and the paper glowed and dimmed.

"Quickly!" Mia rushed me as I opened the map. The letter had faded and in its place was the writing, "The stars will illuminate everything the sun cannot."

"There!" I pointed to the silver dot.

Mia closed her eyes. "We can't go there."

"Why not!" I was confused.

"It is too far away, we could get caught."

"Morphius knows we are here, what could be more dangerous?" I laughed at the stupidity of this.

"He won't attack us here, he is far too weak," Mia stated.

"Is it sensible to really go far away from Mulbeta when we need to be waiting for the star stream?" Hendric sighed; I hadn't seen much of him. He usually just disappeared a lot.

I thought about this. "We need whatever my mother thought would help us."

"We need to train this army first and try to kill Morphius. That can be the back-up plan if we fail."

I nodded. "Morphius is weak. If we can find him, we can take him."

Mia nodded in approval. "Let's get started on the training. I'll split the groups. Even with the attack, we still have more men than we did before." Mia held Diran's hand. "Trainers better pair up." I bit my lip.

We explained to Fredrick and Otius about the map and how we were going to train the men.

"Won't it be better to move out of the camp?" Fredrick looked worriedly at me.

I shook my head. "He's weak. He won't return." Mia tossed a piece of burnt wood. "So we have to find him."

"B—but that will b—be e—easy." Otius looked at Mia; he seemed confused. "W—well the star s—stream has always hit M—Mulbeta."

"That's perfect!" I hopped up and down. "Just before the star stream, he will be at his weakest then." Mia smiled at my new found enthusiasm.

Chapter 21
A Little Competition

Five months later . . .

Jamie joined in to be trained, but I didn't really care anymore. If all the while he was bickering about me and ready to beat Dunstan up like a fish when the end of Rezta was close, then he might as well just stick himself with a knife.

"Shana!" Fredrick strode up behind me. "I've made some progress with most of my last group, and most of those lived. Seeing as you've got them all in your group, I'll go with you." He smiled and set the group in order, pairing them up and teaching them to land a fatal blow.

Any magical soldiers had been killed in the fight, so I had little else to do except to be a second-hand Fredrick. I used my powers a lot to do simple things, such as moving water and setting fire to things without going completely demented.

I hadn't spoken to Jamie or Dunstan about the fight. I kept the conversation civil and loose. Jamie was put into my group for training, but I let Fredrick teach him. It was strange seeing Jamie with a sword. I remembered him being a great athlete at our school. He ran for every charity event and came first in the school's sports days. Now he was training to kill men and to put an end to Morphius. He had also made friends with an angel and found his dead ex-girlfriend.

I had broken up with him before I went into seclusion. Things had gotten steadily worse at home, and seeing him made me sick, just like I felt when I saw myself kissing Morphius. I dropped the water I was practising with; the thought made me lose my concentration.

The group stopped practising to look at the huge puddle I had formed. I'd forgotten how much water I was using and that I could expand it.

"Sorry." The group went back to training and Fredrick came over.

"Are you all right?"

I bit my lip and nodded. "No." Fredrick sat beside me, and my head dropped into my hands. "What are the chances?"

Fredrick took my hands off my face, and I looked up at him. "The chances are whatever we make of the situation. We have an army that's training hard and getting better still. We have you, a powerful Reztarian and daughter of the great Krystith. Our chances are good."

I smiled a little, "thank you."

Fredrick pulled me up. "You're working too hard with your magic. Go and look over the other group. We might just manage to have some fun tonight if they can all at least hold a sword upright."

My smile was a forced one. "Are we going to have a competition?"

He chuckled. "It's what they need."

I peered over at the group. They all seemed dusty. They had done the routine so many times they were probably sick of it.

"I'll go see if they're all game."

Mia and Diran were doing well with their group. There were far ahead of me and Fredrick. They were ready for tonight. Otius's group was the strongest out of all the groups there were.

"Your brother had the idea of having a competition tonight to give them all a bit of fun." Otius looked confused. "I know it's not really appropriate considering the situation, and if you don't want to, that's okay." Otius looked behind me.

I looked over my shoulder. Dunstan was helping a solider to swing his sword. I remember that was what he taught me when I flung my sword into the tree. "You'll h—have t—to check w—with Dunstan."

He turned away. I put my hand on his shoulder and halted him. He faced me and looked scared.

"What's wrong?" I asked. "Have I done something?"

He took my hand off his shoulder. "Y-y-your e-e-eyes—they're g-g-going r-r-red."

I reached automatically to my eyes. How? I hadn't lost control of myself. I wasn't even angry.

I ran over to the water and dropped on the ground. I lifted the water into the air to form a flat circle. I was horrified by what I saw. My eyes had gone completely red, a tinge of black shot around the outside. I panted frantically. My eyes shot to a disturbance behind me. His face was smiling at me. Morphius sneered and bellowed. I dropped the water and shut my eyes.

I opened my eyes. I was scared. I couldn't escape these powers. They were a curse that threatened to destroy everyone I loved. They were powerful enough to take out Morphius.

"Shana, are you okay?" Fredrick was standing in front of me, and I hadn't even noticed him.

"Yes." All the air in my lungs gushed out of me in a flurry; I hadn't realised I was holding my breath.

"You need to rest." He stepped towards me.

I backed off and put my hands up briefly. "No, um . . ." I looked around me. Jamie was frowning at me and Fredrick. "I need to fight—to train, I mean I need to train."

Fredrick looked bewildered. "You can train over here with me if you like, or I could pair you with one of the group."

I was already shaking my head. "No thank you. I need someone I know." (And who better than myself?)

"Dunstan!" Fredrick beckoned him over, but I was already wandering away to a water supply.

The water looked cool and fresh. I had been experimenting and trying to create different objects with water. Recently I had found a way to give the water a minute or two of its own life. I had tried making animals from the water, and now I was going to shape it into my own form.

I touched the pool of water with my index finger. It rippled outwards till it touched the edges of the bowl. I lifted my finger off the water surface and towards my heart. The water knocked me over and gushed passed me.

I hurtled upwards and turned to face the forming water. It pooled on the grass and worked its way up facing me. My eyes boggled as I faced the figure. It wasn't me, and it was certainly the last person I ever wanted to see.

My father took the sword out of his belt and smiled a sickly wicked grin. My breathing slowed. I dropped my sword and stumbled clumsily away from him. Through him I saw Jamie run towards me. My father turned round and stretched his arm forward, and a torrent of water churned towards Jamie. It knocked him through the air, landing on Mia.

"Come to have fun, bitch?" He turned slowly round to face me. I looked at my sword and back to the watery figure.

"Burn in hell!" I thrust my hand forward, and I watched as his body evaporated. The boiling water spat at my face; I let it slam into me.

"Whore!" He screamed the words at me.

"You're nothing to me! You don't even own the title of being called my murderer." I raised my hand, and he disappeared in the vapour.

Dunstan ran up to me. His sword was drawn. He ran behind me and hurled me around.

"Well done, Shana. I thought it would have been harder, but at heart you're more like me than you are them." Kim sneered at me.

She stepped out of the dimness of the forest. Her once-golden hair was now thick and black. Her eyes were blacker than Morphius', and no twinkle was to be found in them.

The dull brown leaves scattered, blackened and shrivelled at her touch. "Kim, what are you doing here?" I looked around for an army.

"Simply came to see my friends," she sneered. "Rather I snog your dad?" she cackled and walked out to me.

Dunstan moved towards her and away from me. I felt my heart crushed. "Go!"

Kim smiled. "Dunstan, care to hug a friend?" Kim opened her arms and pouted. Dunstan raised his sword higher. "Funny, you were eager to do more than that to me at one stage of our relationship." Kim smirked at me.

"Get out of here, Kim." I yelled at her. My soul shattered into splinters. I was pretty sure everyone in Rezta could hear my heart fall to the ground and shatter as easily as glass.

"Oh dear, have I upset your new fancy?" Kim smiled at Dunstan as soon as she said this. My eyes pricked with tears. I stared at Dunstan, his eyes were apologetic. He didn't defend himself against the insinuation that they were once an item.

I looked at him to Kim, and my voice shook. "That's why she didn't kill you."

Kim laughed. "So easy to hurt, like a puppy! You don't deserve your mother's gifts. You didn't deserve your father either."

I heard nothing except silence.

Then the floor started to boom around me. It was like a steady beat. Kim looked at the ground.

The Earth around her began to break and crumble; roots shot out of the ground and grabbed her legs; a wave of roots rippled out of the woods and clung around Kim. They pulled her violently to the floor.

"If you think my father was so great and worthy of someone better, than you can go and wait for him"—my eyes flared and burnt like a million suns—"in hell!" I shot my arms down to the ground, and I heard Kim's screams fade away as she was dragged under the ground.

The earth sealed itself with an ear-splintering crash. I couldn't believe what I had done.

"Shana, wake up!" I felt something shake my shoulder. "Shana, what happened?" My eyes fluttered open. I was lying in a pool of water. Dunstan was leaning over me. He was pale, and his eyes were flashing like beacons.

"What happened? Is Kim dead?" Dunstan looked confused, but Mia snuffed a laugh.

"You can tell what she's hoping for." Mia was fighting a smile.

I leant upwards. My head was pounding, and the field spun like a merry-go-round. "Dunstan, did you ever do anything with Kim that she could hold over you?" (And me.)

"What, where the hell did you get that idea from?"

My head flopped to the floor. Dunstan caught it and laid it down gently.

"She might have concussion." Hendric's face loomed over me.

I closed my eyes again. It was a nightmare. I could sleep easy knowing I hadn't lost him to her forever. I loved him, too much for me to live knowing he wasn't mine.

"Tonight's game will test how far you've come in your training." Fredrick stood next to his brother while he shouted the rules. "You will each fight the nominated one, Jamie, and if you beat him, then you will stay on and fight the next person I call out."

Jamie nudged me. "Are you gonna fight?" His dark eyes were gleaming in the dark.

"No, I'm a little tired." And my head hurts—a lot.

"Oh, that's a shame." He sighed and swaggered away slowly. "I could have beaten you."

Damn it, he knew I was competitive!

"Fredrick, put me down for a fight" Fredrick smiled and shot a look at Jamie.

"You can take him!" Mia skipped up beside me. "And if not, I can!"

We sat on the grass in a circle, all watching to see who would win.

"Are you fighting then?" I asked.

She gave a wide toothy smile. "Of course."

"Shred Mile!" Fredrick called out the first name. A huge brawny beast walked out of the crowd and faced Jamie.

"Any bets?" Diran scooped his head between me and Mia. "I'm on Jamie."

Mia snickered. "Bet you he won't do anything" I bit my lip, trying so hard not to laugh at the innuendo.

They shook hands. All the time I had been here, I hadn't figured out if there was currency in Rezta.

"What are you betting?" Diran walked to the people sitting next to us and continued to take bets.

"You bet any possessions you might have, such as a sword, dagger, food, water." She shrugged. "I just bet my favourite dagger."

I hadn't been concentrating on the fight. A huge thud made me look up. Shred had fallen to the floor; he looked dazed.

"And Jamie wins!" Fredrick announced, and everyone clapped and cheered.

"Mia Green!" I laughed and smacked her on the back lightly.

Fredrick looked over as I announced her name. Everyone cheered and clapped Mia. She glowered at me with a twinkle in her eyes.

"Have fun!" I yelled after her as she walked up to greet Jamie. He had gone rather pale and wide-eyed.

"Any bets?" I turned my head, expecting to see Diran. Dunstan was taking his place beside me and looking adamantly at me.

"You fighting?" I asked. Dunstan smiled and nodded. "Good!"

"So who do you think is going to win?" Dunstan asked, I watched Mia and Jamie dance with their swords at each other's throats. Mia had a glint in her eye.

"Mia, definitely Mia." Dunstan laughed at my certainty. "Who do you think?"

Dunstan cleared his throat. "I have fought with Jamie. I got halfway through fighting him, and, well, you know . . ." I sunk my head into my shoulders. "He's good, at least half decent. I think he could take her."

I scoffed. "No way! If you've seen Mia fight even once," I nodded in conviction, "you'd know there was no way."

Dunstan put his hand forward and I grabbed it, not thinking about what I was doing.

"I bet a walk in the woods that Jamie will win." I gulped dramatically at his proposal.

"You sound like a murderer" I giggled at him "I bet my . . ." I frowned at myself. "I don't know what I want to bet."

"I know what I want." His other hand brushed against my cheek, stroking my lips. My heart beat faster. "It's worth a bet."

"You're on!" I gave a wide smile and lowered my hand. He set his hand on top of mine and intertwined our fingers. I smiled at him. It was what I wanted too. In truth, right now I wanted Mia to lose.

"You are convinced she's going to win." Dunstan frowned at Mia, I wondered if he had seen her fight before. She fought in the brief battle between me and Morphius but I don't think he would have been looking at her. I pursed my lips and looked at Mia. She was throwing her sword at Jamie. He was struggling to avoid her blows. She threw her sword to the ground and raised her arms as Jamie charged her. Jamie was flung up into the air and, I won't lie, I was getting endless amusement from this.

A cold blast of wind shot into my back, I looked behind me. Nothing was there. I looked at the skies above Jamie's head.

The stars were brighter than I had ever seen them. They seemed bigger and brighter. "Shit!" The silent curse did not go unheard. It was like they were moving. I stood up and looked at the sky.

Dunstan stood beside me and looked at the sky with me.

"It can't be. It's too early." I grasped his hand. There was a huge thud and a groan, which I ignored completely. Jamie spat and got to his feet.

"It's started." The cheering died away.

In a second the entire camp was turned around. The soldiers ran silently through the woods, and as planned, they all took different directions in groups. Dunstan, Jamie, and I were left scurrying with our group. The plan was to get me or Mia close enough to Morphius and Kim so we could attack. She was going to scour the left side of Mulbeta with her men and I was to scour the right. Thankfully, the camp wasn't that far away from Mulbeta, though it felt like the other side of the world in the time it took to get there.

Chapter 22
Rise and Shine to all Armies

In Mulbeta none of Morphius' guards had been posted outside as anticipated by Mia. In fact the streets were empty. The only people I saw were men from our own army. Maybe Morphius hadn't noticed the star stream was early. That would be a great advantage to us, but it seemed unlikely now Kim was on his side.

"Shana, stop!" Dunstan pulled me around the corner and behind the wall. "Take this." He pulled a pearl and gold-hilted dagger out of his boot and handed it to me. "If I'm not around, use it." His eyes were like rock, but it caught the ever growing stars like a net would catch fish.

"If you're not around, then I don't want to be either." I pressed the sword back into his hand. He didn't take it.

"If anything happens, the map is all that's going to matter." He put the dagger against my side. "You're going to survive tonight, Shana. I'll make sure of it."

Silence cut through the atmosphere. The only sound audible to me was my own breathing, when a huge thunder erupted through the sky. The stars shot steadily like a beating heart down to the ground; they got faster and faster until they streamed like liquid.

I ran with Dunstan through the streets. Jamie and the group were all over Mulbeta scouring the streets. Everyone was running to the same place at once.

I rounded the corner and froze to the spot. Morphius was standing in the middle of the light. In front of him Kim was using a knife to slice his face and body apart. He was bare to the stars.

I silently took out my sword. Mia curved around the corner opposite me; we nodded at each other. Our plan was now in action. We all charged Kim and Morphius. A huge clicking noise simultaneously rumbled through the street. Kim turned round with the knife. I stopped running and signalled everybody else to stop as well.

In the windows of the houses, men were pointing crossbows at us, all pointed with the strings pulled back. You could hear the strain of the string.

"Just try it, Shana." She lifted her knife and turned back to Morphius. He seemed far away from where he was. His eyes were rolling back as his red blood oozed from him. His blood was red—it wasn't too late.

"I'll kill them all!" She thrust the knife into Morphius' chest, and he sighed in pleasure.

"Kim, stop it! This isn't what Spencer would want." Dunstan pulled me back to him. "He will have died for nothing if you do this, if you let Morphius win."

She laughed hysterically and turned around. "Like I give a damn about Spencer! He was a whining arse. He deserved to die. He couldn't even avenge the death of his parents and siblings. Let him rot!" I was horrified. I thought she cared. "You seem to have been attracted to my pathetic side, so I'll give you a chance. Kill your friends and live as my friend, or die right here by my hand."

I lifted my sword. "Neither!" I raised my arms as quick as the stars flowed, and the windows slammed shut. Streams of arrows were shot, but only one made it out and pierced my side.

"Charge!" A flurry of men dashed forward. I tore the arrow out. Dunstan stood by me.

"Are you all right?" His eyes were alarmed.

"I'm all right." All the men were thrown back. They each slammed into the floor. Jamie landed beside Dunstan, and Dunstan helped him up.

Morphius sighed. It sounded like a pleasurable action to him. Kim turned instantly back to him.

Where were Fredrick and Otius? They were supposed to distract her. I shared a frantic look with Mia. She closed her eyes and bit her lip. When she opened her eyes, she looked sad, almost in despair. She raised her hand at Kim. I started to run forward to stop her, but Dunstan grabbed my waist. I kicked at him to let go.

Mia blasted white ash at Kim. Kim raised her arm. The ash was blasted by black ribbons of mist. Kim smiled wickedly at Mia. I tried to raise my arm, but Dunstan held it down.

"She has to do this. It's a distraction," Dunstan whispered frantically into my ear.

I panted frantically. Kim stepped away from Morphius and raised both her arms. The gravel shook around Mia. Diran was standing opposite Mia. He tried to run forward but was held back by some of his men.

I took my chance. Dunstan let me go, and I ran forward behind Kim. I heard screaming. I saw Diran run in front of me as I stopped in front of Morphius, and I followed to where he ran. Mia was lying facing the sky. Her golden hair was sprawled out behind her, and her eyes were glazed over.

Kim oiled her way towards me. I saw Hendric behind her.

"For Krystith!" I had forgotten that my mother died in his arms. Kim shot her arms out at Hendric and sent him catapulting to the windows. They had been firmly shut by my magic, and I had taken extra precaution and locked the doors with ice.

I took the dagger out of my boot and sent it whistling at Kim while her back was turned. It landed in her stomach as she was turning to face me. Her screams filled the air, and a huge white light shot out of her. The white light shut us in a white dome with Morphius. Her eyes were dripping white blood, and she smiled and clenched her stomach, closing her wound. I turned to Morphius and fell to the ground, my arm blistered when I touched the light. His cuts were closing, and the blood that seeped through was now turning from scarlet red to light pink. It rapidly turned white.

His head snapped down towards me. "It's over!" The white dome shot into Morphius and blasted out as icy wind knocking the army over. I saw Dunstan fall to the ground. My heart was shivering as if someone was dancing on my heart's grave. Morphius' arms were flung open, as if he was about to hug me.

The angels gushed through Morphius. He laughed loudly; his once-slack skin was now a shiny metallic beacon of evil. His eyes were icy black, glistening like wet pebbles. The blood on his face was now white; he had become an angel—but not just any angel, the angel's leader.

Kim was in awe, marvelling at the angels. I scrambled to my feet and ran to Dunstan. I pulled him up. Jamie was lying on the ground next to him. Dunstan hauled him up. The rest of the men were already fleeing from the angels as they flew out of Morphius and paraded into the air. Their white wings were coated with straight feathers, and their black eyes had a single red dot pressed into the middle of them. They shifted all over the city. I looked over the way; Mia and Diran had gone.

Fredrick and Otius were nowhere to be found, and now the only hope of getting out of here was to run like your lungs need for oxygen didn't matter. Dunstan, Jamie, and I all sprinted down the streets we had come from. None of us looked at back. None of looked at the sky.

We sprinted into the cover of the woods. We ran until morning, far away from Mulbeta, with no inkling as to where Mia or Diran were and no idea when it might be safe to stop.

"I have to stop." I panted, leaning against a tree. Nothing was in the sky. There was no noise except that of the wind and the rushed breathing of Dunstan and Jamie.

I sat against the tree and reached my hand into my boot. I stored most things down there now. I pulled out the map. Dunstan and Jamie were looking down over my shoulder. The map zoomed into a wood. The trees were thick, but I could make out myself and Dunstan and Jamie. The map zoomed back out and placed us all central to the map, and a silver dot appeared in the far left corner this time. I panted and looked at the dot. It was in the middle of a rather large lake and across a lot of woodland.

"We have to go there now." Jamie had regained his breath, but I was still panting.

"I need to walk. I can't run any more. You may be an athlete, but I hate running." I slapped the map into Jamie's chest and drifted through the trees.

Jamie turned the map around, trying to figure out where we were going. "This is so confusing. The map keeps moving, like it's following us." He slammed the map at Dunstan. "You try!"

Dunstan picked up the map. He looked at it and frowned. "Shana?"

I took the map. It immediately zoomed in to us and then zoomed out. "Get my dagger please." Dunstan pulled the dagger he gave me out of my boot and handed it to me. I took the dagger and sliced my finger open. Dunstan and Jamie looked at each other.

"Don't worry. I'm not suicidal." I held my finger on the map. The drops of blood dripped over the map. They ran along the map and into its centre. I walked forward, and the blood vibrated a little forward. I gave the map back to Jamie. He wiggled the map but the blood didn't move.

"How did you know how to do that?"

I smiled a little at his surprised tone. "My blood is the key to many things."

Dunstan was standing by my side, looking at the map. I looked down at his gaze. A pool of blood stained my dirty top. It was where the arrow had hit me. It didn't hurt. But there was still some wood poking out, which meant the arrow head was still in there.

"Stay still." I walked hastily away from Dunstan. "You'll have to let me get it out sometime."

"No, no way." Dunstan caught me and turned me around. "You are not yanking the arrow head out of me."

"Shana, just let him take it out. It could be a whole lot worse."

I pivoted round. Diran walked out from behind a tree. In his arms Mia looked pale and deathly, but she was smiling.

I dashed forward. Diran set Mia down on the ground. I hugged her but let go when she inhaled like a spitfire. "Sorry, sorry." I saw her wound; a huge gash had been set in the middle of her chest where her heart was. "Oh god!" I stared horrified at Diran. "She is too weak to heal herself and I don't have the magic to do it."

"I want to but I can't, I just—"

"Don't worry. I'm safe now." She clenched my hand. I inhaled and seethed. Suddenly I fell back on my butt. Dunstan was waving a bloody arrow head at me.

"It needed to come out." I looked at my wound. It was hurting a lot. I stuck my finger in the cut.

"I need something to stop the bleeding." Dunstan threw the arrow away.

I closed my eyes at the pain the arrow had left in my side.

Jamie huffed. "Well, use this because I can't read it." Jamie dropped the map on my lap. The map zoomed into us all from the tree tops. I saw something black move across the edges of the map. My eyes shot up to the sky. Black eyes poked out of the trees. The scarlet red dots were as small as pin pricks, and entirely focused in on me.

It shrieked at us and flew to the ground. It knocked Jamie over. Dunstan ripped out his sword. The angel landed gracefully on the floor. I grabbed the map, covering our destination.

"Someone wants you." He pointed an arched black-boned finger at me. Black fire shot towards me. I lifted my arm; white light ate the fire and sent it back to the angel. The angel was pushed into the tree. I put one hand on top of each other and pressed them in the angel's direction. The angel burst into black dust that scattered over us all. I felt a stabbing pain in my chest. I looked down. A huge blade was poking out of the back of me. Dunstan was standing behind me holding the hilt of a sword.

My soul was shattered, and blood gushed from my mouth. Mia laughed, and so did Jamie and Diran. Tears swept down my face. I fell to the ground and watched my friends laugh at me dying as my father had done.

I opened my eyes. Dunstan was sitting over me. He was brushing my head with a cool wet cloth. I shot up and pushed him away. "Stay away from me!" The cloth dropped to the floor.

"What's wrong?" Dunstan's voice sounded hurt and confused. I looked down at my stomach. There was no wound, no blood. I lifted my shirt—no scar.

I dropped my head into my hands. "What's wrong with me?" If anyone had answered that truthfully, I would have rammed a sword into them.

"Nothing is wrong with you. You're perfect." Dunstan lifted my head in his own hands; he stroked my lips with his thumb.

"Mia won the fight." I smiled at him.

"I don't care." Dunstan leaned forward, and I started to close my eyes. A loud throat-clearing noise came from behind me. I sighed and turned round to see Jamie.

"We need to go." His voice was flat. He looked like a hurt puppy as he stormed from the woods. Dunstan scrambled to his feet and pulled me up. Mia leaned against Diran.

"Help her," I said. "I need to speak to him." Dunstan held my hand a second longer and let me go.

I walked after Jamie. He was waiting two metres away. "Jamie, we need to talk."

"About what?" He looked at the map as though nothing was wrong.

"About your mother." Jamie turned around and frowned, confused at my answer. "Before you came to Rezta, Kim visited your world. She told you it was to find the gem, but it was to be the angel she created in herself. She helped people who were in trouble. Before she left for Rezta, she helped your mother. Your mother's kidneys are fixed." Jamie went numb.

"What? She saved my mother?" I smiled, and tears pricked Jamie's eyes. "My mother's going to live!" He ran forward and swung me around. He hugged me and kissed my forehead.

We hugged, letting his happiness lighten my day.

We all travelled together through the woods all day. I was so tired, and we stopped occasionally to rest Mia, who looked like she was at death's door. She had broken out in cold sweats and began breathing heavily. We stopped every time she got like that. She protested, but it was that or stay behind with Diran. She soon became reasonable at the thought of not seeing my mother's life work.

Dunstan held my hand tightly, and I walked with my head on his shoulder. It felt right, but the memory of kissing Morphius haunted me.

"It's close." We had been walking now for several days. "This time for sure."

My head swayed against Dunstan. I was dead on my feet. "She needs to rest." His arm curled around my waist, taking most of my weight off my feet.

"So does Mia." I let my head droop to look behind me. Mia was covered in soaking wet clothes. Her face was pale and deadly. I halted, and Dunstan and Jamie turned around.

We all sat down. I cuddled closely up to Dunstan, who wrapped me in his bear-like arms. I closed my eyes as his heart beat down my ear. It was like a lullaby. That night I dreamt.

My mother's lullaby drifted in my head. I welcomed it. It made me peaceful, and her sweet voice honeyed every word. The lullaby accompanied the image of me sitting a field with Dunstan. We were laughing and watching stars shoot by.

"Let her sleep." Dunstan's lips moved. I frowned at the dream Dunstan.

"No, we need to go to the point." Jamie's voice echoed round my dream. My eyes opened, and I was staring into Dunstan's black top.

I sat up and looked around. It was fairly light. Mia was fast asleep next to Diran. Jamie was sitting beside me. Dunstan's head was up and glaring at Jamie.

"She's awake. Let's go." I sat up.

"Don't wake them. We'll be back before they wake up." I stood up, helped by Jamie. Dunstan was giving him a hell-fire look.

"I've already written a note," Jamie said as we ran through the woods. I felt fresh and awake even though I had just slept a few moments.

We exited the woods, and a huge lake stretched out in front of us. Glossy mountains reached high behind the trees just over the lake. I looked at the map. The blood was less than a millimetre away from being on top of the silver dot. I sighed. The lake looked freezing, and I took my sword out of my belt and took off my boots. I took my dagger with me, who knows when I might need it?

"You can't go in. You'll catch your death!" Jamie looked horrified as I took my top off. My vest was threadbare, but it was better than getting my other top wet as well. Jamie stared at my chest. "Um, I guess I can come with you." I blushed and looked away. Dunstan had already taken his belt off and his sword. I took the dagger out of my boot and placed it in my belt. I didn't know what was going to happen down there.

"If you run into it, it might not feel as cold." Jamie dropped the map. We all ran forward into the lake and dived.

The water nearly stopped my heart. I couldn't see a thing, but I kept swimming down. I shot a ball of light in front of me. A huge arch sat at the bottom of the lake. I swam to the arch, Dunstan swam underneath me and to the arch; he swam through it and looked confused. I swam to it. "Your blood is the key." My mother's voice echoed around me. I took the dagger out and sliced the palm of my hand. I pressed against the stone column. Jamie swam up beside Dunstan; he looked blue and was slowly turning purple. The water rippled around the column, and a huge blue shimmer passed through the arch. Tentacles shot out and dragged the three of us into the arch. The air was slammed out of me as my chest was crushed onto solid ground. Jamie and Dunstan were sprawled on the ground in front of me.

I looked around. We were back on the surface. I coughed out water. "What happened? Was that meant to happen?" Dunstan got up next to me.

"I don't know—" I got knocked backwards, but I kept on my feet, though. The water rippled and the entire lake shook. I saw Mia from the corner of my eye running up to me.

"Shana, what's going on?" I didn't turn to Mia. Instead I was squinting at the water. Millions of single ripples shot across the surface of the lake. I stepped forward. Jamie had only just scrambled to his feet when a jolt was sent through the earth. It was a steady beat, as if someone was walking.

A head popped out of the water.

It was clear that it was a figure made of water. A whole row of water heads popped up and moved up the water and towards the bank. We all stood frozen. The front row of water figures stepped out of the water and walked towards us. I backed away as the second row appeared out the water.

"Shana, get back!" Dunstan jumped beside me. He had picked up his sword from the ground. The water figures drew swords.

"Drop your sword, Dunstan!" He stared wide-eyed at me. "Do it!" He dropped his sword, and it clattered on the floor.

The water men put their swords away. "It's great," said Jamie as he stepped up beside me, "Water men! You can't destroy water at all!"

"You can evaporate it." I walked up to the army of water men. "My mother's life work was giving water the ability to stay alive for more than a moment."

"Shana Hale, we are at your command." I looked along the bank. The army was stretched so far along the bank that I couldn't see the end of the line.

"Confirm blood presence." I strode forward and pressed my palm to the head of the spokesman.

He nodded and stood to attention. "Blood presence confirmed!"

We marched the army into the woods, after picking up our equipment from the ground, sending them on patrols all around the base camp. "Does anyone know what happened to Fredrick or Otius?" They all shook their heads.

"I assume they went to the castle to warn their father and sister." Mia sat up and panted. She looked worse. "It makes sense."

One of the water men turned around. Diran looked sick with worry. "You need help," said the water man. He knelt down to Mia. "I can help." He pressed his hand to his chest. Diran's eyes were wide. He looked ready to throw up. The water man gently pressed his hand to Mia's chest, and she writhed. Diran touched his sword's hilt. I shook my head and crawled across to Mia.

The water man's eyes glowed bright blue. Her wound began to close, and it disappeared without a scar. Only the dried blood was proof of any wound. Mia smiled; it was the first time since the angels took over Mulbeta.

Diran relaxed. "Thank you!" He hugged Mia closer to him and nestled his head into her hair. "Thank you!" Diran's eyes drooped. "What's your name?"

The water man took his hand away from Mia. "My name is Nohnsan." His voice was gentle and calm. He got back up on his feet and disappeared into the shadowy wood.

Chapter 23
Mothers legacy

It was mid-day but everyone was so tired, we had spent the day analysing the water men to see if we could trust them.

Mia and Diran were fast asleep. Their heads dangled like a ragdoll's. Their snores resembled those of a piglet. I couldn't sleep. Every time I closed my eyes, I had a nightmare about Dunstan. Was it me or was it him? Either way it was worth losing sleep over not to have his character besmirched by my head.

I cuddled my knees and rocked myself. It was cold out, and we had no food, so Dunstan and Jamie went out hunting with some of the army. The darkness folded quickly over the woods. I got to my feet. I needed to walk round. My body was getting numb.

"Where are you going?" Nohnsan's dusty voice brushed gently with the wind.

"I just need a walk." He stepped forward, but the leaves didn't move. They didn't even rustle as he stepped over them.

"I have been entrusted to stay with you." He stood behind me, like a lap dog with no happiness.

"Who gave you those instructions?"

"Master Dunstan." My heart grew heavy. "He was worried about you."

I gave a pinched smile. "Okay, well, I hope I won't bore you, but I probably won't talk."

"I was only instructed to keep you safe."

I lightly stepped out of the make-do campsite. The trees were densely packed together, and the sunset was beaming through. It was more of a stretched beam of light against my face than a proper sun.

The woods looked thinner in the distance. I walked slowly out of the packed wood. A huge field stretched far in front me and a little waterfall was the only feature to be seen. It was too open for my liking, but I walked into the field anyway.

The waterfall fell into a huge pit, which contained a gigantic pool. The current flowed back into the waterfall. There must be a cave. I stepped back and got ready to take a jump. Nohnsan grabbed my wrist. A frown creased his otherwise perfect face.

"No jump." His lips thinned and his grip loosened. "I take you."

I thought about this. "Why can't I jump?"

"Because I was instructed to keep you safe." He hurled his body into me, and I squealed as the water consumed me.

I watched out of the water. I bobbed closer to the edge of the pit. I looked up and saw Nohnsan's chin. I was inside him.

He jumped off the edge of the pit. I closed my eyes. The water was cold, but it was the closest I had come to a relaxing bath for a while. I swam deeper. The water felt lovely against my skin, and it got warmer as I swam to the bottom. I stopped and looked around. The pit walls were all visible except one. A huge blackness covered my vision in front of me. I shot a light ball forward, and it lit up an entire cave. I followed the light into the cave and saw that drawings coated the wall.

The drawings told a story. Bubbles of air burst from my mouth. I didn't have much time. I continued to swim. The light stopped at a wall and rose to the surface. It shone like a sun above the water. I swam up. The surface was more like liquid concrete rippling around me, and I coughed out the water.

The ceiling was covered in huge murals, carvings of pictures spread wide all over the roof of the cave. The images were of a young girl. Three boys stood on either side of her; the boys all had crowns on their heads.

I swam to the cave wall to get a closer look. The girl was Krystith. She was younger than I had ever seen her, but it was certainly her. A water head popped up. The light shone on him, amplifying his deep-set eyes.

"You are safe." It wasn't a question, more a way of reassuring himself. "Brought help." I closed my eyes and sighed. I wanted to be alone right now.

"Who did you bring?"

"She said she was your friend and she had been searching for you."

My eyes widened. "What does she look like?" My head darted over the surface of the water. I was frantically looking for Kim.

"She had blonde hair and fair skin." I slammed against the water and held out my hand, waiting for someone to pop up. "She said her name was Anna." I dropped my hand.

"Anna?" She was alive! "Was she with a man?"

"No, all alone was she." I giggled at his grammar.

Bubbles of air broke the surface. Anna's head popped up, and she gasped in the air.

"Shana, please let me talk." I waited. Nohnsan had a blank expression; she posed no threat. "I didn't tell you because I was ashamed at what I had done . . . ." She struggled for

319

words. "I still loved him, even after I knew what he had done."

I didn't speak. She had been the reason I left them at the time, and now I couldn't care less about her.

"What do you want me to say?" She looked like she had just been slapped. "Do you want my forgiveness?"

"No, I want you to understand." She edged closer to me. "I want you to know, so you don't think of me as a bad person."

I let loose a short laugh. "For loving a murderer?" I thought about this. "I know how strong love is. I know how powerful it is. It is entirely your business, unless it involves any more family disputes over my head. I cannot judge you." I faced the wall again. "I have done more than my fair share of bad things." Vivid images of me and Morphius kissing crossed over the wall.

"Do you know who these men are?" I brushed my fingers on the men's images.

"Have you not read your mother's diary?" She asked me.

"Some of it" I replied as if wasn't a big deal that I was ignorant.

"The three lost princes of Rezta. They're buried in this cave, above our heads actually." I looked at the ceiling. "Your mother was in a world that knew no civility. They wanted the realm to themselves, so each of the kings were killed, but before they were killed they all had sons they hid over Rezta. Krystith was sent all over the realm with a friend to track down these princes and fight for their thrones. Hendric, he was the one to help her."

I turned round in a flash. "What? I just thought he saw her the time she returned to Rezta. I never knew." I shook my head. "I saw her, my mother. I saw when I swam across the lake. But she's dead."

Anna laughed. It was the first time I had ever heard her laugh. It was melodiously charming to listen to. "She did it. She came back. Just like she said she would." She swam to me and put her hands on my shoulders. "We have to go back to the lake."

I shook my head. "Bad idea! Joshua said he sealed off the entrance to the tunnel leading into Morphius's castle. If he didn't . . ." I was still shaking my head. "I don't want to be part of a surprise attack."

Anna threw her arms up into the air. "But don't you see? If you give your mother's spirit your powers, then she can return."

My eyes widened. I looked at the young girl on the walls. "I could have my mother back?" I nodded, convincing myself. "Let's go, before any other crap happens."

"The lake we were at is at least two week's walk away," Anna stated. I bit my lip. "We haven't got anything to lose."

My eyes boggled and my nostrils flared. "We have everything to lose. The entire reason I fight is to keep innocent people alive. Two weeks! By that time they would all be at death's door and still being tortured." The crying Johnsons passed before my eyes.

"Shana, I didn't mean it like that." She started panting in front of me. "It's just that we've lost so much already. We need to get a strong enough army before we even think to attack again." She backed off. She was weary and tired. Black heavy sacks sat under her eyes. She looked like she'd been crying.

"Where's Grint?" Anna burst out crying. I stayed away from her.

"Dead. Detrix killed him. Joshua stabbed him in the back, and then Detrix blasted him into a million tiny pieces." She squeaked the last words. "If you want to save people, then we need your mother."

I felt like someone had slashed my ego in two. "Fine!"

I dived back through the cave, and Anna swam beside me. We surfaced and looked around the pit. We were surrounded by tall walls and shrubbery. "How do we—" I was blasted into the air, cut off in mid-sentence. Anna and I screamed as we shot through the air. We landed like rocks on the surface.

I was completely winded. I felt vomit coming up.

"You are safe." Nohnsan rose from the pit and landed gently on the surface.

I clenched my stomach. "Yes, thank you."

Anna spluttered the words I could not. "I need to sleep."

I faced Anna. She was nodding, and her eyes were growing heavy as well.

My head drifted to the side and my eyes began to close. I shot up and slapped myself. "No, I can't!" Nightmares were not worth rest.

"Shana, just sleep. It won't matter." Anna's drowsy voice made my head swoon.

I pushed myself to my feet, but I felt my legs give way. Nohnsan swept me off my feet.

"Must keep you safe." (Didn't that cross your mind when you winded me?)

He carried me through the woods, and Anna followed awkwardly. We came through to the makeshift campsite.

Dunstan was standing in the middle of camp. He had arms wrapped around his waist. He was groaning and sighing. Wings spread out from behind him. Nohnsan drifted away and left me standing alone. Mia's and Diran's necks had been slashed almost to the point of decapitation and their bodies were strewn across the camp. My heart wept as Dunstan turned around. Kim was locked solidly in his arms.

"No!" I screamed at them, but they didn't hear me. Dunstan's eyes shot up to me. He smiled mockingly at me. His tongue lapped up Kim's lips. I fell to my knees, and tears screamed down my face. "No!" I whispered the word to myself.

"Shana!" I heard a voice scream around me.

"*No!*" I screamed at Dunstan and Kim. The tears saturated my face. "Please!" I begged them to stop. "Kill me!" Anything to end this.

Kim jumped into Dunstan's arms.

"Sorry!" I looked around for the voice.

I sat bolt upright. Mia pulled her hand off my cheek. "Mia?" I cupped my stomach, and my head was swaying. The memory of them made me sick. "Was it real?" Anna sat beside me against a tree.

"Which part?"

I shook my head, so that part was real. "Dunstan, and . . ." I gulped and shook my head. "Nothing."

Mia sighed and sat back. "What was it about?"

Mia sat back on her butt opposite me. I looked around. I was sitting in the camp. No one was about. Diran was still asleep, and Anna was lying against a tree, her eyes drooping.

"Nothing," I sighed. "Get some sleep."

"No, Shana, please tell me." She reached for my hand, but I flinched away. "Why did you want to die? Why are you afraid of sleeping?"

In all my life I had never been so afraid of sleeping as I was now and never had I had someone to talk to about it. I blubbered. Mia wrapped her arm around me. I cried into the leaves. My cheeks were already wet.

"It's my nightmares. They torture me with him."

"Who?" Her voice wasn't prying; it was caring.

"Dunstan. Whenever I close my eyes, I see him, and he's breaking my heart." My voice was strained and wrecked by tears. "And her—she's always with him. He's always there for Kim instead of me."

"They're nightmares. They bring your worst fears into your mind. You've lost so many people that the thought of losing him destroys you."

I sobbed and sat up. "I love him, Mia." I gulped the air. "I love him more than I have ever loved anyone." I thought of Nathan. "It's wrong but I can't help it."

She grasped my hand. "You can't help who you love, and it doesn't hurt to move on. Nathan is gone. You can remember him and love him, but at the end of the day, he's gone."

I sniffed back the tears. "I know, but I can't sleep with these dreams."

Mia nodded. She went into her bag and brought out a bottle. "Use this. It knocks you right out, and I promise you no dreams." She placed the bottle on the ground next to me.

"What is it?"

"I made it from herbs. I used when I was ill." I gulped and nodded. "I need to sleep, but you should use it." She crawled back to Diran. "It's not worth crying over lost sleep."

I smiled at her. "Thanks!" I picked up the bottle and shifted it in my hand.

Mia drooped her head on Diran's neck.

Hendric was gone, and I never knew he had been my mother's companion. I let him die for me. I let Nathan down, leaving his parents in Mulbeta. Fredrick and Otius were missing, and Kim and Morphius had released angels into Rezta.

"If I can do anything else wrong, it won't be tonight." I unplugged the bottle and chugged it. I placed the bottle on the ground and crawled back to the trees.

My head drooped. I heard some leaves crunch around me and the sound of deep friendly laughter. I slept with a smile on my face.

The smell of bacon wafted up my nostrils. My eyes opened to the sound of my stomach groaning like a savage bull.

"Hungry?" Mia jumped to my side waving a chunk of meat in my face. I gagged and held my nose and mouth.

It wasn't bacon. "What is that?" I watched Jamie pick at it and chuck bits away. He pulled a face like a prune.

"Um, I think it best if you don't ask." He closed his eyes and shoved it in his mouth. I heard a squelching sound and few cracks come from his mouth. Dunstan had his back to me. He was leaning over the small fire putting a damp blanket over it.

I fake vomited and stood up in a rush. My head swayed independently, and I rested my back against a tree. "I can live without it."

Dunstan turned round and gave a heart-breaking smile. He looked sad. "It's not bad if you don't smell it or look at it." Mia wiggled the thing in front of my face.

"It'll be even better if I don't taste it." I pushed the thing down to her hip and stepped away to the sleeping Anna. I shook her shoulder.

"Anna, wake up!" She groaned and waved at me. I rolled my eyes. I turned to Mia and pointed to the thing I was supposed to eat. She chucked it at me, and I caught it. "Anna, wake up." I tried a calm voice.

"Go away!" She snapped.

Fine! I slapped the thing around her face. It slopped goo all around her face.

Mia burst out laughing. Anna's eye opened completely. She wiped the goo off her face and looked at the thing I had dumped in her lap—"breakfast", I think.

My head swayed. I crawled to the tree next to her and relaxed against it.

Today's agenda: travel for two weeks to give my dead mother her powers back so she could kick Morphius' butt.

My head was light, but I didn't want to make a fuss. "Come on, Shana." someone shouted at me, I sniffed lightly and got up.

The rancid meat had all gone—good riddance! I missed the age I didn't know up from down, but that was only because I had no memory of it, probably for the best. My stomach growled. I clenched it and looked around. Dunstan and Jamie were talking to Anna. Mia and Diran had disappeared out into the woods. The army of water men trooped loyally after them.

"Can I help you?" Nohnsan stood in front of me.

"Have you got any food that won't make me yack?" Nohnsan nodded sharply and reached into his stomach. His hand disappeared. It was so strange; his body appeared see-through, but when his hand pierced it, I couldn't see it disappear and drag out a dead fish.

"Fish are not originally from your world."

I smiled and took the fish.

"Thank you, Nohnsan."

He bowed and walked after everyone else. I clenched my fist over the fish; smoke slowly rose from the fish. I chewed on the fish as I caught up with everyone else. Nohnsan was lingering behind.

"Are you okay now, Miss Shana?"

"Yes, thank you for the fish." I was still hungry, but it was much better than before.

"That isn't what I meant." I looked confused. "I heard you talking to Miss Mia last night." I stopped walking. "I took the liberty of informing Master Dunstan of your nightmares." I stopped breathing. Anything else he might say would stop my organs all together.

"You did what?" I kept my voice low.

"He asked me if everything was okay, and I told him no. He asked why, and I told him." Nohnsan turned round and walked away.

I slowly regained my breath: Why? Why? *Why?* Would someone do that? Oh bugger! What must Dunstan think of me?

"Anything wrong?" Mia walked in front of me. I was pretty sure I looked like I was about to heave all over the ground.

"Nothing." I regained my voice and the use of my legs. I walked with her, traipsing behind. I didn't tell her what

Nohnsan had done, but she didn't ask why I was ready to pass out.

"Did you have a good night's sleep?" Mia inquired.

"Yes I did, but I drank the whole bottle."

Mia rolled her eyes. "Don't worry. I have one more bottle. You only need a drop, though." She reached back into her back and pulled out a bottle. She handed it to me, and I stuck it in my pocket.

"Thank you."

"Mia!" Diran shouted from in front of us. She rolled her eyes and ran away from me.

The rising sun sparkled through the treetops. Each step I took seemed to jolt the sun beams. I bent down into my boot and pulled out the map. It zoomed straight into me. Nothing flew in the sky as it zoomed out, and the blood was still there. It zoomed to where to where I was, and another silver dot appeared directly to my right. It wasn't that far away. In fact it was only a few steps away in a field of some sort.

Another dot? How was that possible? We already had the army. What else could there be?

I turned away from the marching crowd and followed the map to where the dot was. The woods stopped suddenly. I stared at a huge field with nothing in it. An enormous cliff wall stood tall at the end of the field. According to the map,

I was supposed to be standing right on top of the silver dot.

I ambled forward with the map in front of me. "I don't under—" The ground rumbled, and I dropped the map. "Crap!" The map blew quickly away from me. I ran for the map as the ground crumbled beneath me. I wobbled and struggled to regain my balance. The map blew back behind me and into the woods.

The ground began to shatter all around me like glass falling into the earth. The ground jolted even harder, knocking me to the ground. At that moment the ground gave way beneath me and fell into the earth.

I didn't scream. The wind was flowing past me so quickly that I struggled to even breathe. The sky above me slowly disappeared into a dot above me. I looked down.

The ground rushed towards me. I spread my hands at the ground. I don't know what I was hoping would happen, but whenever I fall I automatically put out my hands.

I slammed into the ground, but instead of being flattened, I sunk half way down in mud. I kept my hands above my head. "Help!" I screamed at the surface, but no one would have heard me.

I shot a light ball into the air. I was in a small room with nothing around me. The ball darted out of the room and into the sky above, lighting up the way I came down.

The mud popped around me. Don't struggle, and don't make any sudden movement.

The mud squirted in my face, and I was dragged under. I slapped onto solid ground. The air was knocked out of me. The ceiling above my head was rippling mud. I heard a whisper around another room. "Who's there?" The whispers grew louder.

I cast a light around the room. A huge arch was carved into the wall. The whispers ceased. I sent a ball of light over to the arch, and I got to my feet and dragged out my dagger. The cut in my hand from last time was coated in dried blood. I sliced the flesh open. The pain was more intense. Must be something to do with the fact I wasn't under water.

I walked slowly over to the arch. The ground was still trembling, or was that just my legs? I stood in front of the arch. It was exactly like the one in the lake. I pressed my hand up along the arch, and the blood smeared obediently onto the rock wall.

The arch shook, and dust fell from all around the ceiling and walls and off the arch. I dragged my hand away, and the arch trembled violently. The inside of the arch burst, completely covering me in mud.

I rubbed it out of my eyes. I looked in confusion at the field I stood in. Dunstan, Mia, Diran, Anna, and the water army stood in the wood. Diran had the map in his hand, and my other light ball shone at his side. They all looked as confused as me. The ground gave a short tremble.

It came from underground and travelled behind me. I turned to the cliff. It was gently vibrating; Cracks appeared all up the cliff. I stepped closer to the cliff. Was it moving? A hand shot out of the rock, and I jumped back. Dunstan shot to my side and pulled me slightly behind him.

"What happened?" His voice was cold and flat.

"My mother's work." It was clear that this was another army.

A stone soldier burst from the cliff, and another ten men followed out of the cliff in a neat row. More men streamed behind each of them.

A stone man stepped in front of the rest and stood in front of me, his eyes were moving slowly and dropped.

"Confirm blood presence." There was icy cold. Each of them looked unique, but all were as expressionless as each other.

I pushed gently past Dunstan and held my hand to the soldier. I pressed against his chest where his heart should have been. Dust fell from his face.

"Blood presence confirmed."

The ground shook again. A hand shot out the ground and grabbed Dunstan's leg.

"Don't move!" I held my hands up to him. Dunstan looked alarmed. His sword was inches away from the hand. The water army didn't move, so it was clear to me we were under no threat or in any danger.

I knelt down to the hand and gripped it. The blood dripped down the hand. I yanked at the hand and pulled up an arm. Dunstan helped to pull. A huge mud man stood before us. He marched to the stone army and stood facing me. "We are at your service." The flesh was scorched around the cut; they took a little more than blood it seemed. More mud men rose from the ground and joined the ranks of the stone men.

Chapter 24

Fire, Water, Earth, Air and the Beast

Thankfully, there weren't as many stone and mud men as there were water men, or we might not have managed to get them all into the woods.

Diran shook the map. "I don't understand." I stepped over to him and looked at the map. "There's another dot." He shook the map in frustration. "Look!" Another silver dot had appeared, but it seemed smaller than the other two. "It's so far away. We are never going to get there and manage to go and save Krystith."

"I don't think my mother wants saving." They all looked at me confused and shocked. "Well, look at the facts. My mother was miserable. She hated her powers, and when I saw her, she never told me anything about saving her. We don't have much time to waste."

"If any!" Jamie snatched the map away from him. "We have to get back to Mulbeta. We have to fight. We have a strong army of water and earth men."

Mia's head popped up. "What did you say?" Jamie looked at Diran and then at Mia. "That's right." She took the map and looked at it. "Yes, that's right."

"What? Can you please tell us what is right?" I was getting a little touchy.

"The elements."

I snapped my head round to the men. A water man and men that came from the earth.

"This next spot here"—she pointed at the map—"is a region greatly known for strong wind."

Jamie frowned. "Elements?" His eyebrows rose.

"Of course, the elements!" Dunstan slapped his head. "Why didn't I think of that? Elements cannot be created or destroyed. If we had an army of element soldiers like these"—he gestured to the soldiers—"we would be indestructible, able to take out the angels and Morphius and—"

"Kim!" All their eyes shot round to me. They all looked guilty, as if I was a mother scolding the naughty children.

"Shana, I know you two were close, but . . ." Mia bit her lip. "She's gone. The Kim you knew has gone." My nostrils flared.

"No, Kim isn't dead. Unlike Nathan, Kim isn't dead, and I have to believe she can come back." Mia stood quietly. Dunstan shrivelled when I mentioned Nathans name.

I stormed out of their sight, grabbing the map from Mia as I went. Kim wasn't gone. She couldn't be. She was like my sister. I wouldn't let her go—not when I could do something about it. I stopped walking.

What could I do? I tried reminding her of Spencer, and she couldn't have cared less. What else? What made her change before?

"Why me?" I shot round. Dunstan was leaning against a tree. He looked in pain, as if I had stabbed him through the chest. "Did I do something to hurt you?"

"No, it's just . . ." I blinked back tears at the memory of my dream. "It's what you could do." His expression went from pained to angry.

"You think I would do that to you? Stab you? Laugh at you? And Kim?" He shook his head, baffled.

"I can't help my nightmares, but it doesn't matter if they're nightmares or memories. They still hurt. In my nightmares, I see you. I know whatever I see in my nightmares isn't real, but it's so clear that I wake up screaming and crying." I shook. "It's my past. Everything in my past has followed me to this world. Every shred of pain and of anguish has followed me here, even to a different world!"

Dunstan stepped forward. His eyes had shrunk. He looked annoyed, but he continued. "Whatever happened on that world has stayed there. The only thing that followed you was Jamie."

"Exactly!" I shouted at him. "I never dumped Jamie because of what my father did to me. Jamie was an escape from him. I saw Jamie having sex with my best friend. He didn't even see me. When I asked him if he had anything to tell me, he said no. I asked my best friend, Sarah. She said no."

Dunstan's eyes melted as I shouted my painful past at him. "And my father, he hurt enough to make me want to kill myself, whenever he could manage to get drunk enough to drag me to the basement, and when I ran away, he killed me with a bottle. As I lay there dying, I watched him laugh at me as if it was the highlight of his life."

Dunstan stepped forward. "Shana, I am not Jamie and I am not your father. I will never hurt you, no matter what happens." He took my hand. "I am never going to leave you. Your father ruined his life. Don't let him ruin yours." He stroked my cheek. "As for Jamie, well I currently feel the urge to try and ram my sword through his heart and see if anything comes out."

I laughed weakly at his sick humour. "It doesn't bother me like it used to. Only you can hurt me. Everyone else can just scar."

Dunstan hugged me tightly to him. "Never!" He whispered the words with such certainty that I felt that they were the last words I was ever going to hear.

"Shana, Dunstan, are you here?" Mia's voice interrupted us.

I pulled away from Dunstan. He rolled his eyes and yelled, "We're here!" Mia came bouncing through the woods. She was out of breath.

"Come quickly!"

Dunstan and I ran hand in hand through the woods. Mia ducked behind a log at the end of the woods. We ducked beside her and looked over the log. A small village lay in the distance, and a few trees covered the path into the village. Dark figures drove over the village, and blood curdling screams rose into the air. A tiny drop of blood landed on my cheek. I wiped it away.

"We have to go in and stop them." Mia stated.

"Where are the soldiers and everyone else?" I asked.

She looked guilty. "I kind of set them around the village ready for an ambush." She grinned cheekily.

"What are we waiting for, then?" I piped up at the chance to test the new soldiers.

Mia stood up with no concern about being seen. "*Charge!*" Her voice boomed all around the surrounding area. A huge wave of men swept into the village. I ran alongside Dunstan and Mia into the village. Dunstan gave my hand a quick squeeze before dragging out his sword. I whipped my sword out, and for the first time the gems glowed. Not an orange colour but a light blue colour.

The angels dived like bombs down to the ground. Water blasts and rocks were thrown at them. An angel slammed on top of me, scraping my collar bone. I screamed and writhed. I pressed my hand to his face. I felt the cold blackness chill my hand, but I held on. I squeezed my fingers tight over his head; it slowly turned colder and more solid. My hands slipped from his head. The angel's head was completely frozen solid. I punched the head, and it shattered into pieces, scattering over the whole floor.

I dived up and grabbed my sword. Blood dripped like a fondue fountain down my body—both white and red blood.

Looking around the village, each angel was fighting at least two of my soldiers. An angel landed in front of me. It was the angel from my nightmare.

He shot black fire at me as quick as he had in my dream. I flung my hands on top of each other and shot white light at him. The black fire shot back towards him. He screamed as he broke into tiny black pieces. I was panting ferociously. The cut over my collar bone was making it harder to breathe.

I heard a scream, not an angel scream. Oh god, Mia!

I shot a gaze over the small area I was fighting in. Mia stood across from me, fighting an angel. Everyone else was completely involved in their own fight.

The angels shot up into the air, and we all followed them with a stare of hatred. They shot through the air and soared high above the village. I clasped my ears and dropped my sword. I heard the scream again; it coursed through me like an electric shock. The angels flew away; the wind glided noiselessly through their wings.

The screams stopped. My head swooned. The village seemed to be moving in circles. Then the scream sounded again. This time I fell to my knees, clenching my head. The screaming was like a full blast siren in my head. The village spun around me like a spinning top.

I felt hands on my shoulders, and I felt my body lie down on the ground. I looked at the sky as it swerved above me. Dunstan stared down at me. I focused in on his eyes. The sky stopped spinning around me. I felt tears drip down my cheeks, but I didn't feel like I was crying.

Dunstan's eyes were sparkling like mini-gems in a lake. "Can you hear me?"

My eyes drooped. "Yes, why?" My voice was no more than a whisper.

"Stay awake, Shana!" Mia's face entered my vision. "Hold the cut closed. I need to stop the blood." I writhed as the cut across my collar bone was pinched closed. A numbing cold stretched along the cut. Mia was freezing it shut.

My eyes closed and my body shook.

"Shana, wake up!" My eyes remained shut. They were too heavy to open.

"May I?" I recognised Nohnsan's voice.

The light shone through my eyes. Cold water was being funnelled drip by drip into my mouth. I coughed when it went down the wrong way. I sat up and spluttered. Jamie was holding a hollowed piece of wood with some water in it.

"What happened?" I moved my hair out of my face.

"The angel you fought carved you up like a turkey. Mia froze the cut, hoping it would stop the bleeding. Then Nohnsan came along." Jamie shivered. "His eyes glowed bright blue. He touched your wound, and he quickly covered you in a watertight seal. Your wound healed." Jamie looked sad. "It left a scar, though."

I looked down. A slim line ran across my collar bone, but it didn't hurt.

"Where's Dunstan?" No one else was around except soldiers; we were back in the woods.

Jamie bit his lip.

"Jamie, where is he?" I leapt to my feet.

"He, Mia, and Diran went with a couple of men to the next dot."

"What!" I screamed at him. "Are they crazy?" It was a rhetorical question.

"They said it was going to save time." He stood in front of me.

"They need my blood to open every arch. The blood confirmation needs some of my flesh to be in contact with it."

Jamie's eyes bulged. "What? They thought it was just blood. They only took a dribble of blood from your hand." Jamie looked horrified. "What's going to happen to them?"

I stormed out of the woods and tapped a stone man on the shoulder.

"Excuse me, sir." The stone man turned around. "What would happen exactly if the blood confirmation wasn't successful?"

"You would have been executed according to the rules of the Krystith blood pass." He stood with a straight back.

"What's a Krystith blood pass?"

"Only a descendant of Krystith may use the army." He stood obediently, waiting for my next question.

"Can you take me to the next spot?"

He nodded. "Yes."

He flung me onto his front and Jamie onto his back and ran full speed through the woods. The trees dashed past us in a blur. I sank my face into his neck and clung on for dear life.

The soldier stopped, and I was whipped off his front by a gust of wind.

"Shana!" Jamie yelled after me.

I was hurled to the ground and landed on my front. I turned round and crept up onto my knees. The wind stopped suddenly and then started again faster than before. Ground was ripped out from all around me and I was tossed casually through the air and onto the ground.

The wind stopped, and Dunstan, Mia, Diran, and Nohnsan fell next to me. They began to be blown away from me again. I grabbed Dunstan's hand. He jumped and looked at me.

"What are you doing here?"

"They need my flesh as well as my blood." Dunstan's eyes went wide. Had he already done it?

The ground around me was mainly dust and sand. The air was dry and painful to breathe in.

"Blood confirmation unsuccessful."

A blast of wind slammed into Dunstan, knocking his hand out of mine. I shot to my feet. A huge man stood in front of me. He was so tall! I slammed my hand onto his chest, and the wind slowed down.

"Blood presence confirmed."

The wind ceased completely. Dunstan was lying on the ground. He looked as if he was having a seizure. He was struggling for air.

"Help him!" I shot a death stare at the wind man. He strode to Dunstan and waved a hand over him. Dunstan's breath came back to him instantly. Mia and Diran were further back behind Dunstan. Jamie was already there helping them up. Nohnsan stood next to the stone man. The wind man marched steadily up to them both and bowed. They bowed back. He stood beside them. Blasts of wind shot through me, and all the sand blew up around me. A wave of men appeared behind me. All of them were grey and misty, and their expressions were clouded over and dull.

"Take them back to the rest!" I ordered the soldiers. They all nodded and turned around at the same time. They marched through the woods, followed by the wind men. The wind was gentle as they moved out of the area.

I moved my hair out my face. This place was like a desert or the harsh savannah with strong winds blowing from every angle. I frantically ran to Dunstan. He was scrambling to his feet.

"Are you okay?"

Dunstan's eyes focused on mine. "Yes." He was panting. "At least we know what they can do. Can't wait for the men of fire!" Dunstan pulled me close; his eyes were intense and alluring.

"Shana!" Diran was waving the map. I looked back at Dunstan. "We need to go!" Diran's voice was stressed.

Dunstan laughed. "That couple have a sweet way of ruining moments."

I walked slowly to Jamie, Diran, and Mia. Dunstan's hand was folded neatly around mine. "At least we have an army now."

"How many men did we lose in that fight?"

"None." Dunstan gave a little smile. "We can take Morphius and the angels."

"I am so glad you said that." Mia grabbed my hand and yanked me away from Dunstan. "Shana, we should leave it."

I was confused. "Why? We need the last part of the army."

Mia was shaking her head. "Not where this leads us, no."

I looked at the map. "It's the prison hold where the girls were kept." Morphius' pet, the room, the wall. I sighed. I saw the arch carved into the wall. We needed to go back down there. "I know where the arch is. The beast is dead, so it won't be a problem to get to."

"Shana, it's dangerous, and besides, how on earth are we going to get to the well again? Mulbeta is taken, and we shouldn't use this army until we have the men of fire."

The waterfall. I could remember the tunnels and the drop from the top. How would we travel up the waterfall and into the tunnel entrance?

I bit my lip. The water men! Nohnsan had shot me and Anna out of the water pit. Maybe he could get us all to the tunnel entrance, but we'd have to be careful and grab the ledge to the tunnel.

"Are you going to tell us?" Mia looked frustrated and slightly confused as she stood in front of me watching my face slowly turn into a smile.

As we sprinted through the woods, I told them about how we were going to get in through the waterfall. I didn't tell them that the arch was above a pit or that I was going to climb a skyscraper of a wall to get to it.

"Shana, wait. How are we going to get to the waterfall in enough time to make this count?"

I spotted a stone man as we headed to the camp. I ran up to him and jumped on his back. I whispered the instructions to him. "Men, form ranks!"

Anna was waiting at the camp. "Where the hell have you been?" she shouted loudly. The guards moved in; they sensed danger. Mia quickly hosed her down with the story.

Anna nodded. "And you expect me to ride these men?" I sat posted on my man and looked dumbly at her.

Anna, Dunstan, Diran, Mia, and Jamie each jumped on a stone man's back. Nohnsan ran next to me.

"What is it that you need us to do?"

I explained how I wanted him to help us get into the underground streets.

"Of course, Miss Shana, but maybe you would like us to also help you get through the tunnels as well. We could freeze the water, allowing you to move safely."

"Yes, that would be great."

The sun was starting to rise again. We had been travelling all night. I was exhausted, but I didn't want to complain because we had done none of the running.

The men stopped running. "We are here," Nohnsan stated.

I jumped off the back of the stone man and ran for the lake and the waterfall. Looking up at the waterfall, there wasn't any rocks to climb up, so we were just going to have to climb through the cascading water.

Nohnsan stepped up beside me. He raised his hands to the waterfall. The noise stopped slowly. All the water stopped moving; the rippling lake stopped moving, and the splatters of water dropped into the lake.

"Thank you."

Nohnsan bowed. He led the way over the lake. He didn't plunge in, but instead he glided over the lake.

"Um, Nohnsan!" He turned round halfway over the lake already. "Can we cross the lake, or are we going to fall through?"

"You may cross."

Jamie walked forward after Nohnsan, and he didn't fall through. We all followed his lead. I wobbled slightly on the lake, and it felt unnatural under my feet.

"Dunstan, I need to tell you something." The memory of kissing Morphius was weighing heavy in my head. It made me feel so sick. It was too closely linked to the nightmare of Kim and Dunstan, the betrayal was the same. I didn't want Dunstan to feel the way I did when I thought of Kim and him.

"What?" Dunstan held my hand and helped me to walk across the lake.

"It's about Morphius." He frowned at the floor and walked forward after everyone else. "When I was climbing the trees . . ." I struggled for words. My head felt heavy and my stomach knotted. I stopped walking.

"Shana, we have to go!" Mia yelled from up front. "Come on!"

Dunstan and I ran under the waterfall. There was no other way. The wall was completely vertical, thoroughly worn down by water. I put my hand on the wall.

"We must climb. I shall stop the stream above."

Nohnsan climbed up the wall with little effort. I knew I could climb a wall, but it looked so slippery. Dunstan jumped high on the wall and grabbed it. He stuck his foot inside a gap and scrambled up after Nohnsan.

I grabbed hold of the wall and pulled my weight up. I didn't think too much about where to put my hands—just enough to keep them moving and pulling me up. I could see the gap I fell from. No wonder I slammed myself so hard on the water; it was so high up. Dunstan and Nohnsan had disappeared above me. Dunstan's head poked over the edge of the gap. The water had stopped flowing out of the gap and dropped below me.

Dunstan put his hand out, and I grabbed it firmly. Dunstan pulled me up without any sign of struggle or distress.

"What did you want to tell me?"

We walked over the water in the tunnel. Dunstan's hand covered mine. Mia and Diran trudged behind us. I could hear the stomping of the army over the water, their feet thudding loudly.

"I don't know how to tell you, but . . ." I struggled for words to make this easier. "When I was on the tree, Nathan appeared on the branch below me and helped me when the branch I was standing on began to break, and we kissed."

Dunstan frowned. "Nathan never left camp." His eyes widened. "You kissed him?" He let go of my hand. Tears pricked my eyes. "You kissed Morphius?" He whispered the words. It was like a nightmare, but I knew this one was real.

"I didn't know it was him until he showed me."

Mia and Diran walked past us. Mia grabbed my hand and dragged me away. Diran walked with Jamie and Dunstan. His face was paler than a piece of paper, and his eyes were rounder than an owl's.

"Sorry." I whispered the words as I was dragged away.

"What are you sorry about?" Mia walked beside me cautiously.

"Nothing. It doesn't matter."

"If it doesn't matter, then there is no use crying." I brushed my eyes. "Where is this tunnel?" I stopped walking and looked up.

"There." We all looked up into the tunnel. "Nohnsan, can you get us up there slowly enough for us to grab the ledge?"

"Yes, Miss Shana." Nohnsan nodded.

My ears burnt red hot when I saw Dunstan look at me. He was completely speechless; he was like a blank canvas; he had no expression.

"I'll go first." I couldn't look at Dunstan. It broke my heart.

Nohnsan raised his hand and I shot up, quicker than I expected. I slowed down. The ledge was just a little above me. I jumped into the gap as I passed it. "I'm here!"

"Okay, we're right behind you." Mia shouted up.

Someone dived and rolled into the tunnel next to me. I stared at Dunstan. His eyes had gained their spark again, but not the spark I loved in him. It was fierce and sharp; it was more like the dangerous spark I saw in him when he fought.

"Dunstan, I'm sorry." Dunstan didn't say anything.

I heard someone else enter the tunnel behind me. I didn't stop to see who came up. Instead I crawled hurriedly through. "Shana?" Anna's voice timidly shook through the tunnel.

"This way." My voice was small and trembling.

I crawled out of the tunnel and into the street. The blankets of the girls were still strewn across the street. I didn't wait for anyone. I walked straight down the street, pulling out my dagger. I walked up the stairs and saw the gate I had blasted when the girls gushed out. I walked straight across the room and to the stairs. Rubble and chunks of rock were scattered everywhere.

The smell of the rotting girls knocked my breath away, but I still walked straight into the room. The pit lay across the room, and above it carved into the wall was the arch. Rumbling shot through the room, and the pit started to smoke. I walked up to the edge of the pit and looked in. Fire shot up from the pit. I quickly dragged out my sword, the dagger still in my other hand and stood defiantly there, waiting for the beast. It wasn't dead; it was hungry.

"Shana!" I heard his voice from behind me. I turned round and saw my friends. Dunstan, Mia, Diran, Anna, and some of my army were all in the room. I looked at the wall.

"We can take him!" Dunstan had gained his powerful voice back, but his face was still warped.

I threw my sword and scabbard at them and put my dagger into my boot. I sprinted to the wall and pulled myself up. I felt a blast of heat shoot past me. I looked down. The beast had arrived and had started the attack on my friends. I looked back to the wall. It was steeper than the waterfall, and with no one to pull me up at the top, it was taking more effort.

The arch was directly across from me. I heaved myself along the wall. I stretched down to my boot and pulled out my dagger, and I slit my hand. I put the dagger in my mouth. I felt something heavy slowly slip out of my pocket. I looked down. My mother's diary was slowly exposing itself to the outer world. I shoved it back in and iced up my pocket.

I slammed my hand on the arch. Fire shot out of the arch. Men flew out and landed on the ground below. Water men blasted the beast, and stones were hurled at its head. Gusts of wind extinguished any flames coming out of its mouth.

"Confirm blood presence."

Mia looked up and pointed. They fire men didn't look up.

Directly below me were the pit and the beast.

"Confirm blood presence."

The room started to fill with heat. I heard a faint chuckle, and I looked behind the beast. A flicker of darkness shot back into the cave behind the beast.

One way down! I hope this would work. I let go of the wall and jumped. I landed on the beast's head and stared directly into its eyes. They were the pebbles of hate, black holes only to be filled by blood. I shot black lightning through its head. I turned and dived off its head. A gust of wind caught me and let me land on the ground. The shrill from behind me drew my heartbeats closer together.

I ran to the man standing in front. He was completely ablaze. This was really going to hurt. I plunged my hand into his heart. I screamed as the flesh melted and shrivelled on my hand.

"Blood presence confirmed."

Hands appeared on my arm and yanked my hand out.

Dunstan was panting. His brows were turned up and were knitted closely together.

"I don't care that you kissed him."

"Shana, Dunstan, we have to go now!" Mia screeched as she bolted down the stairs with Diran and Anna.

I ran to the stairs with Dunstan. The beast shrilled louder than before. Fireballs whizzed through the air and set it on fire. I stopped at the stairs. The men were making a retreat, but I watched the beast writhe in agony. I raised my hand, and white light shot into the beast's chest, directly into its heart; beams of light shot through its eyes and mouth. Its head was hurled back. Dunstan pulled me, by the non—burnt hand, I followed him out the room and down the stairs.

We ran through the staircases and rooms; we dashed into the street, dodging the rubble. "This way, hurry!" Mia beckoned me and Dunstan to the narrow tunnel.

We shot through the tunnel after Mia, she scrambled through quickly. Mia scrambled out on to the narrow ledge, Dunstan and I stopped in the tunnel.

"Mia, why aren't you going?" I yelled out at her, as she stood on the ledge.

"The water," she bawled back at me. "It's running again."

"Just jump," Dunstan shouted.

There was a whooping sound and Mia was gone, she had jumped off the edge and into the running water.

Dunstan and I clambered out of the tunnel and stood looking down at the running water. "Wait!" I ducked down and looked back in the tunnel.

"Fredrick!" Dunstan reached out a hand to him. Fredrick took Dunstan's hand and was pulled onto the ledge. This was a small ledge and I was pretty much falling off it.

"What the hell happened to you!?" I bellowed at him.

"I went to go and warn my sister and father." He was shaking his head. "They weren't there." He looked like a lost boy. "Otius, I lost him." Fredrick looked at me, he looked as if he had been cut open, he was completely exposed to sorrow.

"We will find him." I spoke quickly, knowing this place was going to collapse. "Jump."

I pushed him on the back and he toppled over the edge, I jumped after him.

The water was icy cold; it was as much of a rough landing as the last time. "Shana!" I was being swept down the tunnel when I heard someone shouting my name.

I looked at the end of the tunnel. "Not again." I slammed my eye lids down as I fell off the edge into the waterfall and plummeted back down to the lake. But the drop didn't come; I rose out of the water, as if by magic. Nohnsan lifted me into him, I looked behind me. Dunstan was being lifted out the water by another water man. He smiled at me, I never thought he would again but he did.

Chapter 25

One last problem . . . I Hope

That night, we once again camped in the woods. It was different though, not just because there were four armies of element men with us making it cramped. But because for the first time in a long time we all felt hopeful, the element men had given us a chance of hope.

"Today was interesting." Dunstan sat beside me as we toasted our food over the back of a flame man, who hadn't noticed what we were doing.

"It was." I took my mother's diary out of my bag. "I've been reading up." Dunstan took the diary from me and started to flick idly through the pages. "There is someone in there that can help me."

"What help do you need? We have an indestructible army." Dunstan looked sceptically at me.

"I am going to need to be the one to kill Morphius, only I have that power." I winced; my hand was twinging a bit.

Mia, with her sixth sense was, on me in a moment. "Maybe next time, don't stick your hand into fire." She took hold of my hand, at once it started to cool.

"Anyway." I began talking again; trying to ignore my dysfunctional hand, "The person I was reading about in the diary can help me kill Morphius without losing myself to my darkness."

Wind scattered leaves around me, I smiled to myself. I looked up, the leaves rattled delicately at the top of the trees. Jamie and Fredrick were talking in excited tones with Nohnsan; Jamie was getting great pleasure from knowing something that someone else didn't for once.

"Who is it?" Dunstan kept flicking through the pages; he stopped and looked at a page. "Wow," Dunstan exclaimed.

Mia snatched the diary off him and looked at the page; her eyes grew wide. "Wow."

Diran wandered over to us and plonked himself next to Mia; he started to read the diary. "Wow."

I stood up. "That is who we are going to find, if we can." I started to walk away. The wind started to pick up speed around me, the leaves started to gather quicker.

I could feel the disbelief oozing from Dunstan, Diran and Mia as I walked into the woods.

I sauntered steadily away from the camp and into the quiet of the forest. I stopped at a particularly wide tree trunk.

The only thing my mother told me before she left was one thing: to get to the top and never look back.

I grabbed onto the tree truck and dug my feet into the cracks; I jammed my nails in and started to climb steadily. I was barely off the ground when I heard a ruffle behind me. "Race you." I smiled at Dunstan's voice.

"You're on." I giggled as I started to scramble up the tree.

Dunstan climbed on the opposite side of the trunk, he was fast. But I was faster.

Once we were at the top I stared at the view. The moon was full and brighter than ever, I was standing on a fairly thick branch. "You're fast." Dunstan scrambled up onto the branch with me; he wrapped his arms around my waist and cuddled me into him.

The millions of stars were clustered tightly together; they lit the night sky so brightly it was like looking at a thousand fairy lights.

"Promise me one thing." I didn't look at Dunstan as I spoke.

"Anything." Dunstan whispered into my ear.

"You aren't Morphius right now." Dunstan laughed; I knew his voice so well by now that it couldn't be anyone else's. He thought it is a joke, but it was a serious question.

"I promise." Dunstan cuddled me tighter. I turned my back to the trunk so I could see him.

"In this whole messed up situation, there is one good thing that has come from it." I spoke softly, moving in closer to Dunstan.

"What's that?" Dunstan's voice was almost a murmur.

"You." I had barely spoken the words before Dunstan and I were locked in a passionate and unbreakable kiss.

So much has happened to me, so much is unclear. Morphius, Kim and the angels were all loose in Rezta and were going to try and kill everyone and everything I love. They know nothing of my army or of the man that was going to save me from myself as I try to kill Morphius. My mother didn't give him a name; she just referred to him as the magician in the stars.

About the Author

My name is Amy Flashman. I started this book when I was fourteen years old. I wrote this book around my school work but I wanted to write it as a release, a way of coping with the work I guess.

I actually went to Edgbarrow School. Sadly there was no Jamie, all the characters are fictional, but there was a scary amount of sporting activities.

I live in Crowthorne—an unusual name but a nice place. I spend my time on the gorgeous heath. That was what inspired some of the scenery. I used to love climbing trees. That's where I got the feeling for tree climbing, but I stopped after I heard my best friend fell out of one and landed on her butt on solid concrete! Julia Elizabeth Manning you are the best!

My friends did inspire some of the characters; Mia especially wouldn't have her edgy temper if it wasn't for one of my friends. Miss Golhar I am talking about you. Jess and Phoebe, I thank you for my addiction to Doctor Who.